PLAYGROUND

Dear Reader,

Before you dive of "Playground: Cyprus you of a few things. First and foremost, this story is a work of pure fiction. The characters you'll meet, the twists and turns they encounter, and the intricate webs they weave are all figments of my imagination. If you think, "Hey, that guy sounds like my old math teacher!" or "I know someone just like that!" — rest assured, it's purely coincidental. Or perhaps it is a testament to my ability to create relatable characters!

The opinions and viewpoints expressed in this novel are mine alone. They might wander through the corridors of politics, skim over the ponds of morality, or dance in the fields of social commentary. But remember, they're just one person's musings and shouldn't be taken as gospel (unless, of course, you find them particularly enlightening).

Now, about the setting of our story — the beautiful island of Cyprus. This enchanting Mediterranean jewel is not just a backdrop for our tale but a character in its own right. The locations described are real places that I've had the pleasure of visiting. From the sun-kissed beaches to the historical whispers in the narrow streets, Cyprus offers a blend of history and beauty, making it the perfect stage for this drama to unfold.

Lastly, I wish to impart a thought. Stories like these remind us of the importance of striving for peace and understanding in our world, full of conflicts and

shadows. "Playground: Cyprus" might be fictional, but the underlying hope is real and earnest. Let us all play our part in making the world a better place, free from the scars of war and the shadows of terrorism.
With a twinkle in my eye and a hopeful heart,

Mitchell Lanigan

Chapter 1

The polished silver wings of the Cessna Citation XLS sliced through the cerulean sky before descending upon the tarmac of Paphos International Airport in Cyprus. The private plane's arrival was marked by the clock striking fourteen hundred hours. Gliding towards a secluded terminal parking area, the aircraft came to a halt before its door swung open to release a wave of sultry heat and the palpable heaviness of Cyprus humidity.

From the luxurious confines of his leather seat, Nikolai Gromov emerged, his senses awakening to the familiar scent of the humid Mediterranean air. Stretching his limbs, he barked orders to his dual-hatted bodyguards and personal assistants.

"Secure the suitcases and ensure they remain untouched. Our esteemed friend, Stelios, awaits our arrival!"

Stelios, a prominent Cyprus Border Control figure and successful low-tier real estate developer was the proud proprietor of a quaint network of a few small coffee shops scattered across the island. In Cyprus, it is customary to wear many hats, and Stelios was no exception. With the ripe age of fifty-three approaching, he had one eye on a comfortable retirement, his government position serving as a convenient vessel for his pension and the reins of his business likely to be passed down to his undeserving descendants.

The Cyprus government's modest salary was quite a contrast to the lucrative dealings with wealthy Russians who would descend upon the island in their private jets with their cargo holds filled with caviar, cash, drugs, and beautiful women. For Stelios, the nature of their goods was unimportant - personal pleasure was their sole purpose, never for sale. The Russians came to Cyprus not to generate income but to lavishly spend it, and Stelios was more than willing to facilitate their indulgence. The standard remuneration of ten thousand euros per plane was the agreed-upon price for his invaluable discreet services.

In truth, Stelios knew little about the intricacies of Nikolai's illicit business operations back home. The venture has flourished in recent years due to the crippling sanctions imposed upon Russia by the international community. The items Nikolai smuggled into Russia were far from the conventional. Instead of the usual smuggler business stuff, his cargo consisted of European cheeses and fruits, predominantly sourced from France and Spain. In a peculiarly Russian twist, these seemingly mundane items were transported to Belarus, repackaged in Gomel with ironic "Made in Belarus" labels, before being clandestinely brought across the Russian border tax-free. The merchandise was then sold to Nikolai's acquaintances, owners of sprawling supermarket chains, and the proceeds split between them. It was an operation reminiscent of Nikolai's early days in the smuggling trade.

With its convenient banking system, Cyprus provided Nikolai with the perfect sanctuary to stash his illicit gains. What he referred to as an "alternative landing strip" was a contingency plan should Putin's regime tighten its grip or should the threat of incarceration loom on his horizon. His world was one of the impromptu decisions, and transactions concluded with haste. Long-term plans were a luxury he could never afford. A million euros today was infinitely more valuable than a hypothetical hundred million five years later. Nikolai could be dead, imprisoned, or out of business by then. Cash was king, and Cyprus was his fortress. His security detail, consisting of two bodyguards, was more a status symbol than a reflection of any genuine concern for his safety in Cyprus.

Stelios wouldn't know what was in those suitcases that he eagerly helped to log in the shipping manifests as personal items for relocation. But he had seen enough in his work to recognize when someone was hiding something. He chose to look the other way, happy with the generous "bonuses" that Nikolai's visits brought to his otherwise unremarkable bank account.

Labeled as "special," this visit saw Nikolai transport eight million euros in cash encased in three cumbersome black suitcases. With Stelios by his side, he was confident that the contents of his luggage would escape scrutiny as they had always done.

"Nikolai! Welcome, my friend!" beamed Stelios as he wrapped Nicolai in a hearty hug.

"The heat's unbearable," remarked Nikolai, wiping his brow. "So, I've brought you a nighttime treat," he added, presenting Stelios with a bottle of the renowned Russian vodka Beluga.

"Much obliged, Nikolai! Tell me, how fares Moscow these days?"

"The same old utter madness."

The entire customs process lasted a fleeting minute, and soon, Nikolai, flanked by his bodyguards, was en route to his destination in a sleek Mercedes Vito. As Stelios waved them off, the ten grand in cash was comfortably nestled inside the Beluga box.

After leaving the airport, Nikolai retrieved his phone and dialed a familiar number.

"Nikolai, have you touched down in Cyprus?"

The words were a formality—a hidden question probing the success of Nikolai's latest venture.

"Yes, I'm here and all set. Ready to proceed," Nikolai replied with a voice as smooth as aged whiskey, rich with undertones of a man used to getting his own way.

The voice on the other end belonged to Demetris, a fellow entrepreneur with whom Nikolai had struck a deal to purchase a small 22-room hotel in Paphos, intending to invest some of his cash in real estate. The agreement was a 3-million-euro official sale, supplemented by a 5-million-euro under-the-table cash transaction. Nikolai had already transferred the official sum from his Cyprus company's account and brought the remainder in cash to uphold his side of the bargain. The suitcases contained not just the five million for the hotel purchase but an additional three million to be concealed in the vault at his Cyprus residence.

"A minor hiccup," interjected Demetris. "My meeting in Belgrade ran over, so I won't be back in Cyprus until tomorrow night."

"Fine, I'll be waiting for your call then," responded Nikolai.

"And the additional funds will be delivered as discussed?" asked Demetris.

Silence filled the air between them. Nikolai's silence was his power, demonstrating his control over the conversation and the deal.

"Demetris, when have I not delivered on my word? Rest assured, our arrangement stands firm. I have with me what is required."

Nikolai spoke of millions with the ease of someone discussing the weather. The cash, a heavy secret in his carry-on, was viewed as a tool, a means to an end.

"Very well, Nikolai. I'll arrange for our meeting as soon as I'm back. The paperwork for the hotel is ready. I'm sure it will be a fine addition to your portfolio."

The hotel was a front for Nikolai's labyrinthine dealings. In this place, money could rest as quietly as tourists wandering its halls, oblivious to the structure's true purpose.

"Excellent. Make sure everything is in order. I don't need to remind you of the... implications should there be any... irregularities."

The thinly disguised threat was delivered pleasantly, hinting that Nikolai's affable businessman persona was just one facet of a much darker and more complex character.

When Nikolai ended the call, a text message flashed across his screen: "Police will stop you to check bags." Panic coursed through him.

The message originated from Stelios' phone, a precaution taken after learning of the potential customs issue involving Nikolai's suspiciously frequent flights. An anonymous call about Stelios' covert operations involving Russian planes alerted the police, prompting the dispatch of a special team to investigate. Fortunately, the squad had been delayed, working in their favor as Nikolai managed to slip through customs unscathed, thanks to Stelios' help.

Stelios had used his burner phone, strategically hidden in the airport's restroom, to inform Nikolai of the situation, acting on a tip-off from his contact with the police.

"Stop the car! We're in hot water. The police could pull us over any second for a suitcase inspection," Nikolai barked at the driver.

His bodyguards, Slavik and Zhorik, former FSB agents with decades of experience, immediately sprang into action.

"Boss, over there!" Zhorik pointed to the Athena Royal Beach Hotel they were driving past. "It's the perfect hiding spot for the suitcases."

"You're right, go!" Nikolai agreed, and Zhorik steered the car into the hotel's parking lot.

"Here's the plan, boss: we offload the luggage, you guard it while Slavik checks us in. Meanwhile, I'll source new suitcases," instructed Zhorik. Moments later, Slavik was already approaching the hotel's main entrance. The plan went like clockwork.

With the luggage safely parked in the hotel lobby and Zhorik off to buy new suitcases, Nikolai felt a surge of adrenaline reminding him of the chaotic 90s, rife with gang wars and underworld machinations.

Slavik returned with the porter, hoisting the suitcases onto a cart and signaling to his boss with the plastic key card. The porter began wheeling the cart down the hallway, eventually reaching room 2145. The standard suite offered no view of the sea. The porter was compensated with a ten-euro bill before swiftly unpacking the luggage, placing one suitcase in the wardrobe and the other two in a corner.

"Stay put," commanded Nikolai. "Should the police inquire about you, I'll call you. I'll tell them you're out grocery shopping or something."

"Understood, boss," Slavik responded, easing into a chair as Nikolai departed the room.

The operation progressed seamlessly. By the time Nikolai reached the hotel lobby, Zhorik was already parking the car, wearing a triumphant grin.

"Mission accomplished. The suitcases, while a little different in style, are still black. They're now filled with swimming and sports gear from a nearby tourist shop. I even threw in some vodka for good measure," Zhorik reported as they exited the parking lot, adding, "No sign of the police so far."

"Splendid," replied Nikolai, though a wave of unease washed over him. His intuition warned him that something was wrong, resulting in an inexplicable surge of panic. Even with the smooth exit from the hotel, the new suitcases, and the well-hidden stash of cash in the suite with Slavik standing guard, Nikolai couldn't shake off the feeling of a disaster coming.

Upon approaching the Coral Bay roundabout, his fears were confirmed as they spotted police flashlights. Zhorik decelerated, and sure enough, they were flagged down by a policewoman flanked by two officers.

"Good evening, gentlemen," she greeted them with a smile. "My name is Alexa Marou, CID. In light of the ongoing anti-terrorism operation, we must inspect your vehicle and luggage. Is that acceptable?"

"Of course, officer," assented Nikolai, allowing the police to proceed.

The trunk was opened, revealing the suitcases. "Would you mind opening these?" an officer asked Nikolai, who complied. The first suitcase was brimming with diving masks, fins, and beach toys.

"My, aren't we the sporty types?" the policewoman commented.

"Trying to shed some pounds," Nikolai quipped, his smile mirroring hers.

"Next suitcase, please."

The second suitcase was similarly filled, plus the two vodka bottles.

"Not quite so healthy," she noted, now gesturing towards the third suitcase.

Before opening it, she asked, "I can't help but notice the absence of personal items. No clothes, toiletries... Why is that?"

Unfazed, Nikolai replied, "Well, I own a property here. So, everything I need is already there."

"I see. Fair enough, you're free to go. Mr. Gromov, I hope you'll remember to declare your luggage at the airport next time."

"Will do. Thanks," he responded, adding, "As you can see, there's nothing to declare."

The policewoman's skeptical gaze lingered on him for a moment longer before turning on her heel and retreating to the police car, the two officers in tow.

Seatbelts fastened, Nikolai and Zhorik drove off, satisfied.

"We did it!" Nikolai breathed out.

"All that's left is to transfer the cash from the hotel," Zhorik pointed out. "I'll rent a tourist car for the job to avoid attention."

"Agreed. But let's assess the situation in the morning. There's no need to rush; Slavik's got the cash covered."

With their plan in place, they entered the gated community of Sea Caves, home to some of the priciest real estate in the area. Approaching the front door, Nikolai was greeted by the sight of Olga, wearing a long, red dress. "Fuck!" was all he could muster in admiration.

She was a sight to behold as his third wife, boasting a youthful glow at thirty-seven, standing eleven years his junior. Nikolai was adamant that she possessed the most exquisite derrière he had ever laid eyes on. His first marital union, a quaint school romance, had endured for six years, producing his eldest offspring, Ivan. Ivan had pursued academia in the United States, eventually settling there. The father and son shared fleeting reunions several times annually, with Nikolai always wanting to extend his support financially or via connections. His second conjugal bond could have been more fruitful, lasting two years, characterized by constant bickering and devoid of kids. Several romantic entanglements later – spanning the gamut from brief live-in arrangements to dalliances with ladies of the night – Nikolai crossed paths with Olga. She was the balm to his restless heart, promptly blessing him with a daughter. The six-year-old resided in Cyprus, and her mother served as the vigilant custodian of Nikolai's alternative sanctuary.

Post a passionate hour interlude with Olga, Nikolai emerged from the house, his spirit tranquil yet his body weary. The night was blanketed in an enveloping warmth, punctuated by a celestial tapestry of stars that appeared almost within arm's reach. His thoughts inevitably wandered to the hefty pile of cash stashed away in that hotel room. Retrieving his mobile device, Nikolai dialed Zhorik's number.

"Check on Slavik. Leave the Mercedes. Take the bike instead."

Nikolai promptly returned the phone to his pocket and ignited a cigarette, its embers glowing in the moonlight. He took a thoughtful drag and exhaled dense smoke before crushing the cigarette underfoot. A lingering inexplicable unease—call it intuition—gnawed at Nikolai's gut. He tried to shake it off, thinking about the second round of the homecoming session with Olga. With sex on his mind, he re-entered the quiet domain of his home.

Chapter 2

Anton awoke with the formidable weight of a pounding headache and backache that felt like he'd been hit by a truck. His makeshift bed, a diminutive and antiquated couch in the corner of a basic hotel room, offered little comfort. Last night's rendezvous with a bottle of scotch only made things worse, leaving him feeling completely wrecked.

The king-sized bed in the room was almost swallowed up by his wife, sprawled out like she was auditioning for a starfish role. Her rhythmic snores provided a peaceful soundtrack, a sharp and ironic contrast to the raucous symphony crashing inside Anton's head. With the determination of a man climbing Everest, Anton pried himself from the demonic grip of the couch. Every twitch of his muscles sent electric jolts of pain through his weary body as if his very being protested against the audacity of movement.

Once upright, he rummaged through his bag and emerged victorious with a pack of aspirin. With a chemist's precision, he dissolved three tablets in a glass of water and downed it in one fell swoop, knowing from experience that relief would wash over him in approximately ten minutes. The interlude was spent brushing his teeth, an activity that allowed him to reflect on the grand calamity that had been their trip to Cyprus.

The trip was a complete disaster, a Hail Mary to save their four-year marriage that crashed and burned. Anton, an IT engineer from Kyiv, was the ultimate nice guy. His resume was spotless, with two master's degrees in mathematics and computer science, and he was the poster boy for politeness and decency.

But underneath that kind exterior was a soft spot that made him easy prey, especially for his wife. She was his polar opposite—a social butterfly and a habitual drinker, perfectly happy to spend her days lounging around. She only emerged from their apartment under the cover of darkness to party with her friends, leaving Anton to wonder how he had ended up in this ironic twist of matrimonial fate.

Despite the glaring mismatch in their personalities and values, Anton had shown a mind-boggling amount of patience with her antics. His dislike of confrontation meant their arguments always ended the same way: with him giving in. His logic was no match for her ironclad stubbornness.

Their trip to Cyprus, away from the usual distractions of friends and family, was supposed to be a cure-all for their failing marriage. Instead, it had exposed just how incompatible they really were. The final nail in the coffin was their latest spat. Anton had tried, in his gentle way, to discuss her drinking habit. It ended, predictably, in anger and accusations, proving once again that even paradise couldn't save their sinking ship.

As the bitter taste of toothpaste mingled with the lingering effects of last night's scotch, a sobering realization struck Anton. The love and passion that had once fueled their union had long since dissipated, leaving a seemingly impossible void in its wake.

The aspirin had begun to work its magic, acting as a salve that slowly dispelled the fog clouding his vision and mind. The previous night's events replayed in his head like a surreal film: the heated argument, his wife storming off to the hotel bar, and his subsequent solitary descent into the amber depths of the scotch bottle. He hadn't heard her return, but the sonorous symphony of her snoring indicated that she had indulged in her usual libations.

Standing in the middle of their hotel room chaos, Anton scanned the scene. His wife's clothes were scattered everywhere, a sign of her carefree lifestyle. A pair of shorts and a shirt lay crumpled on the floor. As he bent down to grab his shoes, his eyes caught on a torn condom wrapper tangled in her shorts.

A wave of nausea hit him so hard that he barely made it to the bathroom before throwing up. His mind raced, desperately trying to find a plausible explanation for the wrapper's presence. Maybe it had been left behind by previous guests and somehow got mixed up with her clothes. But the cold, relentless voice of reason whispered the harsh truth. In his gut, he knew exactly what had happened while he was drowning his sorrows.

Anton's face flushed as his heartbeat thundered in his ears, adrenaline coursing through his veins. He splashed his face with cold water, the chill anchoring him back to reality. Slowly and methodically, he began to gather his belongings. Each deliberate movement brought him closer to the brink of a life-altering decision that would finally end this nightmare.

***

The morning found Slavik in high spirits, buoyed by the previous night's escapades. Still lounging in bed, he recalled the chain of events with a satisfied grin.

His mind had been buzzing with thoughts of the cash stashed in the suitcases, and the waiting game in his room was driving him nuts. So, he decided a drink might calm his nerves. He made a quick stop at a nearby kiosk for cigarettes and then headed to the bar.

The bar hummed with the clink of glasses and quiet conversations when Slavik noticed a woman glued to her iPhone. He approached her with a smile and asked if the bar had the best Wi-Fi in town. "And best booze," she replied, motioning for him to join her. One drink led to another, and before long, they were making a beeline for the bar's restroom for a quick romp, followed by an encore performance in his room. Although she was a willing participant, her level of intoxication was a bit off-putting for Slavik. But he shrugged off his reservations and enjoyed the moment, basking in the thrill of the night's unexpected gift.

Finally, he walked her back down the hallway and left her in the same bar, ordering her another glass of wine for good measure. His return to the room was interrupted by a call from Zhorik, who had cleverly stationed himself on his motorbike behind a bougainvillea bush near the beach, wisely avoiding the hotel's main lobby. Their quick chat reassured both men that everything was under control. With a satisfied sigh, Slavik drifted off into a peaceful slumber, while Zhorik made his way to Nikolai's guest house, mission accomplished.

***

The dawn of a new day brought the comforting sight of the cash, still nestled safely in the suitcases. The golden rays of sunshine streamed through the window, bathing the room in a warm glow and signaling that it was time to initiate the next phase of their plan. True to their agreement, Zhorik had rented a silver Toyota RAV4 with red tourist plates, blending seamlessly with the many rental cars that dotted the landscape. The ubiquitous nature of the vehicle made it an ideal choice for their purposes, allowing them to move around without drawing too much attention.

Once at the hotel, Zhorik called Slavik. "The car's ready; let's get moving!" he declared.

"Great! Get the suitcases downstairs while I settle the bill. Have you scoped out the area?" Slavik inquired.

"All clear. Did a sweep, no sign of any police or tails. I even stopped at a neighboring hotel and had a coffee just to be sure. This is Cyprus, after all, relax. " Zhorik responded, his tone casual and reassuring.

Slavik ended the call with a final nod of agreement and got ready for the departure. Downstairs, Zhorik had maneuvered the car into a spot adjacent to a taxi parked next to the front door, minimizing the distance they would have to walk with the suitcases. Satisfied with his parking spot, he entered the hotel.

***

In a fugue of adrenaline, Anton quickly loaded his small suitcase into the backseat of his white rental car, feeling the pulse of his headache but paying it no mind. The car rolled smoothly out of the parking garage when a realization struck him like a lightning bolt – he had left his phone in the hotel room. He hadn't even bothered to check out, as his wife remained in the room, still wrapped in her drunken slumber. Spying a taxi pulling out, he swerved into its vacated spot by the entrance, leaving the car unlocked as he rushed upstairs.

Meanwhile, Zhorik was involved in his dance of deception, trying to transport the suitcases discreetly via the stairwell to avoid prying eyes. As he emerged in the hallway, the eagle-eyed porter, with the scent of easy money in the air, zeroed in on him.

"Sir, allow me to assist you," he insisted, his voice resonating louder than necessary through the lobby.

Zhorik, though reluctant, didn't have the luxury of refusal with so many witnesses around. Nodding, he agreed, giving directions toward a Toyota RAV4 by the entrance before smartly creating distance from the porter and the suitcases lest he be caught on camera. The plan was simple: let the porter load up the car, get paid, and by then, Slavik would be ready to go too. Sure enough, Slavik was at the reception desk, finalizing his checkout.

The porter soon returned, grinning as he pocketed the ten euros Zhorik handed him. A job well done.

Meanwhile, having retrieved his phone, Anton jumped back into his car and took off. His destination: the airport. Any flight, anywhere, just as long as it took him far away from the ruins of his marriage.

Rage was his only companion, thoughts of revenge his only plan.

Back at the hotel, Slavik and Zhorik emerged to find the empty parking spot next to their Toyota.

"A bit cramped in here," Slavik observed, trying to adjust the seat. He glanced over his shoulder, expecting to see the suitcases piled up, but instead saw nothing.

"Stop!" he shouted. "Where are the suitcases?"

Zhorik hit the brakes, the car halting in the middle of the parking area. Both men turned to confirm the obvious – the suitcases were gone. In unison, they stepped out of the car, shock on their faces.

"That damn porter was supposed to load them!" Zhorik exclaimed, his mind racing.

Determined, they marched back into the hotel and up to the third floor, where they found the porter busily tending to another guest's luggage. Opting for caution, they observed him from a distance, assessing his behavior. Nothing seemed amiss - his smile was genuine as he spotted them.

"More luggage, gentlemen?" he inquired cheerfully.

"No," Slavik replied, moving closer to scrutinize the porter's badge. "George, did you load our luggage into the car?"

"Yes, sir. The white Toyota RAV4 parked by the entrance next to the wall," George responded, a slight frown creasing his forehead. "Is there a problem?"

"Next to the wall? White?" Zhorik interjected. "There was a black Mercedes taxi there, not a RAV4."

George's frown deepened. "No, sir. It was a white RAV4, with another car, silver perhaps, parked next to it."

Zhorik felt his legs give out, and he had to steady himself against the wall. A white RAV4. Not their silver one. Panic clawed at his insides.

"I did exactly as you asked," George insisted, a note of fear creeping into his voice. "The suitcases are in the white RAV4 by the entrance."

"Yes, you did," Zhorik acknowledged quietly, a sense of dread washing over him as he turned and headed for the elevator.

"I need a drink," Zhorik declared, echoing Slavik's internal turmoil. The critical nature of their situation hung over them like a storm cloud. Nikolai, their formidable employer, was not known for his mercy or understanding. Their futures seemed to have plummeted to a watery grave in the depths of the Mediterranean Sea.

"So, what's the plan?" Slavik asked, his mind racing as he grappled with their limited options. "We need to find that damn car. Whoever's driving it is blissfully ignorant of the fortune stashed in the back."

"That's assuming they haven't found it already," Zhorik countered grimly. Using nondescript, lock-free suitcases to avoid arousing suspicion at customs had just backfired spectacularly. "Most people can't resist a peek inside when there's nothing to stop them."

"We'll need to split up. I'll head to the airport—most probably whoever has left in that car is headed there. You stay here, work with the hotel management, check security cameras, get the guest list, and get the info on rented Toyota RAV4s through our friends with the police. And you need to call Nikolai to fill him in. We'll need his help—and additional resources—if we're to have any hope of recovering the money," Slavik decided.

Zhorik nodded, fished out his phone, and began dialing Nikolai's number while Slavik made a beeline for the airport in the rented car.

The call was a stormy affair. Nikolai's initial fury gradually subsided as he processed the information, his mind shifting into tactical mode. The time spent berating Zhorik and Slavik for the loss was time wasted. He knew them well enough to trust they were telling the truth.

***

Meanwhile, Anton had abandoned his plan to head to Paphos Airport. He knew that most flights to Kyiv departed from Larnaca, the main airport in Cyprus, a good hour and a half drive from the hotel. His journey was interrupted by an overwhelming thirst, a by-product of the adrenaline and scotch coursing through his body. He pulled over at a kiosk just outside Limassol and bought two large bottles of St. Nicolas water. No sooner had he stepped out of the kiosk was the first bottle already half empty. He then caught sight of the suitcases in his car trunk through the back window.

A chill of foreboding swept through him. Anton flung open the trunk to find three unfamiliar black suitcases. The truth hit him like a punch to the gut – it could only have been the porter who mixed up the cars.

"Bloody hell," he muttered to himself. "Now I've got to go back to the hotel to sort out this mess."

But then, a thought struck him. Was it really his problem? He could just leave the suitcases at the kiosk and inform the hotel of their whereabouts. Decision made. He reached for the first suitcase, his muscles straining under its unexpected weight. "What the hell?" he exclaimed, a dark suspicion unfurling. The weight far exceeded what any airline would accept. The thought of there being a bomb inside flashed across his mind, realizing his fingerprints were now all over the suitcase.

Curiosity getting the best of him, Anton slowly inched the zipper open and peeked inside. The opening was too small to see much, so he reluctantly widened it further. His jaw then dropped. Neatly stacked inside were bundles of €50 and €100 bills. Anton's eyes widened in disbelief as he opened the suitcase. The sheer volume of cash left him speechless. This was more money than he had ever seen in his entire life. And it was just one suitcase.

With his pulse racing and adrenaline pumping, Anton stood beside the car, the trunk filled to the brim with cash. His first powerful instinct, impossible to ignore, urged him to return to the hotel. The clarity he sought eluded him initially, but soon enough, the fog in his mind lifted, revealing two distinct paths before him.

Option one was to head back to the hotel, park the car, and lie in wait for the rightful owners of the money to claim it. Anton was reasonably sure they were already on his trail. The critical unknown was whether anyone had witnessed his departure from the hotel. He vaguely pieced together the events leading to the windfall, concluding that a porter's mistake was the most plausible explanation. Anton recalled crossing paths with the porter on his way out of the lobby. A lapse of just two minutes had resulted in the cash ending up in his car. There was a strong likelihood that the porter could identify his vehicle and a fifty-fifty chance he had noted the license plate. To make things worse, Anton had a sneaking suspicion that the owners of the money weren't exactly model citizens.

The second option was to flee with the money and take his chances. A gamble that could see him emerge wealthy or dead. Anton moved his car to the remotest corner of the deserted parking lot, pausing to take a few deep gulps of water. As he set the bottle down, his mind began to race, teetering on the edge of a pivotal decision that felt like both an ending and a beginning.

Born on the fringes of Kyiv, Anton's childhood was a patchwork of scarcity and modest joys. His parents' marriage unraveled early, leaving him to navigate a world that seemed to reward those with wealth and punish those without. The crumbling apartment complex of his youth was a striking difference from the gleaming towers he saw on rare trips to the city center. Those trips planted a seed in young Anton—a deep-seated desire for a better life, a life where struggle wasn't a daily companion.

He found comfort and hope in mathematics, where numbers and equations offered a refuge from the instability of his home life. His aptitude led him to the prestigious Taras Shevchenko National University of Kyiv, where he immersed himself in math and computer science, driven by a vision of a future where the constraints of his upbringing didn't define him.

Anton's diligence paid off. He emerged as a skilled software engineer, his talents opening doors that had once seemed permanently closed. He found a decent job, saved diligently, and eventually bought a modest apartment—a far cry from the luxury he dreamed of but still a confirmation of his hard work.

Love, too, seemed to be on his side when he met Natalia at the university. She was vibrant and full of life, an obvious opposition to his more reserved nature. Their romance was swift, and for a time, it seemed to complete the picture of the life Anton had worked so hard to build.

But as the years passed, Natalia's occasional drinking evolved into a dependency that slowly eroded their marriage. The arguments, the broken promises, the nights waiting up for her—all of it culminated in a painful life that left Anton questioning the very trajectory of his marriage.

Anton's efforts to mend their fractured relationship were like trying to hold water in his hands—futile and draining. Each attempt to bridge the growing chasm between them only widened the gap. The trip to Cyprus was his last-ditch effort, a hope to rekindle a spark that had long been extinguished. He had planned every detail, hoping the change of scenery would bring a change in their dynamics. But the trip unfolded as a vivid illustration of their failing relationship—Natalia's indifference to the beautiful surroundings, her growing disinterest in his attempts at romance, and the increasing visits to the hotel bar.

In the midst of his heartache, finding the cash was like a sudden jolt, a rude awakening from his long denial. In the silence of this remote parking lot, Anton finally realized the inevitable truth. Their marriage was beyond repair. It was time for him to let go.

The suitcases full of cash, almost mocking in their unexpected appearance, now symbolized a new beginning. A chance to start afresh, far away from the shadows of a love that had turned bitter. This was his exit door from a life that had become a loop of disappointment and heartache.

As he sat in his rented car in the middle of a foreign country, alone, his marriage in ruins, another moral quandary unfolded in his mind. This fortune wasn't his. He hadn't earned it. It had simply appeared in his life by some unimaginable twist of fate. The ethical part of Anton screamed that keeping the money was wrong, that it belonged to someone else. But another voice, born from years of longing and struggle, whispered seductive justifications.

He knew the money was tainted, a by-product of deeds and worlds he had always avoided, but the allure of what it represented was overwhelming.

He weighed the risks, the palpable sense of danger mingling with a surge of adrenaline. This kind of money came with strings attached, the kind that could pull you into the depths of the underworld. The kind of money that whispered of dark deals and dangerous liaisons. Yet, there was also the promise of a life free from financial woes and limitations.

Anton's mind was a whirlwind of thoughts. In a sudden burst of inspiration, he flipped open his laptop and connected to the mobile internet. His fingers flew across the keyboard as he hacked into the hotel's security system in a matter of minutes. To his relief and amazement, he discovered that the video surveillance cameras were out of order, having recorded nothing during his stay.

At that moment, the decision was made. Anton Gorin, the boy from the outskirts of Kyiv who had clung to dreams of a better life, decided to take the leap. Unknown to him, this choice would catapult him into a world far beyond anything he could have imagined—a world where every step was fraught with danger, but the rewards were greater than he had ever dared to hope. Anton started the engine and set off towards Paphos, his mind weaving the threads of his plan.

***

Several hotels down from Athena Beach was a four-star establishment named Aquamare, complete with a luxurious spa. Anton was familiar with the hotel because his wife had used its spa services a few days prior. He drove into its underground parking lot, extracted a bundle of fifty-euro bills from one of the suitcases, and headed for the elevator.

As Anton strolled towards the reception, he was greeted by the minimalist elegance of the surroundings. Neatly trimmed hedges and geometrically precise lawns offered a manicured welcome, leading to a sleek, airy lobby that hummed with understated luxury.

The interior was a haven of calm, neutral tones, where the artistry of simplicity held sway. The reception desk was a modern design statement, staffed by professionals whose attire echoed the hotel's palette of sand and sea. Soft, ambient lighting complemented the natural light that flooded in, casting a gentle glow over the tasteful furnishings. A subtle scent of citrus lingered in the air, a nod perhaps to the island's abundant groves.

A young Cypriot manned the reception desk with a friendly smile.

"Good evening, sir. How may I assist you?"

"Hi there! I'd like to book a room," Anton replied.

"Of course. We have several available, what type of room would you prefer?"

Anton leaned in, lowering his voice conspiratorially.

"Here's the thing. I checked into the Almira hotel three days ago and ended up hooking up with a girl I met at the bar. She told me she was alone, but as it turned out, she was here with her husband, who is now out for my blood. She even knows my name. I could really use some help. I'd be eternally grateful if you could check me in without any paperwork."

As he spoke, Anton slid a hundred euros across the counter.

The receptionist hesitated, glancing from Anton to the money before breaking into a smile.

"Of course, I can help you. However, I must inform you that the rate will be higher without paperwork."

"That's not an issue. I'm prepared to pay double."

"Very well," the receptionist said, tapping away at the computer. "How long will you be staying for?"

"Four days."

"Done."

Anton handed over the cash, received his room key, and returned to the parking lot. Moments later, he was standing in his room on the fourth floor with the suitcases neatly arranged. A cursory rearrangement of the bed covers, and a few items from his own suitcase created an occupied room.

Chapter 3

Zhorik and Slavik were running against time. Their investigation into the missing suitcases quickly became a masterclass in frustration and dead ends. Their first major setback came when they learned that the hotel's security cameras had been out of commission for a week due to cable damage while renovating lobby parts.

In the dimly lit underground parking lot, they poured over the checkout info they had acquired through a hefty bribe to the hotel clerk. Through their local police contacts provided by Nikolai, they obtained a list of rentals of all Toyota RAV 4 cars in the area within the last two weeks. The cross-check of the hotel registration and the rental lists found three matches– a British couple, a Ukrainian couple, and a German guy. The data sprawled before them pointed to three primary suspects, but without visual confirmation from the cameras, it was like trying to find a needle in a haystack. All three rented a white Toyota RAV 4 and stayed at the hotel. The Brits and the German guy checked out this very morning; the Ukrainians did not.

"The Brits," Zhorik muttered, finger tracing their names on the list. "They're our best shot right now. They did not go to the airport as they listed a local address with the reception, so they must be residents of Cyprus or renting a place.".

Slavik was already on his feet, grabbing his keys. "I'm heading to the town of Polis then. If they have the suitcases, they won't be able to hide them that fast. It's been only two hours since they left."

As Slavik sped toward Polis, Zhorik focused on the German suspect working the phones. The information from Stelios, their great friend at the airport, was a cold shower – the German left Cyprus with only hand luggage. It was disappointing but a clear dead end.

***

In the serene coastal town of Polis, the sun cast a warm, golden glow over the quaint streets. The town, with its laid-back vibe and picturesque settings, was the last place anyone would associate with clandestine investigations. But for Slavik, it was just another day's work in the pursuit of a fortune in cash. He had parked his car a safe distance from the British couple's house, a charming villa sitting among lush gardens. With years of experience in surveillance, he blended into the surroundings like a shadow, his eyes sharp and observant. He watched the couple leave for the grocery store, their behavior casual and unburdened, the very picture of everyday normalcy.

Seizing the opportunity, Slavik moved with a predator's grace. He circled the property, scouting for any overlooked entry points. Finding an unlocked window at the back, he silently slipped inside, his movements as fluid as water.

The interior of the house spoke of a comfortable, ordinary life. Family photos adorned the walls, and a gentle breeze fluttered the curtains, bringing in the scent of the sea. Slavik's eyes, however, were fixed on the couple's luggage from their recent trip, casually left in the corner of their bedroom.

With methodical precision, Slavik examined each suitcase. He rifled through clothes, souvenirs, and the usual travel paraphernalia but found no trace of the cash. The ordinary contents of the bags screamed innocence. As he zipped the suitcase closed, a sense of frustration crept up on him. He then checked every single corner of the house, hoping to find the hidden suitcases. Finding nothing, he cursed. This was turning out to be a fruitless trip.

Stepping back into the sunlit street, Slavik watched from a distance as the couple returned, their arms laden with grocery bags. They laughed about something trivial, their laughter floating in the air like music. To Slavik, they looked like any other retired expats enjoying their golden years in Cyprus.

As he drove away from Polis, the town receding in his rear-view mirror, Slavik couldn't shake off the nagging feeling of hitting a dead end. But he wasn't one to give up easily. He made a mental note to revisit the couple if the elusive suitcases didn't surface soon. For now, though, the trail had grown cold, as cold as the shadows that were slowly creeping over the landscape with the setting sun.

***

Back in Paphos, Zhorik and Slavik regrouped, their energy waning but their determination still burning. They revisited the list of suspects again, and their next target became glaringly obvious—the Ukrainian couple.

Zhorik briefed Slavik with a tone of measured certainty, "While you were canvassing Polis, I gathered some intel. Our Ukrainian couple is still registered at the hotel, booked for another four days. What caught my attention, though, is the woman's habitual intoxication, according to the hotel staff. I've located their rental – a RAV 4 parked just one level below. Checked it inside out. Predictably, it was empty. Their room, 3775, hasn't offered much yet. I haven't seen them in the hotel. Looks like they are inside the room, possibly still drunk from last night. I had a word with the porter as well," Zhorik continued, detailing the conversation. "He couldn't recall the car plates; too preoccupied with his tasks, he operated on autopilot – saw the Toyota at the entrance, loaded the suitcases into the trunk, and moved on. He didn't remember seeing anyone near the car. There were guests in the lobby, sure, but he insisted the area around the car was deserted. He did recall loading the British couple's car, but theirs was parked here in the underground garage. As for that Toyota, he loaded our suitcases into, he never saw anyone drive away. His suspicion did flare up at some point, and he repeatedly hinted at getting the police involved. I downplayed the situation, assuring him it was merely personal items we were after, nothing valuable. I wanted to keep his concerns to a minimum."

Slavik's response carried a renewed vigor, "Alright, that narrows our focus for now. Time to check if the Ukrainians are our missing link to the cash. "And here's my take, Zhorik," he added with a note of caution, "We need to tread carefully with this suitcase situation at the hotel, especially considering our run-in last night during the police check. If this word reaches the cops, Nikolai will find himself in a world of trouble."

As the duo navigated the hotel's corridors, they stumbled upon the very couple they were discussing. Stepping out from room 3775, the pair strolled casually towards the pool area, blending into the mix of everyday tourists enjoying the hotel. Slavik immediately understood who he had had fun with but mentioned nothing to his partner.

***

Anton was back in his original hotel room. His wife lay sprawled on the bed, still snoring loudly, the empty condom wrapper peeking out from her shorts. Meanwhile, the RAV4 was safely stationed in the hotel's underground parking.

Unknown to Anton, at the same time he returned to the hotel, Slavik was conducting a discreet investigation of the British couple in Polis, and Zhorik, stationed one parking level above Anton's spot, was busy coordinating over the phone with Stelios, in an effort to track down the movements of the German tourist at the airport.

Anton sat on the killer couch he had slept on and thought through the possible scenarios. The idea that his car would be searched and he would eventually emerge as the prime suspect crossed his mind. It made his pulse quicken, but he forced calm upon himself.

Anton pieced together his conclusions: the main witness in the lost money situation was likely the porter, who must have had a role in the misplaced suitcases. There was a solid chance the porter recalled the car and its plate number and remembered encountering Anton near the hotel's entrance, a memory that could link him to the suitcases. However, with the surveillance cameras non-functional, it boiled down to mere speculation without concrete evidence. Anton also considered the possibility of unnoticed witnesses, a risk he had to acknowledge. The uncertainty of these variables made his decision-making and planning process difficult. Anton looked into the mindset of the individuals who had lost the money, attempting to blueprint their probable course of action. He envisioned them leveraging the porter's memory to pinpoint the specific car involved. They would likely check the guest registry, correlating car models with guest names and room numbers. Asking the receptionist about guests who checked out that day would be a logical step, as well as considering the possibility of monitoring the airport in case someone reported finding the suitcases.

The risks were immense, and the threat of lethal consequences loomed large. But a peculiar intuition whispered to him, suggesting the feasibility of his daring plan. He knew that the initial six hours upon his return to the hotel were critical. Each passing hour would edge him nearer to a triumph that felt increasingly within grasp despite the daunting odds stacked against him.

He planned to blend in, to wear normalcy like a cloak. If he could come across as just another tourist enjoying the Cypriot sun, maybe he could deflect suspicion. It was a gamble, but bluffing was all he had.

Anton played out the scenes in his mind. If the hotel staff, especially the porter, were to recognize him, he knew his response had to be of utter ignorance. Every gesture and every expression would have to radiate innocence. He rehearsed his reactions, perfecting a look of bewildered surprise, readying his mind to feign ignorance convincingly. The thought of a direct confrontation with those who owned the money sent a chill down his spine. He knew these were not the kind of people who played by any rules. Beneath this veneer of confidence and intuition, a gnawing doubt lingered. What if they didn't believe him? What if the porter had a photographic memory? Each 'what if' spiraled into a darker abyss, but he forced those thoughts away. He needed to focus to be ready for any anything.

With all the stealth of a self-trained operative, Anton tidied up the aftermath of his wife's drunken antics. The discarded condom wrapper had to be disposed of immediately. This was hardly the time for fresh scandals to erupt. After rousing from her sleep, his wife was taken out for a leisurely late lunch followed by a walk along the beach. Anton's motives were clear - he needed her out of their hotel room. With a sly grin, he ordered her a mojito, knowing full well the intoxicating effect it would have on her.

Back in their room, Anton displayed his technological prowess by setting up his laptop in a covert video recording mode, ingeniously concealed behind a paused pornographic movie. He expected those who lost the cash to search his room.

Mojito by mojito, his wife's spirits were lifted, and soon enough, the white wine flowed generously. Her merriment reached a crescendo, signaling it was time to retire to their room. Anton delayed their departure, his eyes glued to his iPhone, awaiting an important message.

When it finally arrived, Anton was taken aback. A seemingly innocuous link in his messenger app transformed into a live video feed from his hotel room. The timer on the recording indicated that it had been motion-activated just fifteen minutes prior, capturing a mere four minutes and twenty-three seconds of footage. What he witnessed on the screen sent shivers down his spine: two men conversing in fluent Moscow Russian. Professional hitmen, undoubtedly.

Maintaining an outward calm, Anton assisted his drunk wife back to their room and tucked her in. Now was the time for action. The video revealed the faces of both men, albeit one more clearly than the other. The man whose face was most visible had, predictably enough, glanced at the laptop screen.

Anton exited his room and surveyed the hallway. It was deserted. He made his way to the ground floor and into the bustling lobby. Sitting by the elevator exit was one of the men from the video. While his heart rate accelerated, Anton forced himself to proceed to the bar. Minutes later, he was comfortably seated in a plush chair, whiskey in hand, when the second man strolled in and took up a position in the corner of the bar. This vantage point gave him a clear view of Anton and the hotel's entrance.

Anton seized the moment and approached a table where two giggling girls were seated. In no time at all, he had ingratiated himself into their company. Shortly, a waiter arrived to take their order. The evening wore on, and eventually, the trio made their way to the elevator. As it turned out, the girls were staying on the same floor but in a different wing. Unable to follow them directly, the second man, Slavik, opted for the staircase and arrived just in time to see them disappear into a room.

"He can't be our man," Slavik reported to Zhorik upon his return. "He's off having fun while his wife's out cold. And she's no great catch either."

"How would you know?" Zhorik inquired, his brow furrowing in confusion.

"I had a go with her last night at the bar's restroom without knowing she was his wife. And then took her to my room for the next round. She was so plastered she was practically dead weight," Slavik revealed with a twisted smile on his lips.

"And you had her in the room with the money?" Zhorik questioned, his tone incredulous.

"Yep. But as you can see, nothing's come of it," Slavik responded unemotionally.

The two men, ex-operatives of the Federal Security Service of the Russian Federation, or FSB, were stretched thin regarding manpower. At present, their team was just the two of them. Their early leads with the Brits and the German guy brought zero results. They struggled to identify other credible suspects among the hotel guests apart from the Ukrainian couple. But even monitoring those two around the clock proved a logistical nightmare. Slavik returned home to catch up on some much-needed rest, leaving Zhorik to keep watch overnight. Help was on the way, as their boss had promised, but it would be at least two days before reinforcements arrived from Moscow.

***

Nestled in Coral Bay's ritzy Sea Caves area, Nikolai's grand villa was a symbol of opulence and exclusivity. Perched precariously atop a cliff, it overlooked the sparkling Mediterranean Sea, a view as breathtaking as the sheer audacity of the estate itself.

The villa sprawled over an impressive expanse, blending traditional Cypriot architecture with modern luxury. Its exterior, crafted from local stone, exuded a sense of timelessness, while the terracotta roof tiles added a splash of Mediterranean charm. Lavishly landscaped gardens embraced the property, bursting with native plants, fragrant herbs, and an array of vibrant flowers that seemed almost as carefully curated as Nikolai's bank accounts.

Stepping inside, one was greeted by a grand foyer that opened into a sunlit living area boasting high ceilings and large, arched windows. The natural light flooded in, illuminating the fine furnishings and pieces of art that seemed more at home in a museum than a residence. The interior decor was a masterclass in balancing elegance and comfort, with plush sofas, intricate fabrics, and chandeliers that whispered "money" with every glimmer.

The heart of the villa was its expansive kitchen, equipped with state-of-the-art appliances and finished with gleaming granite countertops. Designed mostly as a social hub, it featured a large island where guests could gather, sip wine, and marvel at their surroundings while meals were prepared by chefs who likely had Michelin stars to their names.

Each bedroom was a sanctuary of luxury, especially the master suite, which had a vast private balcony with a sea view that could make you forget all your worries—if you had any. The en-suite bathroom was a personal spa, complete with a Jacuzzi tub, a rainfall shower, and marble finishes so exquisite that they made the Mediterranean look second-rate.

The villa's outdoor area was nothing short of spectacular. A large infinity-edge swimming pool seemed to merge with the sea, creating a mesmerizing effect that screamed, "Look at what I've got!" Comfortable sun loungers and a gazebo offered perfect spots for enjoying the stunning sunsets.

Adjacent to the pool, an outdoor kitchen and dining area awaited al fresco meals and evening entertainment, perhaps featuring a private concert or two.

Not one to skimp on extravagance, Nikolai's villa also featured a private cinema room, a fully equipped gym, and a wine cellar that could make a sommelier weep with joy. High-tech security systems ensured that this fortress of solitude remained just that—a bastion of wealth and privacy, where every corner whispered tales of luxury and indulgence.

Nikolai's study, tucked away in a quiet corner of the villa, was a shrine to extravagant living.

Upon entering, the first thing that caught the eye was the imposing mahogany desk that dominated the room. Polished to a blinding shine, it bore the weight of numerous confidential meetings, a high-end laptop, and a collection of Montblanc pens aligned next to a leather-bound planner. The desk faced a large bay window that framed a picturesque view of the Sea Caves coastline, just in case the stress of wealth got too overwhelming.

Behind the desk, a floor-to-ceiling bookshelf showcased an extensive collection of books that were never read, existing only to impress visitors. The room was illuminated by a crystal chandelier hanging from the ornate ceiling, casting a warm glow over the Persian rug covering the hardwood floor. The rug's intricate patterns and rich colors added a touch of comfort because what's luxury without a little coziness?

To the side, a pair of leather armchairs flanked a small but exquisite coffee table made of inlaid wood. This was the spot for deep conversations or quiet contemplation, often accompanied by a glass of aged scotch from the crystal decanter on the table because nothing says "I'm pondering great thoughts" like expensive alcohol.

One of the most striking features of the study was a large, antique globe that stood in one corner, a gift from a friend to remind Nikolai of his global connections and ambitions. Nearby, a small but discreet safe was hidden behind a sliding panel, housing documents, and items of great value and confidentiality. They say that even in paradise, one needs a touch of secrecy.

The study's ambiance was one of power and contemplation. It was a place where Nikolai made his most critical decisions and formulated his most ambitious plans. It served as both a workspace and a personal museum, showcasing a life of success and the delightful absurdity of excess.

The golden morning light bathed Nikolai's study in warmth, contrasting its tense atmosphere. Zhorik, Slavik, and Nikolai gathered around the mahogany table, their heads bent in earnest discussion. The agenda was simple yet ominous – formulating a plot to capture and interrogate a Ukrainian man to uncover his connection to a missing sum of money. At the moment, they saw no other credible suspects.

Slavik was the first to break the silence. "I'm not entirely convinced how to proceed," he admitted. "Abducting and subjecting him to our methods of persuasion is no problem. But it's the aftermath that worries me. His disappearance will not go unnoticed, and it won't be long before the hotel staff reports our inquiries to the police. The trail will inevitably lead to the two of us with all our questions and bribing for the guest names, departure dates, cars rented, and, eventually, you, Nikolai, and your multitude of ventures. In my estimation, the risks far outweigh the benefits."

In a brooding tone, Zhorik added, "Unless, of course, we interrogate and then dispose of both him and his wife. That would buy us at least five to seven days before anyone earnestly searches for them. But, as Slavik rightly pointed out, there's a substantial risk of the police connecting the dots and unearthing our little operation here."

Nikolai leaned back in his chair, "You both raise valid points," he conceded. "The last thing I need is undue attention, especially with my last hotel purchase and our regular shipments to Omar. My public image as a respectable businessman and investor is of paramount importance. But let's remember, we're talking about eight million euros here. It's not a sum to be taken lightly. This time, it is my own money!"

Slavik shook his head, "Boss, we don't have concrete evidence linking this guy to the suitcases. He has been consistent with a man preoccupied with fucking around rather than someone trying to cover his tracks. Our investigation into his laptop revealed some rather...unconventional sex interests. Last night, for example, he was spotted in the company of two Serbian women."

Nikolai sighed, his frustration evident. "But if it wasn't him, who could it have been? Our list of suspects is dwindling by the minute. The Brits in the white RAV have been ruled out, which leaves us only with him as our prime suspect."

Zhorik hesitated before responding, "Well, not necessarily, boss. There's still a slim chance that a local—not even a hotel guest, but someone driving a similar vehicle—could have swooped in and made off with the money without even realizing it. The real tragedy here is that the hotel security cameras were out of order. A freak accident during the recent renovations damaged the wiring, which still hasn't been repaired. Otherwise, we would have had our man by now."

Nikolai swore under his breath, "Damn it, you're right. It could have been anyone. Keep your ears to the ground and your eyes peeled. We might catch a break."

With that, Nikolai rose and exited the room, leaving Zhorik and Slavik to plan their next moves.

Two days later, the Ukrainian couple, their belongings packed, departed the hotel under the watchful gaze of Slavik and Zhorik. They drove to Larnaca airport without stopping, returned their rented vehicle to Avis, checked in, and vanished into the terminal building.

***

Three days of frantic searching yielded no results. The suitcases had seemingly vanished. The atmosphere was thick with tension in Nicolai's camp, the sting of their misfortune – or rather, their monumental blunder – glaring. The hotel deal with Demetris was now in limbo, postponed for another two weeks until the subsequent influx of cash. Stelios was on the verge of a breakdown, his fee skyrocketing to thirty thousand euros. Finally, five million euros arrived on a different aircraft, and the deal was successfully concluded. However, the shadow of their loss loomed large over Nikolai's camp. Two weeks after the deal, Nikolai's spirits had lifted somewhat, although the loss continued to rankle. Losing such a staggering sum was not an everyday occurrence. Still, having faced severe setbacks on more than one occasion, Nikolai was slowly coming to terms with the long search for the cash ahead of him, with his mind idly speculating on the identity of the fortunate soul who had stumbled upon this windfall and planning an imminent revenge. He was never going to let it go. His mind was always busy recycling the events of those days in every possible detail, hoping to spot something they had overlooked.

Chapter 4

Zhorik and Slavik, who found themselves under explicit orders from Nikolai to continue their search, were doing their best.

Their efforts had been exhaustive. The search of the Ukrainian couple's room yielded nothing of note, just the usual tourist paraphernalia and an assortment of clothes. The only oddity was an open laptop perched on the bedside table with the computer screen frozen on a still from a pornographic film. Slavik threw a glance at the screen and immediately recoiled, his distaste evident. The contents were not to his liking; kinky sex was not his cup of tea.

Their surveillance of the Ukrainians continued for the next three days, both in and around the hotel. But they gleaned nothing of value from their efforts. The final chapter of their investigation saw them trailing the couple to the airport, where they observed them checking in with two small, brightly colored suitcases before boarding their flight. The RAV4, now empty of its occupants, was promptly returned to the rental office.

The duo convened in their Mercedes, stationed in the Larnaca airport parking lot, their gaze fixed on the departing Ukrainians.

"Alright, look," Slavik began with a speculative tone. "What if the suitcases ended up in that RAV, and these guys found them? What would they do?"

Zhorik contemplated the question for a moment before responding. "I'm not sure. One would need to find a suitable hiding spot for the suitcases. But where?"

Their exchange continued as they watched the Ukrainians disappear into the terminal.

"What would you do in their place?" Zhorik queried.

Slavik met Zhorik's gaze. "The same," he admitted. "I'd stash them in a new hotel room."

A simultaneous realization dawned upon them. Their focus needed to be better.

The next day, they canvassed all neighboring hotels in search of a possible trace of Anton and Natalia Gorin. They bribed receptionists and porters, all to no success. Their cover story, that of old friends on a quest to reunite with long-lost classmates, proved fruitless.

After three days of unproductive searching, they abandoned their quest. The cash story was effectively dead in the water.

***

At Nikolai's orders, the duo set their sights on Kyiv three weeks after the money disappeared, where they quickly tracked down Anton. The summer heat in Kyiv wrapped itself around the city like a shawl, its presence inescapable. In the heart of the seasonal charm, Slavik and Zhorik blended into everyday life with the ease that only seasoned operatives could muster. They cruised through the energetic cityscape, the air resonating with the faint rumbles of distant thunder, signaling the crescendo of summer.

Their target, an inconspicuous apartment building, was tucked between the lively banter of a street-side cafe and an old-fashioned bookstore, its windows a portal to literary worlds long past. The apartment's facade bore the gentle wear of time, even the names on the intercom had faded to near anonymity.

Slavik and Zhorik avoided the direct approach; surveillance was key. They bided their time, watching from a distance while sipping strong local coffee under the shade of a nearby cafe. Hours slipped by, and with the patience of seasoned hunters, they waited for the perfect moment.

When the dusk began to settle, and the streetlights flickered to life, they saw Anton leave his apartment with a gym bag. The duo slipped into the building with a group of laughing teenagers, invisible in their plainness. The staircase inside was a vertical labyrinth of sounds and smells, a neighborhood that hummed with intimate glimpses into residents' lives.

They found Anton's apartment and paused. With a practiced sleight of hand, Slavik silently forced the lock. The door yielded, and they stepped into Anton's modest world.

The apartment whispered of its occupant's existence: minimalist, functional, nothing in excess. Modest lighting illuminated an old, worn desk with an equally worn laptop—a quiet reflection of a life turned inward. Beside it sat a half-empty mug, the steam long gone from its once-hot surface.

Slavik's eyes swept the room, taking in the spartan furnishings that lacked any personal touch. Anton had stripped away the trappings of his past, now immersed in the binary simplicity of code and screen. Meanwhile, Zhorik checked the modest kitchen, finding only the bare essentials for a simple life.

"Seems she's departed," Slavik remarked, alluding to Anton's wife, Natalia. "There's no trace of a woman's touch here."

"Agreed," Zhorik replied as he inspected the cupboards and closets for any remnants of her presence.

The evidence of a life interruption hung in the air – it was clear Anton lived alone with his wife gone. They left as discreetly as they'd arrived. The apartment gave up no protest as they closed the door, re-engaging the lock with a whisper.

As the men slipped into the deepening dusk, the insights they had gathered offered no leads on the whereabouts of the elusive suitcases or any confirmation that the Ukrainians were indeed suspects.

As for Anton's almost ex-wife, they stumbled upon her later that evening. The bar was a splash of neon in the soft twilight, with music spilling out onto the streets. Inside, they found her, laughter bubbling from her lips with the carefree abandon only strong spirits can provide. Her companion, an old university friend judging by their familiarity, seemed a grounding presence, perhaps a reminder of who she used to be before the turbulence of her marriage.

Slavik and Zhorik watched and listened, absorbing the scene. Her behavior suggested she was oblivious to any knowledge about the money, strengthening their belief that this couple might have been the wrong suspects. Slavik promptly dismissed any thoughts of rekindling their past encounter; she was even further removed from the woman he had met at that bar in the Cyprus hotel.

.A week passed as they completed their observations, finding no sign of unexpected wealth or unusual behavior.

In the cool shade of an old linden tree, Slavik dialed the number that connected them to the world of Nikolai's interests. Zhorik listened intently, leaning against the car, cigarette smoke curling into the dimming light of Kyiv's skyline.

The phone buzzed and crackled slightly as the connection was made, Nikolai's voice came through as cold and expectant as they remembered.

"Report," came the curt command from the other end.

Slavik put him on speaker and cleared his throat, "We've found Anton. He's living a modest life, holed up in an apartment as plain as day. Spends his hours behind a screen, coding for a local IT firm."

There was a pause on the line, then Nikolai asked, "And the wife?"

"That's a story dipped in vodka," Zhorik chimed in, "She's unraveling at the seams, drowning her days in a bar, living it up with some old college flame."

"The picture of marital bliss they are not," Slavik added, a touch of irony not lost in his tone.

Nikolai's response was a low chuckle devoid of any real humor. "And our money? Any trace of it?"

"Not a shadow, not a scent," Zhorik replied, flicking the butt of his cigarette into the twilight.

"Then we should keep digging in every direction, including double-checking on the Brits, the German guy, and others," Nikolai instructed.

The line went silent for a heartbeat before Nikolai's voice cut through again, this time with a calculated edge. "But let's imagine it was, in fact, Anton. He might have played the long game here. If he took the money, he knows he can't move it over the border without someone's help in Cyprus. Then, the cash must somehow find its way into a bank account to be accessible outside the country. It's all too risky for him. It must be stashed somewhere in Cyprus."

Slavik nodded, though Nikolai couldn't see it. "So, you think he'll head to Cyprus eventually?"

"He must. It's the logical step," Nikolai mused. "He'll try to slip through the cracks and make it to Cyprus. And when he does, he'll go for the cash."

Zhorik squinted into the distance, gears turning in his head. "Hold on. If he did hide the cash, the question is where. What would you do, Nikolai?"

Nikolai pondered for a moment. "I've given this a lot of thought and came up with two likely scenarios: one, a public storage facility; two, a rental property. But I've already checked with my police contacts, and there's no official paperwork for anything tied to Anton Gorin. Then again, this is Cyprus. Things can be done discreetly for cash."

Zhorik and Slavik absorbed the information. "So, we wait for him to make a move?" Zhorik asked.

"Exactly. Keep an eye on him. The moment he books a flight to Larnaca, Paphos—anywhere in Cyprus or Europe—we'll know he is heading to retrieve the money." There was a sharpness to Nikolai's voice, a predator's focus. "That's when we close in."

"And if he sends someone else instead?" Slavik asked.

"I don't think he will. Legally, one can only take ten grand out of the country in cash. Imagine how much time you would need to move a decent amount and how many flights you would have to take. Plus, there is a huge issue of trust here involving someone." Nikolai's tone left no room for doubt. "Patience and vigilance are the virtues that will recover my fortune."

The call ended, leaving Slavik and Zhorik with renewed purpose. They would watch Anton with the relentless gaze of hawks circling high above their prey, waiting to swoop down and reclaim what had been lost. The next day, they enrolled a few shadowy local guys who would keep an eye on Anton 24/7 and report back to them.

Chapter 5

Desolation clung to Olga like a shroud. The constant waiting for Nikolai's return from his ongoing journeys, the routine obligatory intimacy that marked his homecomings, and the monotony of her existence in their small local world had all become insufferable. Her days revolved around their daughter Christine's school life and dance classes. Personal fulfillment eluded her - spas and sandy beaches, gourmet meals and gossipy gatherings with girlfriends, strolls along the seafront – none brought her joy anymore.

Each morning, Olga would rise with the dawn to prepare breakfast for Christine and then drive her to school. She preferred the solace of their car rides to the services of Nikolai's family chauffeur, Roman. It allowed for mother and daughter to bond. Olga was able to inquire about her daughter's friendships, academic responsibilities, and the myriad of small joys and sorrows that made up Christine's school life. Olga wanted to be an involved, supportive parent, just as her own had been during her upbringing in Odessa.

Born into a Jewish-Ukrainian family in southern Ukraine, Olga's childhood was marked by poverty and struggle. Her parents, however, had been a constant source of love and support. The collapse of the Soviet Union had brought about a seismic shift in their world, thrusting the family into a dire financial situation. When a dubious local modeling agency extended an offer, she seized the opportunity with both hands, a decision that would set her on a path of untold pain and suffering. From modeling gigs at mafia gatherings to the seedy underbelly of the escort world, Olga's life had spiraled out of control until she fled to Moscow, leaving it all behind.

In Moscow, she found employment as a housemaid, saving enough to return to Odessa and enroll at the university. Each summer, she would return to Moscow, working for the same family to support herself. Upon graduation, her beauty and charisma landed her a job at the port of Odessa, where she soon found herself the object of attention from numerous suitors.

And then came Nikolai. Their paths crossed one fateful summer night at a swanky nightclub in Moscow, and she was swept off her feet by his wealth and persistence. In the following years, she would realize the hollowness of her feelings for him. She respected him, admired him even, but love – that was something that eluded her. By then, however, Christine had come into their lives, and Olga embraced motherhood with all her might.

Relocated to Cyprus as per Nikolai's wish, she found herself in a new chapter of her life that today seemed to be taking a turbulent turn. Recently, Nikolai was anxious, his mood dark and stormy. Olga suspected his hotel venture was on the brink of collapse. Little did she know, the winds of change were gathering, ready to sweep her into a vortex that would challenge the very foundation of her world.

Olga's bond with her daughter, Christine, was the anchor that kept her grounded. But even that was not enough to fill the emptiness that had opened in Olga's life. She missed the connection with her family back in Ukraine and longed for the close-knit community she had grown up in. In Cyprus, she had tried to build a network of friends, but the relationships felt superficial and transactional.

There was Elena, a Russian woman she met at a local spa. She had a similar background and understood the difficulties of adjusting to life in a new country. They often met for coffee and long walks along the beach, sharing stories from their past and venting their frustrations. And then there was Karen, a single parent of Christine's classmate, a British woman who had embraced Olga with open arms, introducing her to local life.

While Olga's childhood had been marked by poverty, she had always been surrounded by love and warmth, qualities that were now missing from her life. When she met Nikolai, she became entranced by his glittering world of wealth and glamour. His status, connections, and willingness to provide her with everything she desired blinded her to the realities of their relationship.

But as time passed and the initial allure faded, Olga questioned the basis of her choice. Was it genuinely love that had drawn her to Nikolai, or had she been swayed by the material comforts he could provide? He proved to be a bad husband and, to Olga's huge disappointment, a lousy father. She had to secretly admit that she had never truly loved him, not in the way she had imagined love to be. She recalled their last conversation, and it made her feel unhappy. She vividly imagined the events of that night, almost a year ago, when she saw Nikolai watching the glittering skyline of Paphos from the balcony of their villa, a glass of aged scotch in hand, seemingly lost in his thoughts. Olga stood in the doorway, the silk of her evening gown whispering against the marble floor as she moved closer.

"Another late night?" she asked, her voice a mix of wistfulness and reproach.

He turned, offering her a practiced smile that never reached his eyes. "Just tying up loose ends, my dear. The life of a businessman never rests."

Olga leaned against the metal railings of the balcony, her expression gloomy. "And what of the life of his wife? Is she just supposed to wait around?"

Nikolai's face stiffened, the softness forced. "Olga, you have everything you could ever want. What is there to be unhappy about?"

"Everything," she murmured, looking out over the city. "Everything and nothing. You treat me like I'm another of your possessions, Nikolai. A prize you've won."

"That's not true," he countered swiftly, yet the conviction wasn't there. "You're my partner."

"A partner?" Olga laughed, but there was no humor in it. "I'm the face you need at social events, the arm candy to your successful I. When did you last ask about my day, my hopes, or even how I feel? You think about me only when your testosterone level increases."

Nikolai frowned, unaccustomed to this line of questioning. "Olga, this empire I'm building, it's for us."

"For us, or you?" she challenged. "You live in a world of under-the-table deals and deceit, Nikolai, and I'm just another deal. The one you've already closed."

He stepped toward her, but she halted him with an upheld hand, a barrier as firm as her resolve. "I married a man I believed I understood, a man I thought I knew," Olga's voice trembled with emotions. "But that man is as absent as the warmth in your touch. I am more than an object of sexual desire, Nikolai. I refuse to be treated as a mere instrument of your pleasure! It's not your wealth I'd been after. It was the dream of a normal, loving family! The dream that never came true." Her words, laden with frustration and a deep sense of betrayal, echoed in the tension-filled room.

"Olga, you're talking nonsense," Nikolai said, his voice low, an edge creeping in.

"Am I?" She looked into his eyes, searching for the man she once believed in. "Sometimes I wonder if you even know me at all."

With that, Olga turned and walked away, her heart heavy. Nikolai watched her go, the ice in his glass cracking under the pressure of his grip, a metaphor for their crumbling marriage. Under his breath, he muttered a vicious, "Ungrateful bitch," his words steeped in scorn. Then, with a swift, bitter motion, he drained his glass of whiskey in one burning gulp. Deep down, he realized she was telling the truth. He knew that he would not be distracted from his underworld activities by her or even Christine. The thirst for money and power was way more significant than some pretty face of a wife or a family. It was true that what Nikolai cared for was having a prize, a beautiful woman nearby who turned heads and sparked envy in his social circles. And pleased him sexually, of course. The fleeting idea of forcing her into sex momentarily flickered in his mind, but it was abruptly swept aside as his phone rang. Glancing at the caller ID, he instantly knew he should postpone the punishment of this wife for later.

***

Eleven months passed, and Olga's mind remained in constant turmoil as she grappled with conflicting emotions. She knew she had to make a choice: accept the confines of her life in Cyprus, be treated like a highly paid slave, and somehow find a way to make peace with herself or take a stand and fight for the life she truly desired—a life where she was free to make her own choices and follow her heart.

Now, with Christine in the picture, her feelings of entrapment grew even stronger. She yearned for Christine to experience a childhood filled with genuine affection and support, not to grow up in the shadow of a loveless marriage where her mother was a trophy wife, subjected to the whims of a husband who saw intimacy as an obligatory service.

But taking a stand meant confronting the truth about her feelings for Nikolai. It meant risking everything she had built over the years, the stability and security that had once seemed so appealing. It was a daunting prospect, and Olga was still determining if she had the strength to face it head-on. She was genuinely scared of Nikolai and what he would do to her should she try to get out of the marriage.

It was on the day of Nikolai's return from his long trip to Moscow when she found herself dreading his return. The very thought of him claiming her body again as his right was now insufferable. The idea of enduring his forceful advances, a ritual that marked every homecoming, filled her with an overwhelming sense of despair and repulsion.

***

The sun had already dipped below the horizon, leaving a cascade of brilliant oranges and purples painted across the sky. Olga stood next to the window, watching Nikolai disappear into the evening shadows, a lit cigarette glowing in his hand. As she watched him go, a solitary tear, heavy with salt and sorrow, traced a slow path down her cheek. She felt a familiar sensation of being exploited, reduced to nothing more than a paid escort. The humiliation and heartache washed over her, leaving behind a deep hollowness that seemed to echo through the silent rooms of the opulent house.

She turned back towards the bedroom, feeling anger within her. As she sank onto the bed, the scent of Nikolai lingered in the air, a reminder of the unwanted intimacy they had just shared. Deep within the emptiness that had become her life, Olga felt the stirrings of change. It was like a subtle, creeping sensation weaving its way toward her heart. The path ahead was uncertain, but she knew she had the strength and courage to face whatever came her way.

She had faced adversity before and had become more resilient. She knew she could do it again. That was the night Olga decided to end her marriage.

***

Two days after Nikolai's return from his trip to Moscow, almost in the middle of the night, Olga went to the kitchen to pick up a water bottle when she heard voices. She stood silently in the corridor, her heart racing as she strained to listen to the conversation emanating from the study.

"I don't care what it takes, Zhorik. Just find them and get the money back!"

Olga edged closer to the study, her bare feet making no sound on the plush carpet. She pressed herself against the wall, holding her breath as she tried to catch every word.

"Nikolai, we've been at it full-time. These suitcases are like ghosts. They've vanished into thin air," Zhorik responded, his voice strained.

"I don't want excuses, Zhorik. I want results. That money is important. I won't let it slip through my fingers. If we need to snatch, interrogate, cut someone's fingers off, or even kill them, so be it. I need that money back! Nobody steals from me!" Nikolai said, his voice rising with anger.

Olga felt a shiver of fear run down her spine. She had never heard Nikolai speak like this before. His usual calm and composed manner had been replaced by a raw, primal rage that sent chills through her body.

She waited until the conversation ended before quietly retreating to her room. She closed the door softly behind her and leaned against it, her mind whirling.

What had just happened? What was this money that Nikolai was so desperate to retrieve? And who were these people that had taken it?

Olga knew Nikolai was involved in shady business dealings, but she had always tried to remove herself from that part of his life. She had convinced herself that if she didn't know the details, she could pretend it wasn't happening.

But now, she realized that she couldn't ignore it any longer. The shadows hovering at the edges of her life suddenly crept in, threatening to engulf her in darkness.

She couldn't sleep that night until the early morning hours, and when she got out of bed with a determined set to her jaw, she picked up her phone and dialed a number:

"Karen, it's Olga. We need to talk."

Chapter 6

The emptiness of the Kyiv apartment felt oppressive as Anton and Natalia Gorin unpacked the remnants of their Cyprus misadventure. This morning's light, which usually bathed the room in a warm glow, seemed to cast a pall over the couple. It had been two days since they landed home, two days filled with silence broken only by the clink of Natalia's bottle against her glass.

Anton watched her, his mind restless, churning with memories of the money, the tension of their escape, and the realization that the woman he had married was now a stranger, eroded by her vices.

"I can't do this anymore," Anton finally said, the words slicing the silence like a shard of glass.

Natalia looked up; her eyes bloodshot but lucid for the first time in days. "Do what?" Her voice was a hoarse whisper.

"This," he gestured around, "Living with... with this constant drinking. I don't recognize you, Natalia. And after what happened in Cyprus…"

She scoffed, a bitter sound, "You're blaming me for Cyprus? It was your stupid idea to go there in the first place!"

Anton's hands clenched into fists, his nails digging into his palms, a physical attempt to hold back the torrent of his frustration. "No, I am not blaming you. But I need you to be present, not just... not like this."

Her eyes flared with a defiant spark. "Maybe I wouldn't need the drink if I had a husband who—"

"Who what, Natalia?" His voice rose, "Who tried to keep you from drinking yourself into an early grave?"

"No! Who would be willing to share my active life, see new places, take me to theaters, take me to a fucking Paris, not Cyprus, and bring some excitement into my world... Not just this fucking screen and a fucking code." She gestured toward Anton's desk.

Anton stood there speechless. The words hung between them, heavy with truth and regret. He realized they saw the world differently. What he viewed as calm and stable, she saw as uneventful and dull. His preference for tranquility and stability clashed with her desire for excitement and nightlife. Anton's unwillingness to be her late-night companion in bars, pubs, and nightclubs had created a gap between them. He knew it had to end now.

A tear slipped down Natalia's cheek, carving a path through the makeup she hadn't bothered to refresh. "I'm going to stay with Lena," she murmured, referring to her old university friend.

Anton nodded, his decision settling in his heart, heavy and irrevocable. Hours after Natalia's departure, he sat alone, the echo of their parting conversation lingering. He regretted the years spent in this marriage. There had been love at the beginning, but it was long gone. Now, the burden was lifted from his shoulders, and he felt like a new chapter of his life had begun.

***

Anton's mind wandered to the rented apartment in Paphos, where he had stashed the cash. He replayed the memory in his mind, every detail crisp and clear as if to reassure himself that the money was safe.

The move had been a blur—a careful operation. He waited until Natalia, intoxicated and oblivious, passed out. Anton knew the men from the video were watching the hotel, but they hadn't watched him closely enough. The night before, he had agreed with the Serbian girls to borrow their car under the guise that his rental had a flat tire. In the pre-dawn light, he slipped through the back door to the underground parking lot, found the car, and drove to a neighboring hotel where he had hidden the suitcases. One by one, he loaded them into the trunk and headed to the address of an apartment he found online and arranged to view. The apartment had been his last act in Cyprus, a two-bedroom flat with a view of nothing but the backs of other buildings.

The Aquamare Beach Hotel had been a temporary vault for the cash—a risk too significant to linger. Anton knew he had to move it, but his options were few. He couldn't deposit it in a bank or use a safety deposit box without triggering inquiries he wasn't prepared to answer. The money needed to disappear, and renting an apartment seemed the only viable but risky solution.

He had scrolled through dozens of online listings before finding a modest apartment advertised for a quick cash rental. The ad was terse, with no flowery language or enticing photographs, just a promise of privacy and no prying questions. It looked perfect.

The landlord, Mrs. Theodora Georgiou, was a woman who carried an air of having seen it all. She wore her skepticism like a second skin, and it was clear she wasn't interested in the stories of her tenants if the rent was paid. Anton called her from a burner phone, his voice steady as he arranged a meeting.

"I need the place for a year, maybe longer," Anton said when Mrs. Georgiou closed the door and let him inside. She sized him up with a practiced eye. She was certain she saw another illegal worker before her, as she had seen many.

"I understand you are going to be working in Cyprus illegally to make some money," she said, "but still, a year's rent, upfront, in cash," she stated, with her arms folded across her chest.

"That's not a problem," Anton assured her, patting the briefcase that never left his side. "I value my privacy."

Mrs. Georgiou nodded, understanding the subtext. "No papers, no names. I see you; I forget you, you forget me," she said bluntly. "This is not a hotel. No cleaning service. No maintenance. You take it as it is."

The apartment was on the third floor of a run-down old building, the hallway outside smelling faintly of fried food and cleaning agents. It was a time capsule of faded wallpaper and linoleum floors, furnished with mismatched chairs and a couch that had seen better days. But it had a solid lock on the door and windows overlooking a quiet back alley.

"It's perfect," Anton said, not because it was, but because it had to be.

"The money," Mrs. Georgiou extended a hand, palm up. Anton opened the briefcase just enough for her to glimpse the stacks of cash inside. He counted out the year's rent, which amounted to twelve thousand euros, and added another thousand on top, feeling the weight of each bill in his hand.

Mrs. Georgiou didn't count it. She just stuffed it into her apron pocket. "Since we have no paperwork, I will need a deposit for all communal charges," she said calmly. Anton got another two grand from the briefcase, which sealed the deal.

He watched her leave, the keys now in his possession. Once she was gone, he allowed himself a moment to breathe, to feel the risk he was taking. The apartment was no fortress. Anyone could break in.

Anton locked the door and scanned the simple setup: two bedrooms, each with a plain but sturdy bed. His mind was a whirlwind of calculations and risks, each scenario playing out its potential disasters. The cash had to be hidden where no casual search would reveal it and where even a more thorough inspection might overlook it. Anton went to the nearest DIY shop and was back in less than fifteen minutes with some tools he thought might be helpful.

He set the suitcases on the floor and unzipped them slowly. The bills seemed to whisper as they shifted, a soft rustle of paper that was now his life's soundtrack. The mattresses were his best option—familiar enough to be ignored yet intimate enough that few would think to probe deeply.

Starting with the first bedroom, he carefully sliced open the stitching at one end of the mattress with a small knife he'd purchased. The incision was just wide enough to allow him to feed the stacks of bills into the innards of the mattress, placing them flatly not to create a noticeable bulge. He pushed the bundles deep inside, spreading them out to distribute the volume evenly. Once the mattress was stuffed to his satisfaction, he used a basic sewing kit to close the opening, ensuring his stitches were as invisible as possible.

He repeated the process with the second mattress, once again ensuring the distribution so it retained its standard shape and wouldn't betray the secret it now held. Once finished, Anton dressed the beds with sheets and blankets, the patterns of the fabric offering the last veil of disguise for the wealth they concealed.

With the suitcases now empty, Anton had to eliminate them. Simply throwing them away was too risky — they could draw attention and potentially lead someone back to the apartment. He decided to dismantle them. He removed the frames using a screwdriver, separating the panels and the extending handles. He then cut the fabric and lining into smaller pieces, removing any tags or distinctive marks. Disposing of the suitcase parts required several trips to different parts of the town. He dropped small amounts into various bins and waste collections to avoid drawing attention.

Once he had taken care of the suitcase remnants, Anton came back to the small apartment. The money was as well-hidden as he could manage. Now, he could only hope that the seams of the mattresses held as tightly as the secrets they contained. He switched off the mains at the electricity box, cut off the water supply at the water meter, locked the door, and left.

***

Sitting alone in his Kyiv apartment, Anton's memories of Cyprus and the feel of the cash were still vivid in his mind. He had managed to hide the cash, but the most challenging part was still ahead. He was a wealthy man now; the only problem was actually getting his hands on the cash and moving it out of Cyprus. A titanic task, indeed.

The sense of being watched was his constant companion, a shadow that loomed at every corner. Walking to work, he couldn't shake off the feeling of eyes tracking his every move. He noticed unfamiliar faces that seemed more interested in him than in their surroundings. Near his apartment block, a car that never used to be there sat idly, its occupants obscured but ever-present.

At his office building, he'd catch glimpses of strangers loitering nearby, their gazes following him as he moved past the windows. They were subtle, but they stood out to Anton's observing eye. They were too still, too focused, and their presence was too consistent to be coincidental.

Paranoia, some might say, but Anton knew better. This was the reality of someone who had crossed a dangerous line. Every shadow held a threat, every stranger was a potential enemy.

He realized that his every step must be calculated, his every decision weighed with the utmost care. The watchers were waiting for a mistake.

He pulled a well-thumbed copy of John Grisham's "The Partner" from the bookshelf and sat in his well-worn armchair. It wasn't just his favorite novel. It was a manual, a source of inspiration. Like the protagonist in the book, Anton knew he had to die—at least in the eyes of the world. He had to craft a new identity as carefully as an author creates a character that could withstand scrutiny and doubt.

Anton realized that sudden changes to his appearance might be a dead giveaway of his intent to disappear. His every move could already be under scrutiny, and anything out of the ordinary would raise immediate red flags. Night after night, he sat in his quiet apartment, his mind racing. He knew he had to move carefully and craft a plan so unassuming yet ingenious that he could vanish without a trace.

Anton felt a strange mix of exhilaration and dread as he pored over maps and timetables. The prospect of starting anew, free from his past and the looming threat, fueled his resolve. He knew his window of opportunity would be narrow, and when it came, he had to be ready to step through it into a new life, leaving Anton Gorin far behind.

Chapter 7

Alexa Marou was in the office, methodically scanning the latest reports on the Border Custom scheme that had landed with a thud on her desk. Her reputation as a relentless pursuer of justice in the Cyprus Police's Criminal Investigation Division preceded her, and for good reason. Her academic pedigree was impressive—a law degree from the University of Athens and a master's from the University of Nottingham—but it was her razor-sharp intuition and integrity that made her the bane of criminals across the island.

Alexa stood out in any room, not just for her beauty but also for the quiet confidence that wrapped around her like a cape. In her early thirties, she bore the hallmarks of her Hellenic heritage and the rigorous discipline of her profession. Her features were a striking blend of classic Mediterranean charm and the delicate finesse of ancient Greek sculptures. Her almond-shaped eyes, a rich shade of mahogany, seemed to pierce through the most intricate covers, discerning truths that lay beneath. A cascade of dark chestnut hair framed her face, often pulled back into a no-nonsense ponytail while on duty.

Her soft olive complexion spoke of generations thriving under the Cypriot sun, complemented by a personality as radiant as the Paphos lighthouse at sundown. Standing at an imposing height, she moved with an almost cat-like elegance, indicating the many hours spent in physical training and martial arts, disciplines she eagerly embraced for her job.

Despite her allure, her intellect intimidated those who underestimated her based on looks alone. As well as graduating from one of Europe's premier universities, Alexa was fluent in Turkish, and English, indicative of the island's complex heritage and her commitment to bridging divides. Her quick wit and comprehensive knowledge of cybercrime were assets that had fast-tracked her career, earning the respect of her colleagues and a reputation amongst the criminal underbelly of Cyprus.

Single by choice, her dedication to her job was not for lack of suitors but rather a deliberate focus on ambition and the drive to make a difference in a landscape often marred by corruption and clandestine affairs. She saw herself as a defender of her island's integrity, a modern-day warrior in a long lineage of formidable Cypriot women who had shaped their destiny through the ages.

Alexa's background was as colorful as the streets of Limassol during the carnival. Daughter to a respected judge and a renowned local artist, she grew up in a household where justice was discussed with the same passion as art. Weekends were spent between courtrooms and galleries, instilling in her a profound understanding of the human condition and the complexities of society. This upbringing forged within her the unshakeable belief that everyone had a story and that, often, the line between right and wrong was as intricate as the filigree patterns on traditional Cypriot silverwork.

Sitting at her desk, Alexa's attention was fixed on the printout of the anonymous call that had initiated the quietly kept investigation into the officer of Cyprus Border Control, Mr. Stelios Georgiou. Her fingers traced the lines of text as she played the tape recording once again, the voice echoing through her office. This wasn't a simple tip-off; it had a personal element. The caller's voice carried a tinge of bitterness, an underlying current of frustration and passion. After a few days of her investigation efforts, Alexa knew who had made that call. She decided to keep it to herself, understanding the sensitivity and potential danger of revealing the informant's identity prematurely to anyone, even her boss.

Her focus returned to the task at hand. Stelios Georgiou, a Border Control Officer with an unblemished record, was now at the center of a potentially huge scandal. If true, the allegations painted a picture of corruption and conspiracy at a high level.

Alexa's office door clicked open, and in walked her boss, Inspector Demetris Savvas, a grizzled veteran of the force whose instincts were as honed as his investigative skills.

"Alexa," Inspector Savvas began, "I've been hearing whispers about Nikolai Gromov's recent antics. Sources confirmed your initial information that his men were up to no good in that hotel. Witnesses saw suitcases—enough to fill a cargo plane—shuffled around like a shell game. And the story about his swimming gear..." He let out a skeptical chuckle. "My feeling is that something strange was going on. Surely, they brought some stuff with that plane, and we missed it. What do you make of all this?"

Alexa leaned forward; her eyes locked with her boss's. "I've dug into it. The hotel staff were more than willing to talk after a little... persuasion. Gromov's men were throwing money around like confetti at a parade. They wanted guest lists and asked for security camera access, offering the manager a grand. The security cameras' wiring had been damaged and not repaired yet, so the manager had nothing to offer. It's more than a little odd—it's suspicious. I can't figure out how and why they ended up in that hotel in the first place. One of them booked a room and stayed for the night. He did have three items of personal luggage, according to my sources. Mind you, when I stopped Nikolai's car in Coral Bay that night, his luggage was full of that swimming gear."

Savvas nodded slowly, his look puzzled. "I was wondering if there is a way to get into Nikolai's inner circle to get some information on what is happening. Olga, Gromov's wife, is living in a luxury villa here while he's running around the world with his schemes. I doubt she's clueless about her husband's businesses."

Alexa's mind flickered to Olga, the enigmatic wife of Nikolai. She had a hunch that beneath the life of luxury and indifference, a well of information might be waiting to be tapped.

"I think it's time we bring Olga Gromova into the fold discreetly. See if she's willing to play ball, or at least if she'll slip up and give us something to go on," Savvas suggested, his eyes narrowing.

"Understood. I'll approach her carefully. If there's anything to find, I'll find it."

"Good. But Alexa," Savvas paused, his expression hardening, "this case is a ticking time bomb. Gromov's connected—politically and financially. Who knows how deep it goes? Be careful."

Alexa Marou knew that Nikolai Gromov's operations extended far beyond the shady dealings in his new hotel. The cash flowing through these schemes had to come out clean on the other side, and Cyprus, with its sun-kissed shores and murky financial waters, was the perfect place for money laundering.

"Alexa," Savvas continued, his tone a mixture of caution and urgency. We need to unravel this thread by thread. If our suspicions are correct, this goes beyond Gromov. He's just the tip of the iceberg. We're looking at potential complicity in our own backyard—government officials, bankers, auditors, and who not. And if the right palms have been greased, we'll find the residue."

Nodding, Alexa had already begun formulating a plan. She would start with the low-hanging fruit—the conspicuous accountants and the too-flexible bankers. A discreet inquiry here, a careful conversation there. Each interaction would be a delicate probe into the murky depths of corruption.

And then there was Olga. She could be the key to unlocking the vault of secrets her husband held. If Alexa could gain her trust, perhaps Olga would unknowingly divulge the needed evidence to bring down Nikolai and the entire syndicate that enabled him and the others like him.

But trust was a currency in short supply, and Alexa knew that to earn it, she'd have to offer something in return.

She thought about her boss's warning: "Be careful." Those words echoed in her mind, reminding her that the stakes were higher than ever. She began to map out the network they suspected—officials who turned a blind eye, accountants who cooked the books with gourmet precision, auditors who 'audited' with their hands tied, and bankers who dealt in numbers that never quite added up.

The connections were like a spiderweb, each strand linked to the next. It was an intricate dance of crime and conspiracy, where the illegal became legal through property purchases, business investments, and the sudden display of wealth that didn't match declared incomes.

She knew one wrong move could destroy the whole operation and her career. Cyprus Government, heavily influenced by long and passionate ties with the old Soviet Union from decades of Communist regime and a more recent overwhelming influx of Russian money pouring into the local banking system, was not very tolerable to investigations into the prominent Russians living on the island. Typically, the Russians would immediately complain through their sources, and the ambassador would call the Presidential Palace and start bickering, eventually triggering the flow of advice trickling from the top down to an investigating officer with a warm but persistent suggestion to drop it. But not with Alexa.

As Inspector Savvas left the room, Alexa turned to the mountain of evidence on her desk. The puzzle pieces were scattered and elusive, but she was determined to assemble them.

***

Olga and Karen sat opposite each other at a table in the corner of the quaint café they'd come to call their own. The soft clinking of porcelain and the murmur of other guests created a bubble of privacy in the otherwise open space.

Karen Winters had that quintessentially British aura about her, a blend of approachability and an undercurrent of resilience from years of solo navigation through life's unexpected turns. Her move to Cyprus had been a fresh start, one marked by the Mediterranean sun's warmth rather than the UK's cool drizzles.

In her mid-thirties, Karen carried herself with the composure of someone who had found balance in the chaos of single motherhood. Her hair was a tapestry of light brown hues, often pulled back into a practical ponytail, a few strands deliberately escaping to frame her empathetic face. Her eyes, a clear sky blue, reflected a mind constantly at work, solving problems with the same deftness she employed in unraveling complex mathematical equations.

Teaching math at the local international school, Karen had a knack for making numbers come alive, weaving them into stories that captivated her young audience. Her lessons were more than math; they were life skills, something she hoped would benefit her students. She was slender, her posture hinting at a time when ballet classes were a fixture in her schedule, now replaced by the playful chases after her daughter and her friend Christine. The children's friendship had been the reason for Karen and Olga's bond—a shared understanding of motherhood's trials knitting them together.

Karen's style was a fusion of comfort and classic English elegance, favoring soft cardigans and intelligent, crisp trousers. A lover of literature, she could often be found with a well-thumbed novel peeking from her bag, ready to steal moments to indulge in her passion for the written word.

"So, what's on your mind, Olga?" Karen inquired, her voice laced with a comforting British lilt. "You seem more... contemplative than usual."

Olga took a deep breath, the kind that seemed to pull from the depths of her soul. "Karen, I've been doing a lot of thinking lately," she began, her voice a whisper. "I've realized something quite disturbing about my marriage... I don't think I've ever truly loved Nikolai. It was all about the escape, the wealth, the security it represented from a childhood filled with none."

Karen's gaze held steady, a pillar of support. "It takes courage to admit that, Olga. To oneself, most of all. What brought you to this realization?"

"It's not just that," Olga continued, her voice gaining strength. "It's his dealings, the secrets. I've overheard conversations, Karen. Dangerous ones, with people who... who are not just businessmen. They're... I don't know, but they scare me."

Karen reached across the table, placing her hand over Olga's. "Talk to me, love. If there's anything this old soul has learned, it's that a problem shared is a problem halved."

Olga's eyes met Karen's—there was fear there, and vulnerability. "I suspect he's involved in dark, criminal things. And I... I'm lost, Karen. I feel like I'm living with a stranger, and his world is so foreign to me."

"There's a strength in you, Olga. I've seen it. You're a survivor," Karen said firmly. "But this—this is about your safety and your child's. Have you thought about what you want to do about it?"

"I want to be free of this life filled with crime and shadows. But the fear of what he might do, or what could happen if these people he's involved with think I'm a liability..." Olga's voice trailed off, and she took a shaky sip of her coffee.

Karen nodded slowly, her eyes never leaving Olga's. "First things first, you need to be safe. We can figure out the rest later. There's no rush to decide right now. But know this," she squeezed Olga's hand, "you're not alone. You have friends, resources… you have me."

The advice was pure Karen—practical, sincere, unfiltered by the emotional whirlwind Olga was experiencing.

"Thank you, Karen. I… I needed to hear that. It's just that I don't even know where to start," Olga admitted, the weight of her situation pressing down on her.

"Start by believing in yourself. Trust that you'll know what to do when the time comes," Karen said gently. "And until then, let's plan. Let's talk about what a safe exit would look like. We can sort out the logistics and figure out the practicalities."

Olga nodded, a semblance of determination creeping into her gaze. "Yes, let's do that."

For the next hour, they spoke in hushed tones. Karen offered clear-headed advice, the kind that comes from intelligence and a life full of ups and downs. They plotted and planned, not with the thrill of conspirators, but with the seriousness of two women carving a path through a thicket of thorns toward freedom.

***

Alexa prided herself on the meticulous nature of her work. She had spent the better part of the day piecing together the puzzle that was Olga and Nikolai's fractured fairy tale. Her sources were diverse, a mosaic of voices ranging from the discreet whispers of the groundskeepers to the low, concerned murmurings of the household staff at Nikolai's estate. The stories gathered painted a picture of a marriage wrapped in melancholy, with Olga often a solitary figure in the luxury surrounding her. Alexa's instinct told her that this solitude was not of Olga's choosing.

The more she heard, the clearer it became that Nikolai's image as the doting husband was another facet of his finely crafted public image. Olga, from what Alexa gathered, was more a trophy than a partner, a beautiful object to adorn Nikolai's arm at public gatherings, but neglected and overlooked in the quiet corridors of their expansive home.

Alexa had learned long ago that emotions were powerful levers, and the growing file on her desk suggested that Olga's unhappiness could be exactly what she needed to unearth Nikolai's covert activities.

The plan was simple. Alexa's agent was discreetly following Olga and reporting her whereabouts. Alexa wanted to meet in a public place without drawing any attention, in case Nikolai's people were also watching his wife. As she made her way to the mall after her agent reported that Olga had been strolling casually past the boutiques, her mind was a whir of scenarios, each pathway in the dialogue mapped out with alternatives should the tide of conversation shift unexpectedly. She rehearsed opening lines that were casual yet pointed, topics that could turn into the probing questions she needed to ask.

Alexa understood the delicacy of the situation. Her goal was not to intimidate but to align, to position herself as an ally to Olga in whatever storm was brewing behind the mansion's walls.

As she arrived at the mall, Alexa took a deep breath, the air flavored with the salt of the nearby sea and stepped inside. Her eyes quickly found Olga, and with a practiced smile, she approached, ready to begin the intricate ballet of building a human connection.

***

Olga was at the local mall's bookshop, trailing her fingers over the spines of new releases when a voice addressed her softly from behind.

"Excuse me, I couldn't help but notice you looking at the crime section. Any recommendations?" The woman was casually dressed, with an earnest smile, and exceptionally good-looking.

Olga turned, a polite smile gracing her lips. "Well, I do enjoy a good mystery. Are you a fan?"

"I am, actually," the woman replied, stepping closer. "Especially the real-life cases. By the way, my name is Alexa."

"Olga," she replied, shaking Alexa's extended hand.

They exchanged pleasantries and chatted about books for a few minutes before Alexa tilted her head towards the café area. "I was just about to have coffee. Would you care to join me?"

Olga hesitated for a moment but found Alexa's company pleasant and unimposing. "Sure, that would be nice."

Once settled in the corner of the café with their drinks, the hum of the mall fading into the background, Alexa's demeanor shifted subtly. She leaned in, her voice dropping.

"I must admit, Olga, this isn't a chance encounter. I wanted to talk to you specifically."

Olga's back stiffened. "What do you mean?"

"My name is Alexa Marou, and I'm with the CID, Cyprus Police," Alexa said quietly, observing Olga closely. "I'm involved in a case that may affect you."

Olga felt her heart rate pick up, a cold sweat forming at the base of her neck. "I don't know what you're talking about."

"I'm investigating a case of illegal smuggling and possible money laundering. Your husband, Nikolai, might be involved," Alexa continued, her tone careful, her gaze sympathetic.

Olga's mind raced. How much did this woman know? "I think you have the wrong person. My husband is a businessman."

"Olga, I understand this is frightening, and you may want to protect your family and walk away from this conversation now. But this is serious. If Nikolai is involved, and I have my reasons to believe he is, you could be in danger too," Alexa pressed gently. "I am sure you have had nothing to do with his dealings, but if he has committed crimes, it will impact your life and your daughter's," Alexa continued.

Olga's fingers tightened around her coffee cup. "And what do you want from me?"

"I believe you may have information that could help us," Alexa explained. "I can offer protection, should you need it."

Protection. The word echoed in Olga's mind. She thought of her child, the conversations she'd overheard, and the gnawing fear that kept her awake at night.

"I... I don't know anything," Olga whispered, a lie that tasted like ash in her mouth.

"Here is my card. If you want to talk about anything or need help, please call me," Alexa said, sliding a business card across the table. The card mentioned only a name and a phone number.

Olga pocketed the card without looking at it. "I have to go," she said abruptly, standing. "Thank you for the coffee."

"Olga," Alexa said softly. "It's not only about the law. It's about keeping you and your child safe. Think about it."

As Olga left, her thoughts spiraled into confusion, each word from the officer echoing like an unstoppable bell. Her heart hammered against her ribcage, a frantic drumbeat in the quiet bookshop. The shelves around her seemed to close in as she processed the seriousness of Alexa's implications— Nikolai, the man she had once viewed as her partner, was entangled in illegal activities that now threatened her family.

Anger welled up within her, a storm of emotion. She despised Nikolai for the shame he brought upon their household and the stain his actions had smeared across their lives. She felt foolish for believing his charming smiles and grand promises, thinking they could lead a normal life.

Her marriage, once filled with hopeful beginnings, now felt like a nightmare. How could she have been so blind?

At that moment, a decision crystallized within Olga. She would do whatever it took to protect Christine, to distance her from the life Nikolai had built on deceit. Olga's future actions would be guided by a single intention: to cut the ties binding her to Nikolai's dark criminal world and forge a new path for herself and her daughter—one illuminated by truth and the promise of a peaceful life.

Even with these thoughts, it took her over two months to agree on the next meeting with Alexa.

Chapter 8

Alone in his apartment, with the city's hum as his only companion, Anton's mind raced with strategy. His plan needed to be believable, blending seamlessly into the fabric of everyday life. He weighed his options, each scenario unfolding like a chess game in his mind. One wrong move could spell disaster.

Then, a brilliant idea struck him. He would craft a narrative so ordinary yet perfect for his skills: an IT job offer in a European country. This would let him move away from Kyiv, throw off anyone watching him, and eventually disappear to Cyprus with a new identity. It was the perfect cover—simple, effective, and, hopefully, untraceable.

The idea was simple and brilliant. He would officially relocate as Anton Gorin and then, at the right moment, abandon his old identity, assume a new one, and vanish.

Anton leaned back in his chair, letting the thought unfurl in his mind. He knew some friends from the tech community who relocated to Czechia. The Czech tech industry flourished, a signal for IT professionals across Europe. Positions for skilled IT engineers, especially in cybersecurity, were in abundance. He could easily blend into this growing sector and become another expat pursuing a lucrative career opportunity.

He began crafting his story, each detail carefully chosen for its plausibility. He researched the Czech tech scene, familiarizing himself with the major players, the latest trends, and job openings that matched his profile.

This plan had a dual purpose. Firstly, it would provide a logical explanation for any changes in his routine, his sudden need for relocation, or unusual activities as he prepared for the move. Secondly, and more crucially, it would divert any lingering attention away from Cyprus, away from the hidden fortune that awaited him there.

He began laying the groundwork by sending out his resumes and setting up Skype interviews with actual tech companies in Prague. Eventually, he received a genuine job offer. Using his true identity for the job application was necessary to build a credible story.

Anton then orchestrated a very public acceptance of the offer by sharing his news on social media. He openly discussed his new opportunity with friends and family, expressed excitement about moving to Prague, and even started taking Czech language classes. His social media profiles buzzed with updates about his preparations for the move, with carefully created posts that showed him packing and studying Czech culture and basic phrases.

He even rented an apartment in Prague, signed a lease, and set up utilities remotely. It was all a ruse, but the digital paper trail it created was substantial, tangible, and easy for his enemies to check.

To sell his new life further, Anton visited the Czech embassy to inquire about integrating into Czech society. He asked questions about taxes, healthcare, and other mundane details that would not interest someone simply looking to vanish. He was pretty sure whoever was watching his moves followed him to the embassy and back.

He maintained his usual routines in Kyiv, careful not to alter his habits or behaviors. To the outside observer, Anton was just another professional excited about an overseas job opportunity, not a man plotting his erasure.

Anton's plan hinged on one critical component: a new identity. This was not a simple task of just forging documents. It required getting an authentic passport that could withstand the scrutiny of any border official. The key to achieving this lay in the underbelly of the Ukrainian judiciary system, a world Anton had reluctantly brushed with during his university days.

Reaching out to these dubious contacts was a dangerous dance. Anton knew he was stepping into dark waters, where trust was a currency as fragile as glass. But necessity drove him, and he was willing to venture into this risky terrain. His contacts were people he knew only by reputation, individuals who could manipulate the system's gears for the right price.

The process was covered in secrecy, with meetings in various locations, cash exchanged in unmarked envelopes, and whispered conversations that left Anton's heart racing. He was aware of the risks. If caught, this could mean prison or, worse, drawing unwanted attention from those he was trying to evade. But the pressing need for a new identity overpowered these fears.

After days of clandestine meetings and nerve-wracking waits, the passport was finally in his hands. A brand-new authentic passport created a new person with a birth certificate and all other details adequately inserted into an all-state Ukrainian database. To any observer, he was now Alex Paniv, a name chosen for its commonness and lack of ties to his real identity. The document was expensive, costing him a significant portion of his cash savings, but it was a necessary investment. It was his ticket to a new life.

With this new identity, Anton took the next step in his plan. He opened several bank accounts across different Ukrainian banks under Alex Paniv. These weren't large deposits – just enough to cover essential expenses like car rentals, accommodations, and daily necessities in the future. The stage was set, and Anton was finally ready to make a move.

***

His departure to Prague was anything but quiet. With a well-crafted fanfare of social media posts and fond farewells, he traveled to the Czech Republic. His studio apartment, sparse and practical, became his operational base, while the busy streets of Prague offered the perfect camouflage for a man seeking to blend into the background.

He settled quickly, adopting the routines of someone eager to assimilate. Mornings were for office work and language lessons with a stern but fair tutor who marveled at his student's dedication. Afternoons were spent walking through the vibrant streets of Prague, immersing himself in the city's rich mix of history and culture.

In Prague, Anton's job turned out to be more than just a cover. He quickly settled into his new role as a senior coder, impressing his team with his efficiency and innovative problem-solving skills. Within the first two weeks, his contributions were so significant that he earned a reputation as a valuable asset to the company. Recognizing his talent and dedication, the company even offered him the flexibility to work from home—a privilege he gratefully accepted. This arrangement provided the perfect cover for his deeper plans while allowing him to stay genuinely engaged in a role he found surprisingly fulfilling.

***

Tucked away in the charming Vinohrady district of Prague, Anton's residence was a quiet note in the vibrant symphony of urban life. This was a neighborhood where the past and present danced in harmony, each corner telling a story with a pulse that was both gentle and lively. Despite the beautiful and carefree surroundings, Anton's diligence unfolded in his studio. Hidden cameras, discreetly purchased from different vendors, peeked out from his bookshelves and behind innocuous knick-knacks, their lenses capturing the ebb and flow of life inside and out. Every evening, as the city dimmed and the streets hushed, Anton reviewed the footage with a meticulous eye, searching for the familiar in a sea of strangers.

About twenty days after his orchestrated arrival in Prague, Anton's past breached his new world with a sudden discovery. A man's face, once captured on video in a hotel room in Cyprus—a ghost from his past—drifted through the crowds in his footage. Anton's pulse quickened. The man lingered on the periphery for seven days, like a vulture circling, never venturing too close but always present. Then, on the eighth day, nothing. No sign of the man. No familiar faces. Just the tide of anonymous lives flowing through Prague's streets.

Even so, Anton kept his watch. Days turned into weeks, and the recordings offered nothing but the mundane existence of urban life. When another month passed without incident, Anton allowed himself a ghost of a smile. The ruse had worked. His preparations could enter the next phase. The path back to Cyprus and his hidden fortune lay open now. But patience had been his most steadfast ally, and he wouldn't abandon it. Prague was still his stage, and he had yet to deliver his final performance.

Anton, or Alex Paniv as he now wanted to be legally known, had carefully laid out his path to return to Cyprus. His documents were impeccable. The birthdate on the passport made him two years older, a subtle change that distanced him further from Anton Gorin's identity.

Alex's departure from Prague to Cyprus was a masterclass in planning and strategy. Every step and every decision was calibrated to ensure his previous self, Anton, remained in Prague with all the necessary formal signs of existence. He diligently paid his utility bills and maintained his employment with the Czech company, working from home. He remained a pillar of productivity and innovation, his presence felt through regular Skype calls and virtual meetings. His work, always punctual and of superior quality, earned him accolades from colleagues and superiors alike.

The company greatly valued his contributions, unaware of the double life he was leading.

He kept filling his social media with selfies captured across the city's picturesque landscapes. These carefully planned and strategically posted images were part of his scheme to maintain the illusion of his ongoing life in Prague.

Alex purchased Wi-Fi-controlled electrical sockets, programmable through an app on his phone. He installed them in his apartment and plugged in desk lamps and bras in every socket. These high-tech devices were switching lights on and off at random intervals to mimic the activities of a living, breathing resident. Even his TV played its part in this deception, turning on each evening, the volume set just loud enough to be heard by anyone who might be listening outside his door.

This charade was vital. It was supposed to buy Alex the time he needed to operate freely as his new persona in Cyprus. The longer he could sustain Anton's existence in Prague, the more time he had to devise a plan to transfer his fortune from Cyprus to Czechia. Once done, he would leave Cyprus forever, never to return.

Alex planned his departure for the early hours of the morning, a time when the city was still engulfed in slumber's embrace. As dawn's first light gently brushed Prague's skyline, he slipped out of his apartment. The streets, usually bustling with life and energy, were eerily silent.

As he made his way to the train station that would take him to his next chapter, his mind was a whirlwind of plans and contingencies. He had carefully arranged for his studio to be maintained, bills to continue being paid, and his employment to carry on remotely to preserve the illusion of Anton's ongoing life in Prague. Mentally, he was checking all the boxes, hoping he had covered all the angles. Now was the time for Alex to emerge.

He traveled lightly, carrying only a worn leather duffel bag that had seen better days, much like the man carrying it. His clothes were plain and simple: a dark denim jacket, comfortable jeans, and a cap pulled low to obscure his features.

Boarding a train heading south, he settled into the rhythm of the rails. The plan was to reach Greece via trains and buses and then take a boat to Cyprus.

The journey to Greece was a collage of landscapes and faces, a world slipping by the window as he embraced his role as Alex Paniv. He found a strange relief in the anonymity of transit, each mile taking him closer to his sun-soaked abyss. His once slender frame had filled out with muscle, resulting from countless hours lifting weights and a controlled diet. Even his hair had transformed, dyed a shade lighter, while his eyes—

once hidden behind glasses—now shimmered with the subtle hue of blueish contact lenses.

The travel was slow, but Alex was in no hurry. He took a train from Prague to Budapest in Hungary and another train from Budapest to Bucharest, Romania, where he jumped on the bus to Athens. Upon arriving in Greece, the air carried the scent of the sea mingled with the aroma of fresh olives and sun-warmed earth.

His next leg was by sea. He boarded a boat headed for Limassol, slipping into the background amongst families and couples. The boat ride was a time for reflection; the steady hum of the engine and the rhythmic clapping of waves against the hull were a soundtrack to his thoughts. The horizon was an unbroken line, a symbol of the infinite possibilities before him. Alex still felt the weight of his old life, an anchor he was desperate to cut loose.

As the boat carved its path through the sapphire waters of the Mediterranean, Alex stayed away from the other passengers, his gaze fixed on the approaching land. Cyprus would be his sanctuary, a place to truly bury his former identity and nurture a new one. The sea air was brisk, whipping his hair and clearing his mind, readying him for the challenges ahead.

By the time the boat docked in Limassol, Alex had been mentally ready to embrace his new identity and his life. He disembarked with a sense of purpose, stepping onto Cypriot soil as if he belonged, as if the ghosts of his past were nothing but a bad dream dissolving in the warm embrace of the island sun. Limassol greeted him with familiar scents and sounds. He filled out the customs declaration, carefully noting the 8,000 euros that would be the seed of his new beginning in Cyprus. This single paper was the only official acknowledgment of his passage, a brief flicker of visibility. He then moved through the streets of the town like a ghost, unseen and unknown.

Alex rented a car using a Ukrainian bank credit card issued to his new name, and finally, he made it to Paphos and arrived at the apartment that housed his hopes for a new life.

Alex stopped and held his breath at the weather-beaten front door that was the gateway to his fortune—or his downfall. His hand lingered on the handle, clammy with a mix of the coastal humidity and his own nervous sweat. The lock yielded to his key as if welcoming him home. As he pushed the door open, the scents of the apartment washed over him: a blend of sea salt carried by the breeze and the musty silence of a space long uninhabited. Alex stepped inside. The apartment was untouched, a thin layer of dust the only sign of the passage of time. He walked to the bedroom, his movements hesitant, his heart thrumming in his ears.

A part of him—the weary part, the part that yearned for peace—whispered to leave it all behind, to walk away from the cursed fortune that had turned his life upside down. The temptation to flee, to return to the simplicity of a normal life in Prague and a well-paid job, was a strong and seductive call.

He stood over the mattresses, his hands trembling as he contemplated the possibility of a clean break. The money, though untouched, felt tainted, each bill a reminder of danger and deceit. For a moment, he was back in his car, stunned by the unexpected discovery of the suitcases, his life turning on its axis.

But then, the steelier part of Alex kicked in. He had come too far and risked too much to walk away now. With a shaky exhale, he reached for the first mattress, his fingers slipping beneath to probe the hidden cavity within.

The fabric gave way to the cool touch of paper. Bill after bill, stacked and untouched, just as he had left them. The tension released in a rush, and Alex allowed himself a brief, grim smile. There was no turning back now. He was in it for the long haul.

A sigh escaped his lips, not of relief but of readiness.

At that very moment, the persona of Anton Gorin, the beleaguered IT specialist, was shed like outgrown skin. He truly was Alex Paniv now, and his new life had just begun. He packed the cash into two large plastic storage containers, loaded them into his car, and set off into his new life.

***

The drive to Nicosia was a meditative transition. With its intimate streets and cozy tavernas, Paphos was a world he needed to escape. The risk of crossing paths with the mobsters was a gamble he was unwilling to take. Nicosia presented itself as a labyrinth of possibilities. It was where anonymity was as easy to come by as a cold glass of Cypriot beer. The city bustled with life and people, its streets a mosaic of faces and cultures—perfect for a man seeking to dissolve into a new identity.

The city was a vibrant mixture of ancient and modern, with Byzantine walls encircling an expanse of bustling markets and contemporary galleries. Street vendors called out, their voices a melody against the clatter of coffee cups in busy cafes, where locals engaged in animated conversation over thick, frothy Cyprus coffee.

Turning away from the main streets, Alex found the neighborhood where he would disappear into the fabric of everyday life. His new apartment, found and rented over the Airbnb during his trip from Czechia to Greece, was on a quiet side street, an unassuming residential building whose exterior bore the warm tones of the local architecture. The apartment was on the second floor, accessed by a set of stairs that cracked with age and whispered secrets of its past inhabitants.

The living space was modest but adequate. Sparse furnishings provided functionality without a hint of luxury: a small table, wooden chairs, an old sofa, worn-out fabric armchairs, and a firm bed that promised restful sleep. The walls were adorned with simple, framed photographs of the Cypriot landscape - a glance at the island's beauty.

French doors opened to a narrow balcony, offering a view of the urban life outside. The apartment was bright and bathed in the golden light of the late afternoon sun, casting long, lazy shadows across the tiled floor. In the distance, the jagged outline of the Pentadaktylos Mountains etched itself against the sky.

Alex moved his treasured luggage up and unpacked his few possessions. The apartment had a small utility room with a built-in cabinet featuring four deep, empty shelves. Alex emptied the containers, as they would never fit on the shelves, packed the cash into black garbage bags, and stashed them on the shelves. He covered the bags with all kinds of household items to ensure the garbage bags weren't too visible. He made a mental note to buy and install a lock for the utility door.

***

Days and weeks passed, and Alex's routine in Nicosia became one of careful construction. He opened accounts in three different banks and deposited eight thousand euros in each, presenting the same currency declaration. It was a small amount, designed to avoid triggering any alarms. It was just enough to establish himself and create a resemblance of a modest income that would enable him to build an air of legitimacy. Alex contacted the Airbnb owner and easily struck a deal. The owner eagerly accepted a six-month advance payment in cash.

His days were filled with routine—grocery shopping, visiting the gym, exploring the city's many cafes and parks. But beneath the surface of his everyday life, Alex's mind was always working, always planning. The cash hidden in his new apartment was a dragon's hoard that needed protection and transformation.

Legitimizing the money was the puzzle he now faced. He kept his eyes and ears open for whispers of a financial advisor or lawyer—someone skilled in turning the shady gains of his past deeds into the appearance of respectability. This person needed to be a little more than competent. They needed to be discreet and somewhat flexible in their ethics.

Alex spent his evenings poring over the business section of the Cyprus Mail, studying articles and ads for hints of the person he needed. He attended business networking events, presenting himself as an investor looking for opportunities in the local market. His cover story was that he was an IT consultant with a startup idea looking for partners and a setup.

The quest for an advisor was less about money and more about survival, building a future where he could be free of the fear that had shadowed his every step since leaving Kyiv. Each night, as he lay in his Nicosia bed, he thought about the path that had led him here, the decisions made, and the lines crossed. But there was not much time for regret. The only direction was forward in the world Alex had created for himself. And forward meant finding the key to unlocking the chains of his past—a key he hoped to find in the sun-drenched streets of Nicosia. Alex knew the downside of his quest: he would need a solid explanation for the source of the funds, and that presented a serious dilemma. Until one night when he had an idea.

***

Alex sat at his properly organized workstation, the hum of his computer's cooling fan blending with the distant chatter of Nicosia life drifting through his open window. The glow of the screen highlighted the determination in his eyes. Before him lay the fruits of his labor: a complex yet user-friendly software capable of performing rapid arbitrage trades across multiple cryptocurrency exchanges. He had worked on a similar thing for a client while employed in Prague.

He had named it "ArbiCrypto Pro," an automated system designed to exploit the price differences of cryptocurrencies. It was a legitimate enterprise, a tool that could appeal to the ever-growing market of crypto traders looking for an edge.

Knowing he needed a bank to back his business to appear credible, he approached his Cyprus bank with a well-crafted pitch. The personal banker, dressed in sharp attire, eyed the figures Alex presented. They were impressive, and the bank, recognizing the potential of fintech innovations, quickly provided the entrepreneur with corporate accounts for his newly registered and promising company.

Now came the part that Alex had cautiously planned for. He needed a partner to create the air of a thriving business and legitimize his cash. Through extensive online research, he had identified a local developer, Michalis, whose reputation for skirting the edges of legality was well-known in certain circles. Alex found his profile on social media and sent him a message.

Michalis was a stout man with a thick beard and a gaze that calculated every angle of a deal. Alex met him in the private board room of a co-working office, away from prying eyes and eavesdroppers.

"Michalis," Alex began, the light from the laptop screen casting a soft glow on his intent features, "I have a proposition you might be interested in." He pushed the laptop across the polished surface of the mahogany table, where the screen displayed an interface of complex graphs and numbers—a high-frequency trading software named ArbiCrypto Pro.

Michalis leaned forward, his curiosity visible. "Explain," he prompted, his voice as textured as the aged leather of his chair.

"This software is designed to exploit split-second differences in cryptocurrency prices across various exchanges," Alex detailed. "It buys low and sells high with such speed that it captures profit before the markets can adjust. It's a tool for consistent earnings, a lucrative addition for those navigating the volatile seas of the crypto world."

A calculated pause allowed Michalis to digest the information before Alex continued, "I'm proposing an exclusive partnership. I understand that you do not need this software, but I need official sales, and you might require a constant influx of cash in your construction business to pay your freelance workers. So, I give you fifty thousand euros cash every month, and you buy these software licenses from my company for forty, pocketing ten for your services. As a bonus, I will teach you how to trade with this software, and I'm willing to provide you with a hundred grand in cash as a deposit against your investment into crypto brokers' accounts. Once you know how to trade and see this software making money on your investment, you will return the hundred grand to me and operate independently.

Michalis' interest was now clearly visible, but his response was tinged with skepticism. "I understand the cash trade system. Your cash in return for my official payments and my 20% profit on every transaction. That's clear. What's the catch with the software?"

Alex leaned in, his voice dropping to a conspiratorial whisper. "There is no catch, Michalis. Put it this way: I am very good at what I do and have been working on this robotic software for months. I have tried and tested it on tiny amounts, and it delivers. All you need to do is push a hundred grand in and sit back. On a monthly basis the software will generate at least 5% return, but it can go as high as 25%. To prove my story, I will give you one hundred thousand in cash to keep locked away in your safe while your hundred grand is working in the exchanges. That way, you are safe if you lose."

The silence that followed was thick with consideration. A man well-versed in the subtleties of the grey market, Michalis recognized the allure of a scheme that promised gains without the usual taint of illegality. He sat back, the shadows playing across his face as he contemplated a future where his financial streams might multiply. Michalis finally nodded, the faintest hint of a smile tugging at the corners of his mouth. "Alright, Alex. You have a deal. But remember, I'm only interested in clean operations. If this blows back on me—"

"It won't," Alex interjected, "I've covered every angle. This is as clean as it gets in our line of work."

"Where did you get the cash from?" asked Mihalis, looking directly into Alex's eyes.

Alex did not frown. "I'm a programmer, right? And I'm a perfect one at that. I produced a few online casino sites for cash for some shady people."

This satisfied Mihalis and made perfect sense to him. The two men shook hands. Alex had taken a significant step toward legitimizing his cash.

***

Alex's life became a careful routine of appearances - he was suddenly the entrepreneur, the innovator, the tech-savvy foreigner with an eye for the crypto market's future. His evenings were often spent in front of the soft glow of his computer screen, refining and updating his software, making sure it delivered what was promised.

The life he had known — the nervous glances, the constant fear of exposure, the weight of hidden cash — was now neatly tucked away in bank accounts, hidden behind the legitimate transactions from Mihalis' company.

Weeks later, Alex's dealings expanded exponentially, his cash exchanges surged to an impressive figure due to Michalis bringing in his friends interested in getting their hands in crypto dealings for free, exchanging their official payments for Alex's cash with a twenty percent profit. Who would miss a deal like that?

It's fair to say that legitimizing Alex's cash would eventually cost him over 20%, considering the taxes on his company's profits. However, Alex quickly invested the money received from Mihalis and his friends into his crypto exchange trading. He was soon covering his 20% cash exchange losses with gains in the crypto markets.

Alex's genius did not end at merely exchanging cash for inflated software licenses. He went further, teaching Michalis and his colleagues the ins and outs of his software. They weren't just buying his product. They were investing in a skill, a way to make their own money. With Alex's discreet guidance, they learned to navigate the volatile crypto markets, using the arbitrage software to earn impressive monthly returns.

***

The sun hung low over Nicosia, painting the café in amber and coral. Alex sipped his espresso, the bitter liquid grounding him as his mind waded through a sea of financial jargon on his tablet. Investment firms, audit services, and offshore opportunities formed a digital maze, a puzzle he was determined to solve.

His concentration broke when he overheard a fluid stream of Russian from the following table. Subtly shifting his gaze, Alex noticed a woman, her profile as striking as it was melancholic.

She was a vision, like something out of a dream, with a grace that was truly extraordinary. Her hair cascaded down her shoulders like threads of dark gold, each strand catching the sunlight that danced through the open canopy. Her figure was a study in perfection, sculpted as if by an artist's hands, with curves and lines that whispered tales of genius craftsmanship. She wore a dress that complimented every aspect of her impeccable form, its fabric hugging her contours in a delicate embrace, suggesting a goddess's physique.

But it was her eyes that held Alex's attention most firmly. They were vast pools of the deepest blue, mirrors to a soul that carried an ocean of sorrow. Within those irises was a haunting sadness, an untold story that overshadowed her outer splendor.

As she conversed softly in Russian, her voice was melodious yet tinged with melancholy. She spoke into her phone with an elegance that matched her appearance. As the call ended, her eyes met his, revealing depths of sadness that struck a chord in him.

Alex initiated a conversation with an impulsive decision after weeks of solitude. "It's rare to find someone who appreciates a good coffee at this hour," he commented in Russian with a casual smile.

The woman offered a soft laugh, her guard lowered by the shared linguistic bond. "I'm waiting for a friend, but it seems I'm destined to enjoy this coffee alone," she replied, a slight lilt in her voice.

They fell into an easy conversation, Alex crafting a narrative of a tech entrepreneur eager to dive into the Cypriot business waters. At the same time, she shared expatriate living stories of Paphos, careful not to divulge too much. The connection was effortless, and Alex was captivated by her beauty and the vivacity she tried to conceal behind her reserve.

As the city's bustle swirled around them, the minutes slipped into a pleasant half-hour of easy conversation. But as quickly as the interlude had begun, it ended when a Cypriot woman approached the tables.

"Olga, there you are!" the newcomer exclaimed in Greek before switching to English. "Sorry, I'm late."

Olga stood, and with a final smile towards Alex that hinted at gratitude and a touch of regret, she joined her friend. Alex watched as they melded into the crowd, the back of Olga's figure imprinted in his mind.

He sat back, feeling an unexpected sense of loss. Indeed, her beauty was remarkable, but her aura, the subtle dance of strength and vulnerability, lingered with him. Alex finished his coffee, the taste bittersweet, pondering the strange twist of fate that had briefly intertwined his path with a woman from Paphos, the place he intended to avoid.

Chapter 9

A few weeks before Alex left Prague for Cyprus, Slavik, who had returned from the Czechia's mission, was called into Nikolai's office for reporting. Gromov's shadow stretched across the intricate Persian carpet as he paced his office back and forth. Slavik waited, his figure almost blending with the dimly lit corners, a patient statue in the game of power and silence.

"Boss," Slavik finally said as Nikolai paused and turned a gaze upon him that could freeze the sun. "The Prague operation has concluded. I've kept Anton under close surveillance for a full week. He's living there under his name, working an IT job for a local Czech company, keeping a low profile. My sources confirmed he is legally employed, and the company is pleased with him."

"And?" Nikolai's voice was a dangerous whisper, each word laced with an edge. "Any trace of the money?"

Slavik shook his head, a controlled gesture. "No, Nikolai. He's clean, at least on the surface. Lives like a modest programmer and keeps to himself. He rents a small studio. No lavish expenses, no car, no unusual movements. If he's hiding something, he's doing it well."

A humorless chuckle escaped Nikolai, his features a mask of cold amusement. "A mouse living in a hole, hoping the cat has grown bored," he mused. "And yet, our cheese remains unclaimed."

Slavik shifted his weight slightly, a ripple in his otherwise still posture. "Exactly. If he did take the money, he's not flaunting it. He's careful and disciplined. Perhaps he's a better actor than we gave him credit for."

Nikolai turned to the window. The skyline of a sleeping city sprawled before him. "Or he never took it at all. Maybe we were wrong about Anton." The contemplation seemed to hang heavily in the air, a rare admission from a man not prone to doubt.

"But the operation, sir," Slavik pressed on, "do we extend the surveillance? Prague could be a stop—"

Nikolai raised a hand, silencing him. "No. Pull back. We have spread our net wide and caught nothing but water. If he did steal from us, he's escaped, and we have larger empires to build than to chase after shadows and dust."

Slavik's jaw tightened, but he nodded. "As you wish. I'll redirect our resources."

"Good," Nikolai affirmed with finality. "Anton Gorin, the man who might have outsmarted us, let him be a footnote in our history. For now, we have more pressing enemies to attend to." Slavik retreated from the office.

Nikolai's decision to pause the hunt for Anton was a strategic move. As the door closed behind Slavik, Nikolai's expression subtly shifted from acceptance to calculation. He hadn't risen to power by being lenient or allowing potential threats to go unchecked.

Sitting behind his grand oak desk, fingers steepled in thought, he reflected on the disappointment of Slavik and Zhorik. They were capable men, but this game required a finer touch—one that Anton played well. Slavik's report hadn't convinced him of Anton's innocence but rather highlighted the inadequacy of his current hunters.

He reached for the encrypted phone in a drawer, its existence only known to a precious few. He had another player in mind, someone whose skills were way sharper than the usual brutes he employed, someone for whom the chase was as subtle and intricate as a dance. This individual would not be deterred by false modesty or clever ruses. This person would uncover the truth if Anton Gorin still held onto Nikolai's riches.

Nikolai dialed a number known only to him, connecting to a part of the world where even whispers held power. "I have a special task," he spoke when the line was picked up, his voice now commanding, imbued with the total weight of his authority. It was time to call in the master to fix the mistakes of the apprentices.

***

Dmitri Orlov was a ghost in the intelligence world—a myth to some, a whisper to others. Born to the chill of Murmansk, his existence was shaped by discipline, hard work, and extensive training.

Dmitri Orlov was born into an intelligent family of officers involved in Soviet military covert operations. Discipline was ingrained in him from the start, and disappearing into shadows was his second nature.

From the beginning, Dmitri didn't seek the companionship of his peers. His childhood games were solo exercises in surveillance and strategy, practiced in the frozen playgrounds of his hometown. During these early years, his ability to detach himself grew, his emotions receding like the tides of the Barents Sea, leaving his mind as sharp as ice.

As Dmitri rose through the ranks, colleagues and mentors watched with a mix of apprehension and respect. His rise was quiet but swift, like a whisper that carried authority throughout the halls of power. There were rumors of moments when Dmitri's decisions had meant the difference between life and death, his orders carried out with precise efficiency, leaving no room for hesitation. In truth, Orlov was a man of principles, deeply devoted to serving his country.

To look into his eyes was to gaze upon the tundra of his soul: vast, barren, and brutally beautiful. The whispers spoke of him as a ghost, passing through the human world, leaving a chill in his wake that was felt long after his silhouette had melted into the horizon.

His past assignments were known to a scant few, their details locked away in files so confidential they were almost folklore. Orlov had been the architect behind the quiet dismantling of a major terrorist ring in Eastern Europe and the retrieval of sensitive materials from under the noses of rival agencies. He was, in every sense, the FSB's unseen blade.

The meeting with Nikolai took place in an inconspicuous dacha outside of Moscow, a place reserved for conversations that were always in its walls. The air was tense, tinged with the aroma of black Russian tea and the faint scent of pine from the open window. Orlov listened, his gaze steady, as Nikolai laid bare the intricacies of the case, his suspicions surrounding Anton's deception, and his frustration with the incompetence that had allowed the situation to fester.

"I have a reason to believe that Anton Gorin is behind the theft. However, it is only my gut feeling. I need your level of skills to know for sure. I can't rely on my own resources, and my people aren't qualified enough for the job."

Orlov nodded once, slowly absorbing the details like a sponge. His mind was already turning, calculating, as Nikolai continued to unravel the narrative that had led them to this juncture. When the story was laid bare, Orlov finally spoke, his voice the aural equivalent of a sharpened blade.

"I will look into Anton Gorin. I will retrieve whatever he has taken if he did. Since this is a private gig, my skills come at a price," Orlov stated, his eyes never leaving Nikolai's.

"Twenty percent of the retrieved funds or a hundred grand if I get conclusive proof Anton is innocent," Orlov said. With a curt nod, Nikolai agreed, knowing the worth of the man before him. "You'll have whatever resources you need at your disposal."

A faint smile touched the corners of Orlov's mouth, not of pleasure but of acknowledgment of the hunt before him. "Then consider it done," he said. "The prey may run, change his skin, name, life... but he cannot hide from his shadow. And I am very good at finding shadows. Especially under the sun."

With a handshake that sealed the deal, Nikolai knew that the game had changed. Orlov was the harbinger of a storm Anton could not possibly anticipate. The chase had taken a perilous turn, one that would inevitably lead to the doorstep of a ghost named Alex Paniv, who once called himself Anton Gorin.

***

As the echo of light conversation faded into the cafe's ambient murmur, Alexa and Olga stepped out into the warmth of the Cypriot sun. Alexa was the first to break the silence.

"That man you were talking to back in the cafe... who was he?" Alexa asked, her eyes scanning Olga's face for any flicker of recognition.

Olga hesitated, her thoughts racing back to the man, "Nobody. I... I don't really know him. We just had a casual conversation. He said he's starting a business here."

"Just casual?" Alexa pressed, careful not to push too hard, too fast. "You seemed quite engaged. It's important, Olga. If there's something more—"

"No, there's nothing more," Olga interjected quickly, perhaps too quickly, displaying a hint of the tension she held within.

Alexa decided to shift gears for now, allowing the topic to rest in the background of their dialogue. "Okay, let's talk about Nikolai's businesses then. The hotel he purchased—do you know why he was interested in that particular property?"

Olga wrapped her arms around herself, a protective gesture. "He said it was a good investment. That's all. Hotels do well here, don't they?"

"They do," Alexa nodded. "But we both know that's not always the main reason behind such purchases. Was there any unusual activity around the time of the acquisition?"

Olga bit her lip, her mind flashing through fragmented memories, snippets of conversations overheard, faces half-remembered. "I... I think he mentioned something about 'making changes for the betterment of the future.' I didn't understand what he meant at the time. I thought it was just business talk."

Alexa observed her closely, noting the conflict behind Olga's eyes. "And the finances for this purchase, did they come from legitimate sources to the best of your knowledge?"

"I... I don't know. Nikolai doesn't share details like that with me. But I can't imagine it's all clean. Not with the people he meets." Olga's voice quivered.

"Listen, Olga," Alexa said, her tone softening. "I know you're afraid, and I understand why. But this is about protecting your future and your daughter's. You have a chance to get ahead of this, to keep your hands clean before the storm hits."

Olga's gaze fell to the ground, a storm of her own brewing in the wells of her eyes. "I don't know what to do," she whispered.

"I can help you, but you have to trust me," Alexa offered, her promise hanging like a lifeline. "We can keep you safe, but I need you to be honest with me about everything."

The weight of the moment was palpable, the choice clear but daunting. Olga's next words and actions could irreversibly alter the course of her life. The safety of her daughter, the desire for a life untainted by her husband's shadowy dealings—these were the scales on which her decision would be based.

After a lengthy pause, Olga nodded. "Okay. I'll tell you what I know, all of it. But you must promise me that Christine and I will be safe."

Alexa extended her hand, a gesture of solidarity and assurance. "You have my word, Olga. We'll do everything in our power to protect you both."

As their hands met, an unspoken pact was forged. Alexa Marou, an officer of the law committed to justice, and Olga, a woman on the brink, about to unveil truths that would ripple through the foundations of her life and beyond.

The evening had given way to a dusky twilight, painting the Cypriot landscape in deep blue and soft purple. In the privacy of Alexa's car, the two women sat in silence for a moment. When Alexa finally spoke, her voice was gentle but firm.

"Olga, I need you to tell me everything you know about Nikolai's activities. Every detail could be vital."

Olga drew in a shaky breath, her hands clasped tightly in her lap. She gazed out the window, watching the fading light dance through the olive trees before she began her tale, her voice a quiet echo of past fears and untold secrets.

"In the nineties, Nikolai... well, he wasn't the businessman he pretends to be now. He smuggled weapons and drugs. It was a different, violent time, and he was... proud of his mafia connections."

Alexa noted every word, her expression neutral, encouraging Olga to continue.

"Now, he claims that he's reformed. But his business... it's still smuggling. Only it's imported food from Europe through Belarus into Russia. It's all done with cash and so much of it. I don't know where he keeps it all, but it somehow makes its way to Cyprus."

Olga's eyes darted around nervously as she spoke of the vault. "There's a vault, a big one, in our basement.

I've never seen inside, but sometimes, I hear the heavy door opening and closing late at night."

Alexa's eyes narrowed slightly at this. "And the talks you overheard about someone stealing from him—"

"Yes," Olga interjected, "he's furious. Says he'll kill whoever is responsible for it. There's a rage in him I've never seen."

"And the local contacts?" Alexa prodded further.

"One of them is Stelios. I met him once. He has an air of danger, but I don't know what he does. And then there's Omar." Olga's voice lowered. "He speaks Russian, but not like us. He's from the Middle East, I think. They talk about the weather, the heat. I once saw him in Dubai. He came to meet Nikolai at the hotel we stayed in. Nikolai often talks to him on the phone. I assume they have some business together."

"Could you ever estimate the size of Nikolai's operation?" Alexa's tone was steady, but her eyes were sharp, missing nothing.

Olga shook her head, her expression one of someone who'd often pondered this question. "No, but it never made sense to me. The amount of cash and his investments here in Cyprus... well... smuggling food can't bring in that much, can it?"

Alexa was silent for a moment, absorbing the information. "Anything else, Olga? Think carefully. Friends, associates, places he has frequented?"

Olga was silent, her mind scouring through years of half-truths and veiled conversations, searching for a clue, any thread that could unravel the mystery of Nikolai's empire. "There are others, shadows that come and go. Men with hard eyes and silence around them like a cloak. I don't know their names, but they carry themselves like predators."

She met Alexa's gaze with a haunted look in her blue eyes. "I'm afraid, Alexa. What if he finds out I've told you all this?"

Alexa reached out, placing a reassuring hand on Olga's. "We're going to protect you, Olga. You're doing the right thing and are not alone in this anymore."

Olga nodded, and a tear escaped, a symbol of fear and hope, tracing a path down her cheek. Alexa started the engine, the car pulling away into the night, carrying them away from the past and into an uncertain but necessary future.

***

Olga stayed overnight at a five-star hotel in the city center. She was too exhausted to drive back to Paphos the same day. Sleep didn't come until the early morning hours. She woke up late, barely managing to get downstairs in time for breakfast before the restaurant closed.

When Alex's familiar figure caught her eye, Olga sat alone, attempting to find comfort in the hotel's breakfast offerings. He was deeply engrossed in conversation, but his attention swiftly shifted upon noticing Olga, and his face broke into a surprised smile.

Their eyes met, and for a moment, Olga felt the chaotic thoughts that were plaguing her mind quiet down. Alex politely excused himself from his meeting and made his way over.

"Olga, what are the odds?" Alex began with a chuckle that suggested both surprise and delight. "I didn't expect to see you here this morning."

She mustered a weary smile, "Neither did I," her voice revealing her sleep-deprived state.

"Trouble sleeping?" he asked, his tone conveying an understanding beyond mere politeness.

"You could say that," Olga admitted, appreciating the empathy in his voice.

"Care for a change of scenery? A walk might do you good," Alex suggested, gesturing towards the sunlight streaming through the open doors of the hotel.

They wandered down the sunlit streets, the unexpectedness of the situation hanging between them like a delicate veil. Their conversation began tentatively, punctuated by the sounds of the city.

"This is strange, isn't it?" Olga finally said, an awkward laugh escaping her lips. "We just met yesterday, and here we are, walking through Nicosia as if it were the most natural thing in the world."

Alex nodded, "Life is funny like that. Sometimes, you bump into someone, and it seems like it was meant to be."

As they strolled, they shared stories of their lives, careful not to dig too deep into the more sensitive details. The air between them was filled with the tentative dance of two people circling the unsaid, the unknown.

Alex and Olga's spontaneous morning walk gradually led them to a quaint little cafe in a quiet corner of Nicosia.

"Would you like to join me for lunch?" Alex asked as they approached the cafe, its windows adorned with flowering plants.

Olga hesitated for a fraction of a second before nodding. "I think I'd like that," she said, the burdens of her mind momentarily lightened by the prospect of simple human connection.

Over a leisurely lunch that seemed to stretch the boundaries of time, they found themselves busy with conversations that ranged from the mundane to the profound. They spoke of Cyprus, its history echoing in the streets they had walked, and its present-day rhythm felt in the buzz of the cafe.

"Life here is... different," Olga mused, picking at her food. "It's like living on the edge of Europe and the Middle East all at once."

Alex agreed, "There's a kind of peace in how the sea meets the land, and the ancient sits beside the new. But I suppose every place has its undercurrents."

They talked about the local culture, the food, and how the sun painted the world gold in the evenings. Olga opened up about her daughter, her hopes for her, and her fears.

"And you, Alex? What's your story with Cyprus?" she inquired.

He sketched a vague outline of a startup owner seeking new horizons, carefully navigating away from the details of his business. "It's the land of opportunity, they say. I'm hoping they're right," he offered with a smile that didn't quite reach his eyes.

As the plates were cleared and the final sips of coffee were enjoyed, the conversation took a more introspective turn. They reflected on their journeys, the choices that led them to this island, this cafe, and this moment.

"It's odd," Olga said, a contemplative note in her voice. "We're both from elsewhere, yet here we are, finding solace in a stranger's company."

Alex nodded. "Sometimes, talking to someone who doesn't know the whole story is easier. There's less judgment, more... space to breathe."

Their lunch ended with an exchange of phone numbers. Olga drove her car back to Paphos with renewed clarity, her spirit uplifted by the unexpected connection. Alex watched her leave, feeling an unfamiliar tug at his conscience, wondering about the crossroads where their lives had intersected and where they might lead.

As the day gave way to the velvet embrace of a Cypriot night, fate's enigmatic design lingered in the back of their minds. There they were, two souls unwittingly entwined in a maze of hidden truths and half-spoken stories. Alex, living under the new identity, had unknowingly stolen a fortune from the same dangerous beast whose shadow loomed over

Olga's life. And Olga, unknowingly seeking comfort in the company of the most wanted man on her husband's list, found a flicker of companionship in the eyes of a stranger. Destiny had played its hand masterfully, drawing them together in a dance of circumstance where every step and turn held the secrets yet to surface.

Chapter 10

Dmitri Orlov moved through the cobblestone streets of Kyiv like a phantom, hunting down clues about Anton Gorin. The city, with its ancient churches and hills full of history, seemed to whisper secrets that Orlov was ready to gather. His presence was almost mythical as he tracked the remnants of Anton's old life with chilling precision.

Kyiv, once the place of Anton's mundane existence, now silently testifies to his disappearance. Orlov walked through Anton's deserted flat, which echoed of a life that had vanished. Neighbors spoke quietly about the unassuming man who disappeared like mist over the Dnipro River. Finding and learning nothing of importance, Orlov headed to Prague.

In the pulsing heart of the Czech capital, he moved with purpose through the city's ancient streets like a man on a mission. His target was an office building sitting among the vibrant cityscape, a hub for transient start-ups and driven entrepreneurs. It was here, in the ever-shifting landscape of ambitious young faces and minds, that Anton Gorin had allegedly set his roots with TechBite, a fast-growing digital start-up.

Orlov stepped into the building's lobby, his gaze sweeping over the occupants with the precision of a seasoned hunter. He approached the reception, where a sharply dressed woman met him with a professional smile. He asked to see Anton Gorin, an IT engineer working for TechBite with offices on the second floor. She phoned the company's receptionist, who confirmed Anton was employed but worked remotely from his home. If a message needed to be left, she was eager to help. Orlov declined the offer and moved to the downstairs coffee shop, which was busy with office employees.

"I've seen many faces here," the barista girl said after Orlov showed her a photo of Anton and presented a fifty-euro bill, her accent subtly foreign, "but this one doesn't ring a bell. It's a revolving door of people; he might've been one of them, but he didn't stand out. What I can say for sure, I haven't seen this face recently."

Her words only deepened Orlov's suspicions. Anton had crafted an illusion of presence, a figure just tangible enough to be real but elusive when pursued.

Orlov checked the company records through his contacts in Czech law enforcement. The records confirmed Anton's employment. The bank records confirmed salaries, utilities were paid and groceries bought.

Next, he turned his attention to Anton's studio apartment. From the street, it appeared normal, lights flickering on and off at regular intervals, suggesting life within. After a couple of days of observation, with no sign of Anton coming or going, Orlov's suspicion reached a tipping point.

Orlov knew that a direct break-in was too risky. Anton, a cybersecurity expert, could have set up sophisticated alarms or surveillance systems that would immediately alert him to any intrusion and thus make him lay low. It was a gamble Orlov wasn't willing to take.

Instead, Orlov opted for a more covert approach. He contracted a local security company, known for its discretion and efficiency, to set up a comprehensive surveillance operation. They installed cameras covering every possible exit and entrance of the building housing Anton's studio. The goal was to capture every movement, every face that came in and out, day and night.

For ten grueling days, Orlov and his team scrutinized the footage, analyzing the comings and goings of residents and visitors. The surveillance was exhaustive, leaving no stone unturned, no shadow unchecked. But as the days passed, one thing became abundantly clear: Anton Gorin was nowhere to be seen.

The life patterns in the building continued as usual, but Anton's presence was conspicuously absent. The smartly timed lighting in his studio, which at first had suggested occupation, now served as silent proof of his absence. Orlov figured that the lights switching on and off had a pattern that repeated every three days. It was a clever disguise that had initially cast doubt but now only confirmed Orlov's suspicions.

Every piece of the puzzle laid a trail that told Orlov Anton was not an ordinary man swept up by circumstance but one who planned his moves with a bright mind. Orlov's instincts, honed by years in the shadows of international espionage, whispered that Anton had been playing a role here, a character written for a specific audience. He hadn't left a job in Prague. He'd just abandoned the stage once his performance was complete.

With this insight, Orlov retreated from the bright lights of the city center to the muted glow of his temporary quarters. There, with maps and scattered notes, he began to weave the threads into a cohesive narrative. Anton's elaborate misdirection was a signature mark of someone who understood the value of confusion. Dmitri Orlov had always been thorough in his methods, which served him well in the world of intelligence. Anton had definitely left a brief trail somewhere as every movement in the digital age cast a shadow, however faint. Orlov knew this well.

Starting with border crossings, Orlov, through his connections, requested logs from Ukrainian nationals exits from Czechia starting from the day of Anton's arrival to Prague. From the struggle of names and dates a pattern emerged: a Ukrainian passport holder, Alex Paniv, moved from Prague to Budapest almost four months after Anton settled down in Prague. This traveler had nothing tying him back to Ukraine—no return ticket, no family traveling alongside, and it sparked Orlov's interest. But the most important thing was that there existed no entry date for someone called Alex Paniv into Czechia within the last five years. Orlov dug deeper but found no history of Alex Paniv's trails in Ukraine.

He traced Alex's movements to Greece. Digital footprints were elusive by design, but Orlov still managed to find a boat ticket under the name Alex Paniv. The boat went to an expected destination—Cyprus. "Bingo," Orlov whispered to himself with a smile and booked the next flight from Prague to Larnaca, Cyprus.

Once in Cyprus, Orlov tapped into the network of local informants that the FSB had cultivated over the years. Paniv had been cautious but not invisible. A car rental here, a cash-paid apartment there—his ghostly outline began to materialize from the fog.

Orlov cross-referenced images using surveillance footage from airports and public spaces with the dates of Alex Paniv's known movements. And there he was, captured in grainy footage at Limassol Marina, a man whose face matched Anton's. This man moved with the confidence of someone who believed himself to be unwatched, unguarded.

Cyprus was a hub for many seeking the discretion of its financial institutions, but even here, the electronic whispers of bank transfers spoke volumes to those who knew how to listen. Orlov collaborated with Cypriot authorities, drawing upon mutual interests to secure access to Alex's financial activity. The trail led to several banks home to accounts opened with precise, even amounts. Soon after, he found Alex's local company registered under his name and the company's corporate bank account.

With each step closer to Alex, Orlov marveled at the man's ingenuity and predictability. For all his efforts to dissolve into the background, Anton, now Alex, could not escape the fundamental truth that to live meant to leave traces. To Orlov, each trace was a thread in a web now drawing tighter around its prey.

In only twenty-three days, Orlov was ready to draw back the curtain on the grand illusion Anton had crafted. He was the storm on the horizon, the unraveller of Anton's carefully woven curtain of lies.

***

Alexa Marou sat in her well-organized office, the glow from her computer screen highlighting the determination in her eyes. The secret service and police chatter had been abuzz with the news of Dmitri Orlov's presence in Cyprus. Her sources, a blend of informants and digital trails, painted a picture of a man far from a tourist soaking up the Mediterranean sun. She sifted through the data, connecting dots that sketched a picture of an FSB operative inquiring about a certain Alex Paniv and interacting with Nikolai Gromov.

Her gaze flicked over to the window, watching the hustle of the city below. Orlov wasn't here for the view. The reports of him having lunch with Nikolai Gromov at the Annabelle hotel, a place known for its luxury and discretion, only added to her suspicions. Alexa prided herself on her instincts, which told her these men were players in a game that could have far-reaching consequences.

The whispers among the local financiers about Paniv's crypto company had reached her ears as well. His software was gaining traction, a legitimate venture but tinged with something unusual about it. Alexa knew the signs of money laundering when she saw them, and Paniv's sudden success was too convenient to be a coincidence.

Inspector Savvas, her mentor and confidant, handed her a slip of paper. "MI6, Jack McBride," he said, his voice low. "He's your man for anything regarding Orlov."

Alexa hesitated, considering the implications of contacting British intelligence. It was a line she hadn't crossed before, but these were not ordinary circumstances. She dialed the number, her heart rate picking up a notch as the line rang.

"Jack McBride," came the crisp British accent on the other end of the secure line. Alexa couldn't possibly imagine how dramatically her life was about to change with the start of this call.

"Mr. McBride, this is Inspector Alexa Marou with the Cyprus Police. I am currently investigating a suspected smuggling network with Russian nationals living in Cyprus being heavily involved. I have just stumbled upon something interesting in my findings. We might have a mutual acquaintance in Mr. Dmitri Orlov who has recently joined a scene here in Cyprus," she stated, getting straight to the point.

There was a pause, and then, "Inspector Marou nice to meet you. Yes, Dmitri Orlov and I are old acquaintances. If I may say so. How can I assist you?"

Alexa leaned back in her chair, locking eyes with Savvas. "I understand you've had history with him. Well, he's surfaced here in Cyprus, and I suspect he's involved in activities beyond the scope of average smuggling criminals. He's been seen with a local business figure, Nikolai Gromov, who is my primary suspect, and he's been inquiring about a Ukrainian national, Alex Paniv. Understanding this man's level and current activities in Cyprus, I assumed it would be best to consult with you on the matter."

The line crackled with the tension of a thousand unsaid words as Jack McBride absorbed the information. "If Orlov's in some kind of play," he finally spoke, his tone betraying the gravity of the revelation, "then it's definitely a high-stakes game. The FSB doesn't deploy their top dogs for small fry."

Alexa listened intently, her mind racing with the possibilities. "We've been grappling with a smuggling suspicion," she admitted, leaning closer to the phone as if it could close their geographical distance. "And I suspect that it's not just trinkets or contraband. We're talking about substantial sums—potentially tens of millions in cash."

The silence on the other end was telling. When Jack spoke again, his voice was laced with a new urgency. "Cash smuggling at that volume... It might not be just criminal. Smells political if FSB is involved. I need to dig deeper into this Gromov character."

Alexa's grip tightened on the receiver. "My gut says it's all interconnected. Gromov's recent movements, the crypto activities... there's a pattern we can't ignore here."

"I'll run Gromov through our databases and see what the UK side of things can flesh out. Anything that ties back to Orlov is a red flag, and we've been tracking certain... financial anomalies that could very well intersect with your situation," Jack said, the sound of keystrokes punctuating his words.

"We could use your insight, Mr. McBride. Cyprus might be a playground for some of these operatives, but we're determined to close it down," Alexa responded, her resolve as clear as the Mediterranean skies.

"You'll have my full cooperation, inspector," Jack assured her. "I'll be in touch when I have something concrete." Jack paused and then added, "A playground, you say... that makes a lot of sense." Those were his last words before he clicked off.

***

The setting sun cast a golden curtain over the expansive courtyard of Nikolai's Paphos villa. The shadows of the date palms lengthened like dark fingers stretching across the stone tiles. Nikolai, the self-styled king in his Cypriot stronghold, paced by the pool's edge, casting occasional, restless glances at the gate.

Dmitri Orlov arrived precisely on time. His silhouette outlined against the fading light as he was ushered through the iron-wrought gates. The man walked with an air of quiet confidence, his eyes taking in the opulence of the villa with a dispassionate detachment.

Nikolai should have used more time on pleasantries. "Well?" he demanded, the single word hanging between them heavy with expectation.

Orlov's voice was calm, unlike Nikolai's barely contained agitation. "Anton Gorin, now known as Alex Paniv, is indeed in Cyprus," he began, handing Nikolai a dossier thick with surveillance photos and bank records. "He's been quite the entrepreneur, setting up a facade of a crypto trading software business. It's clever, really—mixes legitimate operations with his money laundering to mask the flow of," Orlov theatrically paused. "Well, I hate to mention it, but your own cash."

Nikolai snatched the dossier, his eyes scanning the documents rapidly. "This... software scheme. Explain."

Orlov obliged, detailing the intricacies of the business. "Paniv offers a software service for cryptocurrency arbitrage trading, essentially exploiting price differences across exchanges. It's a real service, but he's inflated the price, and it seems he has struck a deal with a local developer. The developer buys licenses in bulk, laundering Paniv's cash through these transactions."

Nikolai's eyes narrowed. "And you have his address? His accounts?"

"Everything," Orlov confirmed, pointing to a section in the dossier. "I suggest surveillance for a few weeks. Understand his routines and his contacts. Wait until he leads us to where the money is kept."

Nikolai threw the papers onto a nearby table, his hands shaking slightly. "I don't want to watch him—I want my money and for him to pay for his theft."

Orlov's gaze was steady, unflinching. "Impatience could cost you everything. A few weeks could mean the difference between partial recovery and regaining all you've lost."

The words hung in the air as Nikolai looked out toward the darkening horizon. The desire for retribution fought with the logic of Orlov's argument.

Finally, he nodded curtly. "Fine. We do it your way— for now. But I want updates. Daily."

Orlov bowed his head slightly. "You'll have them. We'll bring Paniv to justice on our terms."

As Orlov turned to leave, Nikolai called out to him, a hard edge to his voice, "And Orlov, when it's time to move, I want to be there. I want to look into his eyes as his world crumbles."

Orlov didn't look back as he responded with a grim tone of certainty, "Of course. He stole from Nikolai Gromov. There will be nowhere left to hide."

***

Inside the offices of the Cypriot Police Headquarters, the atmosphere was thick with anticipation. Alexa stood before her superior, Inspector Savvas, a dossier of recent findings under her arm. Her expression was one of intense focus.

Savvas beckoned her to the chair opposite his large oak desk. "Alexa, it looks like you've pulled at some dangerous threads. What is the latest update?"

Alexa sat down, placing the dossier in front of them. "Boss, we have a developing situation with Dmitri Orlov. He's been seen with Nikolai Gromov again on numerous occasions, now including a visit to his villa."

Savvas' interest was visibly heightened. "That is really interesting, they are definitely up to something."

"I'm still not certain what it is, though," Alexa affirmed, her voice steady. "Moreover, Orlov has been traveling between Paphos and Nicosia back and forth. He is still on this Ukrainian guy, Alex Paniv, who runs a crypto software operation."

Savvas frowned, the gears turning in his head. "You know, Alexa, that crypto thing is a perfect smokescreen for money laundering or worse."

"Exactly," Alexa said with a nod. "And there's a peculiar aspect to it. Paniv's primary clients are local property developers with no apparent background or interest in cryptocurrency. It's as if they're using the software as a front."

Savvas stroked his chin thoughtfully. "Interesting, but for what purpose?"

"There's more," Alexa continued, "Jack McBride returned with the information on someone named Omar, stationed in Beirut. He's believed to be a financial linchpin for extremist groups throughout Lebanon, Gaza, and Iraq."

"And Inspector, here is the most important and final detail," Alexa continued, drawing Savvas' full attention "The name 'Omar' actually came to me before the Brits, directly from Olga Gromova."

Savvas looked up sharply, his expression a mix of surprise and intrigue. " Nikolai's wife?"

"Yes, she's been cautiously cooperating," Alexa explained. "She has overheard her husband's conversations multiple times. Omar's name came up regularly, and it wasn't just passing chatter. She sensed Omar was important to Nikolai's operations."

Savvas nodded slowly, processing the information. "That's a direct link and a whole different story, Alexa. We could be looking at an international crime syndicate or, worse, a terrorist plot. If Olga Gromova is willing to share this with us, it could mean she's either desperate or genuinely wants to distance herself from whatever Nikolai is involved in."

"She's frightened, I could see it in her eyes," Alexa said. "She's aware of the gravity of her husband's dealings and the danger it presents to her."

"Her cooperation could be invaluable," Savvas remarked, his tone considering Olga's delicate position. "Keep her close, Alexa. Ensure her safety. If Olga is willing to talk, we must offer her all the protection we can."

"I've assured her of our support and the possibility of immunity from prosecution if she cooperates fully," Alexa confirmed. "She's on edge, though. It's clear she's never been on this side of the law before."

"Understandable," Savvas acknowledged. "We're dealing with highly volatile individuals. Olga's cooperation could be the key to exposing Nikolai's network and understanding Omar's role within it."

153

"I'll continue to work with her and see what else she can provide us with," Alexa assured him, feeling the weight of the responsibility. "She could very well be our best shot at untangling this web."

"Very well," Savvas concluded. "Keep me updated, Alexa. Every small detail could lead to a breakthrough. And be careful. If Gromov suspects we're onto him, we never know how he might react."

Savvas' eyes darkened at the mention of the name. "The plot thickens. These elements could converge into something far more ominous than we anticipated. Nikolai, Omar, this Paniv character—threads here could weave a very grim carpet."

Both officers fell silent for a moment, contemplating the intricate web of crime and espionage that was starting to reveal itself. Alexa finally broke the silence.

"We need to move carefully but swiftly," she said. "The connections are there, and I believe we're on the cusp of unraveling a major conspiracy. Gromov's obsession with finding his stolen money, Orlov's sudden interest, Paniv's curious client list, and Omar's financial ties. It all paints a worrying picture indeed."

Savvas leaned back, his gaze fixed on Alexa. "Alright. Keep your investigations under tight wrap. With a determined nod, Alexa gathered her papers.

"Understood, sir. I'll dig deeper and keep you informed."

***

Agent Dmitri Orlov, with years of experience in surveillance and intelligence gathering, knew the value of patience and precision. Upon Nikolai's approval, he initiated a discreet but comprehensive surveillance operation on Alex Paniv, whom he believed to be Anton Gorin.

Orlov established a covert surveillance team that operated in shifts, ensuring that Alex's apartment and his movements were constantly monitored. Utilizing a mix of traditional fieldwork and advanced technology, including long-range cameras and electronic listening devices, the team was poised to capture every minute of Alex's daily life.

Throughout the week, Orlov documented Alex's routine. He noted that Alex had a strictly professional lifestyle—departing early for his office, attending sporadic business meetings in city cafes, and even occasionally visiting local tech stores for equipment that seemed to be for his software development business. However, it was the late-night activities that drew Orlov's interest. Alex often spent hours into the night in his home office, the glow of computer screens spilling into the dark Cyprus nights. Orlov didn't attempt to sneak into Alex's apartment, knowing that

Alex could digitally secure the space and receive notifications of any intruders. Dmitri had no intention of being recorded on cameras.

Suspecting that the remaining cash was hidden in the apartment, possibly within a concealed safe or an architectural blind spot, Orlov reported back to Nikolai with his findings.

Meeting again at Nikolai's estate in Paphos, Orlov laid out his report. "He's careful, I'll give him that," Orlov said, handing over the photographs and video stills. "But everyone has a pattern, and his revolves around his home office. I believe that's where he's hiding your money."

Nikolai, gripping the edge of the table, looked over the evidence with a hawkish intensity. "Could it be in the walls? A hidden safe, perhaps?" he suggested.

"Possibly," Orlov replied

Nikolai's eyes burned with a mix of anger and anticipation. "How soon can we move in?" he asked, his voice low but tinged with impatience.

Orlov held up a cautioning hand. "We mustn't rush this. We should wait for a new transaction to appear in his company's bank account. That would mean he exchanged the cash for a wire payment. The key is to carefully analyze his movements to locate the possible hiding spot for the money. Once we confirm that it's in his apartment, I'll let you know."

Nikolai considered this, his jaw tightening. "Very well, keep your men on him. I want to know everything—every call, every visitor, every breath he takes."

As Orlov nodded in agreement, the surveillance operation continued, each day tightening the net around Alex Paniv—a man unwittingly caught in a dangerous game of cat and mouse with one of the most influential and ruthless men.

***

Jack McBride was not easily ruffled. His tenure in MI6 had seen him plan operations from the favelas of Rio to the deserts of the Middle East. But Cyprus presented a unique combination of a criminal enterprise that intrigued even his seasoned mind. Jack's thoughts raced to analyze again in detail how this story unfolded. He was in his office in the heart of MI6 headquarters in London, poring over the latest intel that hinted at a nexus of shadowy finance and illicit Russian activities on the Mediterranean island.

A report caught his attention on Omar Sayed—a name that sent ripples through the intelligence community. Omar, a Libyan national, educated in Moscow and currently based in Beirut, was a mastermind financier, his fingerprints on the financial streams that fed the most radical and dangerous cells across the Middle East with a possible shadow of FSB or SVR. The traces were there, but the dots weren't fully connected—until Cyprus came into the picture.

When Jack followed up Alexa Marou's request on Dmitri Orlov, he shared a detail of the intelligence report about the dealings of Omar Sayed in Beirut. Alexa immediately recognized and confirmed that the name Omar came to her from Olga Gromova, the wife of Nikolai. It sparked McBride's interest as Omar was a cash man for the extremists in the Middle East, and Nikolai was under suspicion of smuggling cash into Cyprus. Suddenly, it all started to make perfect sense to Jack.

He had heard Alexa Marou's name even before she called him the first time. She was a well-known figure within the Cyprus Police. Over a secured line, Jack called her again, excited by the interest in a possible connection between cash smugglers and Middle East terrorist operations initially fueled by Omar's Russian education background and his current rumored status as a critical money man. They discussed their cases at length.

The mention of Omar in the same breath as Olga Gromova, the wife of a significant Russian player in Cyprus, was the catalyst that solidified Jack's resolve. It was no longer just a matter of tracking financial flows. It was about uncovering a potentially explosive link between Russian organized crime and financial operations supporting extremism. The final information provided by Alexa that intrigued Jack the most was the appearance of a top FSB man, Dmitri Orlov, in Cyprus. It could not simply have been a coincidence; Jack was sure of it. Something was brewing on the island.

Jack packed his bag, ready to travel to Cyprus. His mission ahead was clear: to infiltrate, observe, and expose the dangerous liaison between money, mafia, and mayhem.

As Jack boarded his flight, the London skyline receded into the background, giving way to the azure expanse of the Mediterranean Sea. The upcoming rendezvous with Alexa Marou would be the first step in a dance of diplomacy and danger. Jack McBride was heading into the fray, and the game was about to change.

Jack's first encounter with Alexa Marou in person was under the bright fluorescent lights of a poorly furnished conference room within the Cyprus Police Paphos headquarters. The atmosphere was charged with urgency as the two operatives, each a guardian of their nation's security, prepared to share their intelligence.

Jack laid out the snippets of information he'd gathered about Omar and his connections to Cyprus. As he spoke, his eyes couldn't help but take in Alexa's poise, the way her determination emanated from her very being. There was a fierceness in her gaze that spoke of battles fought and won, and it stirred something within him—a mixture of respect and an unexpected flutter of attraction.

Alexa, in turn, listened intently, her mind cataloging every detail Jack presented. She was accustomed to the company of men who wielded power, but there was something different about Jack McBride. He exuded a quiet confidence that didn't demand attention; it commanded it. While her focus remained on the task at hand, she couldn't deny the subtle, inexplicable pull she felt towards him.

As the meeting progressed, they pieced together the fragments of their separate investigations. The phone calls between Omar and Nikolai, the untraceable funds, the whispers of a deeper conspiracy—all pointed to a collaboration beyond mere criminal enterprise. It quickly became clear – the situation required a joint operation.

Jack walked away from the meeting with a newfound resolve. When out of sight, he reached for his phone, his fingers deftly composing the message that would bring his MI6 team to the Mediterranean island.

As he awaited his team's arrival, Jack allowed himself a rare moment of anticipation. Not just for the operation ahead but for the chance to work with Alexa Marou, a woman who impressed Jack. He didn't know that Alexa mirrored his sentiments, her thoughts drifting to the enigmatic British agent as she prepared to face whatever dangers lurked in the shadows of Cyprus.

***

Their first move was simple but risky: they needed to introduce a listening device into the lion's den—Nikolai Gromov's luxurious estate. The usual cleaning crew, a trio of local Cypriot women, would be their unwitting accomplices. Among them was Georgina, whose unsuspecting routine access to the most private quarters of the estate made her an invaluable asset.

Jack, with his team laying the groundwork, enlisted Alexa Marou's assistance. Alexa, whose connections in the local community were as deep as they were discreet, reached out to Georgina's family. Under the veil of night, in a quiet location away from prying eyes, Alexa met with Georgina and her husband, Nicos.

The scene was tense, with shadows dancing across the walls as Alexa laid out the plan. Georgina, a sturdy woman whose hands were accustomed to hard work, listened intently, her eyes betraying the fear that gripped her. Nicos, protective yet understanding the seriousness of the situation, placed a reassuring hand on her shoulder.

"We need your help," Alexa began, her voice low but firm. "Your access to Gromov's study is crucial for us.

Georgina, we promise your involvement will be kept under the strictest confidence. No one outside of this room will ever know about it."

Georgina's heart raced at the thought of deceiving her employer, a man known for his ruthless disposition. The danger was there, but so was the sense of duty that Alexa's words ignited within her.

After what felt like an eternity, Georgina nodded. "I'll do it," she whispered, more to herself than to the officer before her.

The next day, as the sun cast its golden glow over the estate's manicured gardens, Georgina went about her duties with the added weight of the mission at hand. With nimble fingers trained in the art of stealth by Alexa's team, she planted the listening device—a tiny beacon of truth in a sea of deceit—within the luxury of Nikolai's study.

As she left the room, her heart pounding, she allowed herself to breathe again. The deed was done, the die was cast, and the gears of justice began to turn, all thanks to the courage of an ordinary woman who dared to do her part in the shadowy dance of espionage.

***

Sitting in a dimly lit room, Jack stared at the live feed from a sophisticated listening device they had planted in Nikolai Gromov's study. The room buzzed with the tension of anticipation. The device, a marvel of espionage technology, was discreet and undetectable and had already begun transmitting crucial intelligence. The scratchy sound of a dial tone ended abruptly, and Nikolai's deep voice filled the room.

"Stelios, it's me. The shipment from Moscow will be here in three days. Be ready," Nikolai's voice was stern, carrying the weight of an order that expected no argument.

There was a pause, a crackle of static over the line before Stelios responded. His voice was weary, tinged with a nervous energy that spoke volumes.

"Nikolai, the CID, they're sniffing around. It's getting hot here, I don't know if…"

Nikolai cut him off, his voice a low growl. "I don't pay you to think about the CID. I pay you to get the job done. Fifty thousand euros, Stelios. That should be enough incentive."

Stelios's voice was barely above a whisper, the sound of a man cornered. "It's not about the money, Nikolai. They're onto us. If we get caught—"

"Then don't get fucking caught!" Nikolai snapped back. "You've done it before. You'll do it again. And don't get scared by local police clowns. If the worst comes to the worst, we will always buy our way out. Fifty thousand for you this time, Stelios, do you hear me? Are we clear?"

There was a tense silence, a void filled with unsaid words and unvoiced fears. Then, finally, Stelios's resigned voice came through. "Clear. I'll get it done. But this is the last time, Nikolai, please."

The line went dead, and Jack McBride's mind was racing in the room's quiet. The pieces began falling into place, forming an incomplete picture, but every new fragment added depth to his understanding.

He turned to his team, "We need to find out what's in that shipment. If it's what I think it will get us to Omar and possibly the whole FSB's Middle East scheme behind."

One of the younger agents, a tech wizard named Sophie, piped up. "I'll cross-reference Stelios with recent and past flight plans. We'll see the pattern if he's been moving something for Nikolai."

Jack gave a curt nod, his mind already moving to the next step. "And keep an eye on Orlov. He's the key to this whole thing. If he makes a move, we need to be two steps ahead."

As the team set to work, the whirring of computers and the low murmur of voices filled the room. Jack

McBride stood at the helm, a conductor orchestrating an espionage symphony, each noting a vital beat in the heart of their operation.

***

Unknown to Mr. Orlov, McBride's team carefully and silently recorded his every step. Jack's agents were phantoms within the spy world, skilled at operating invisibly even under the gaze of those as wise as Orlov.

Their operation was surgical. The British agents employed various tactics, from signal interception to physical tailing. They kept a watchful eye on Orlov, recording his rendezvous, the ebb and flow of his interactions with his own surveillance team, and even capturing the frequency of his encrypted communications back to Moscow. In a rented apartment that served as their makeshift command center, walls papered with surveillance photos and strings connecting various points of interest, the agents poured over every detail. Their tech specialists worked tirelessly, deploying algorithms and forensic software to crack into Orlov's secure channels.

They reconfirmed Alexa's initial information that Orlov's investigation was narrowing to an individual —Alex Paniv. It became a priority to understand why an FSB operative was so keenly focused on a man who had, until now, seemed like an odd figure in this whole story.

One evening, one of the British agents in a municipal worker uniform slipped past the window as Orlov sat at his workstation in the ground-floor apartment used by the Russians as a temporary headquarters. The agent, wearing a weed killer spraying tank and equipment on his back, was using a unique device silently siphoning data from Orlov's wireless network.

Back at their own base, the British agents combed through the data. They scrutinized the timings of Orlov's surveillance shifts and the patterns in his subject's behavior.

"Look at this," one of the agents whispered, pointing at a string of encrypted messages that had been painstakingly deciphered. "He's onto something to do with hidden or stolen assets."

Chapter 11

Alex Paniv's instincts had always served him well. He had carefully maintained his anonymity since arriving from Prague, always making sure not to let his guard down. But the man who had just walked past his car for the second time, a plain-looking figure, had tripped silent alarms in Alex's mind.

The first pass could be dismissed as a coincidence. The second time, with the man's hand subtly sliding something under the car's trunk, confirmed Alex's suspicion. He had seen enough in his former life to recognize surveillance when it was happening.

He had installed a tiny, almost invisible battery-operated mobile camera over his parking spot. He received notifications to his smartphone when the camera picked up anyone close to his car, so Alex could then follow up and check the recordings. There it was, as clear as the Cypriot sun: the man just planted a tracker on his vehicle. Alex's lips pressed into a thin line, confirming that they had found him.

He sat back in his chair, allowing the adrenaline rush to subside into a cold, calculating resolve. Panic was a luxury he couldn't afford. They expected him to run, to make a mistake, but he would not oblige them.

Alex knew that touching the money would be like sending up a flare. His accounts would be monitored, transactions flagged, and the noose tightened. No, his next steps would have to be off the grid, invisible to the prying eyes he now felt crawling over his life. He couldn't know for sure if his cash was safe now, but he understood by the mere fact that if they planted a tracking device onto his car, the odds were high that they had no idea where he kept the money. Alex's mind rushed back to his hiding place.

***

He had always been a planning man, and his latest venture was no exception. The plan was simple yet ingenious, designed to evade even the most prying of eyes.

A few months ago, Alex reached out to a man named Yannis, a friend of Mihalis, whose moving and storage business had seen better days. The business was slow, and the man was eager for work, so Alex's request couldn't have arrived at a better time. With a firm handshake and a wad of cash that smelled of promise, Alex secured Yannis' discretion and services.

"Yannis, I need to store some old furniture items for a long while. They're not mine as I'm renting the place, but I can't use them. They're so old and uncomfortable." Alex had said. "I must return them once I'm done renting the place."

Yannis nodded his understanding. The storage facility he operated was a labyrinth of forgotten treasures and dusty memories. It was the perfect place for Alex to hide his valuable burden.

As the day started fading into an early evening, they moved the old, worn sofa and matching armchairs, along with other old items, to Yannis' storage unit. To any onlooker, they were just pieces of outdated furniture, relics of a bygone era. But within the bowels of the sofa, nestled between springs and stuffing, lay stacks of crisp euro bills - the weight of Alex's future.

Yannis handed Alex a key. "A year in advance, all paid up. You can come and go as you please and bring more stuff if needed," he said.

In the following weeks, Alex visited the storage unit under the guise of bringing an old lamp and a stack of books for storage. Each visit allowed him to withdraw the necessary funds to sustain his growing business venture with Mihalis and his gang. The cash flowed from the depths of the sofa to the legitimacy of bank accounts, all under the watchful eye of Alex's brilliant arbitrage software. In a world where trust was a rare commodity, he had found a way to navigate the treacherous waters of his predicament, one clever move at a time.

***

Alex gathered a small bag with essentials — clothes, some cash, a laptop, other useful devices, and a few personal items that meant something to him. Each movement was deliberate and controlled. The bag had been prepared since the day he arrived in Cyprus, a grim but necessary measure. Alex understood that he must cut communication with everyone now, including his collaborators and loyal real estate developers turned crypto gurus. He had to disappear and lay low for a while. The cameras would remain, his digital eyes on the life he was about to leave. Should anyone enter his apartment after his departure, he would know about it. It was time to go, to blend into the crowds of Nicosia, until he became just another face and then vanished altogether.

Alex locked the door to his Nicosia apartment with a click that seemed to echo ominously in the deserted hallway. His eyes darted back and forth, his every sense on alert for the sound of footsteps or the creak of a floorboard. He had planned his escape, playing it over in his mind like a game of chess, anticipating every possible move of his pursuer.

Moving swiftly, he took the back stairs, avoiding the lift, which felt like a trap. At every landing, his hand rested on the cold metal of the railing, his other hand inside his jacket clutching the handle of a concealed knife—just in case. At the end of the staircase was a utility room window leading to the utility room itself.

Alex had made sure the window could be easily opened long before his escape. He went in and through the utility room before emerging into the humid night air on the other side of the building, his heart racing, not from the exertion but from the acute awareness that his life hung on a knife's edge.

With his collar turned up and his cap pulled down, Alex melted into the city's shadows. He moved with purpose but without haste, avoiding the main streets, choosing his route with the familiarity of someone who called the city home. He reached a taxi stand that was busy enough to be anonymous but not so crowded as to draw attention. Slipping into the back seat of an idling cab, he asked the driver to take him to the airport. He decided that his first destination should be Larnaca Airport, where he bought a ticket to Frankfurt, paying with his credit card. He never intended to use the ticket. He just wanted to buy time and send the wrong signal to his pursuers. As the night drew, he bribed his way for the no-ID check-in at one of Larnaca's three-star hotels and fell into a restless sleep.

***

As dusk settled over Paphos, Dmitri Orlov's silhouette loomed against the backdrop of a failing light. He had always prided himself on being two steps ahead, but this time, Anton Gorin, or Alex Paniv as he was now known, had vanished. Orlov's reputation was on the line, built on a foundation of successful operations and the quiet fear he instilled in those who crossed him. He stepped into Nikolai Gromov's study, the tension palpable. Nikolai, who had been pacing like a caged animal, turned sharply. "Well?" he demanded.

"He's gone," Orlov admitted, his tone even, betraying no emotion. "But not for long. He cannot have gone far."

Nikolai's fury was a tangible thing. "You promised me this would be handled! You assured me he'd be found!"

"And he will be," Orlov's response was firm and unwavering. He's clever; I'll give him that. But everyone leaves a trail."

The forced entry into Alex's apartment had yielded nothing. The money was nowhere to be found; there were no safe, false walls or hidden compartments. It was a ghost, like its owner. Orlov watched Nikolai as he barked orders into his phone, dispatching Zhorik and Slavik like hounds to the airports. Orlov left and drove away.

Nikolai fumed at the situation when his phone rang, cutting through the air like a knife. "Omar," he whispered before answering. The brief conversation ended with Nikolai saying, "It will be ready as always."

***

In the quiet confines of a back corner table at the cafe, Jack McBride spread out a thin folder in front of Alexa, their coffee cups steaming gently aside. The murmur of the cafe visitors around them was a comforting white noise, a bubble of normalcy in the undercurrents of intrigue.

"Omar's call to Gromov was intercepted. He's cautious, but we caught a break. The content was coded, but the gist is clear—there's a shipment coming in," McBride's voice was a low drawl, laden with the weight of implication.

Alexa leaned in, her sharp eyes scanning the printouts. "Do we know what 'goods' he's referring to?" she asked, using air quotes for emphasis.

"Not in detail, but given Omar's connections, we can assume it's either cash or something that'll lead us to a larger network," McBride answered, watching her closely.

Alexa's mind raced, piecing together the fragments of information. "And this 'agreed spot' Omar mentioned... any leads on where that could be?"

"We're combing through surveillance as we speak," McBride confirmed. "It's a needle in a haystack, but Omar's not exactly a ghost. He leaves echoes."

Alexa's posture was resolute, her determination etched into the lines of her face. "We need to proceed with caution without tipping off Gromov or Orlov. If we aren't careful, we could spook Omar and lose him."

McBride nodded, his expression matching her seriousness. "I propose a two-tiered operation. Surveillance from a distance—no direct interference unless necessary. And a secondary team ready to move in on Omar once we have a lock on the location."

The idea resonated with Alexa. "It's risky. We can't afford any slip-ups. The stakes are..." she paused, "... higher than we anticipated."

"Exactly," McBride's response was clipped. "This operation could unravel more than just a local crime syndicate. We could be looking at international implications. We need to play the long game here."

Their conversation continued with a blend of strategy and speculation. They dissected every angle, aware that their intelligence was as dangerous as it was crucial. The intercepted call was their best lead yet, and they both knew it.

As Alexa finished her coffee, her gaze locked with McBride's. "I'll coordinate with the local team. We'll need to be discreet, efficient, and absolutely silent."

McBride's smile was a thin line. "Silent as the grave, Alexa. We're not just hunting a criminal. With Orlov in the picture we are stepping into a dangerous zone of the espionage world."

They stood up, the folder now tucked securely under Alexa's arm. "Let's catch ourselves a terrorists' banker," she said, her voice low but fierce.

The air was thick with the salt of the sea and the weight of their mission as Alexa and McBride parted ways. McBride watched her stride away, her confidence as evident in her walk as it was in her strategic thinking. There was a fire in Alexa, one that spoke of more than just professional competence. It was a passion that mirrored his own—a drive that went beyond the call of duty. As she disappeared into the crowd, he felt an unexpected stir of admiration, not only for the officer she was but for the woman he was beginning to see.

Alexa felt the meeting's intensity linger like an aftertaste. There was something about McBride that went beyond his dossier. Yes, he was dedicated and sharp, with an understanding that matched her own, but there was a depth there she hadn't anticipated. As she walked through the crowds of tourists and locals alike, she replayed their conversation, not just the words but the unspoken understanding that seemed to pass between them. Was it just professional respect or something more? She shook her head, a wry smile playing on her lips. Now was not the time for such thoughts, yet they clung to her as persistent as the Mediterranean breeze.

***

The next day, Alex woke early and took a taxi to Limassol, where he spent a couple of early morning hours wandering about the old town, checking his tail, and having numerous coffees. He emailed and then called an Airbnb host, using his newly acquired anonymous phone, who had advertised a place to rent in Latchi, a small but picturesque village on the other side of the island, right on the shores of the sea. Alex made a cash deal over the phone to rent the flat for a week. An hour later, he took another taxi and was on his way to his new home.

He allowed himself a moment of respite as the taxi wound through the quieter streets. His mind, however, refused to quiet. Latchi was not a random choice. It was a picturesque escape where the tight grip of his current life could loosen, if only for a moment. It was a place to think, to plan, and to disappear.

The landscape began shifting as the taxi veered off the main road. Gone were the city's bustling streets, replaced by the open embrace of the countryside. Olive groves passed in a blur of silvery green, punctuated by the occasional flash of a red poppy or the deep purple of wild thistles. The air grew tangy with the scent of the sea mingling with the earthy perfume of the fields.

Latchi emerged on the horizon like a portrait of Cypriot serenity. The small fishing village was a mix of natural beauty and quaint charm. The harbor, a crescent of crystal waters, was lined with boats bobbing on the gentle swell, their masts a forest of slender white against the azure sky. Nets lay sprawled on the docks, drying from the day's catch, as fishermen mended their webs with the deft, calloused hands of tradition.

The village seemed to grow organically from the land, its buildings a cascade of terracotta and white, huddled together as if for comfort. Bougainvillea draped over balconies and walls in a riot of pink and purple while the paved streets wound lazily towards the beach, as though meandering to the water was a daily pleasure.

Alex's eyes were drawn to the horizon, where the sun began its descent, painting the sky with strokes of orange and gold. The sea reflected this spectacle, each wave a moving canvas, capturing the fading day's light and shadow. He could feel the tension ebbing away, replaced by a sense of peace he hadn't realized he was seeking.

As the taxi slowed to a stop, Alex paid the driver and stepped out into the embrace of the tranquil evening. The air was cooler here, the breeze a gentle caress, and the distant laughter of children mingled with the rhythmic clapping of the waves.

The studio he rented was modest, a simple dwelling among the locals' daily lives, just as he wanted it. A brief meeting with the owner ended fine, with him getting cash and bogus personal details from Alex without even bothering to check his ID.

As Alex settled into the sparse room, the adrenaline that had fueled him began to melt away, replaced by an all-consuming fatigue. He was safe, for now, but the solace was a cold comfort. The studio walls closed in on him, a tangible reminder of his isolation.

His thoughts drifted to Olga, the only person he knew outside his Nicosia circle. Should he call her? Perhaps she could help him hide. But could he take the risk of involving her in this twisted game of cat and mouse? He pondered with the phone in his hand, weighing it like the decision itself. He knew that calling Olga could mean dragging her into the depths of his trouble, but the human connection, the need to hear a friendly voice, was overwhelming.

As his laptop screen's soft glow filled the rented studio, Alex navigated through social media platforms. Driven by an inexplicable urge, he typed "Olga Paphos" into the Facebook search bar, unsure of what he might find. His innocent curiosity about the mysterious woman who had crossed his path was about to take an unforeseen turn.

Profile after profile appeared on the screen, a parade of strangers' lives unfolding before him. He paused at pictures of beach outings, family barbecues, and smiling faces, wondering if any of these glimpses of normalcy would ever be within his reach again.

Then he saw her: Olga Gromova. A pulse of recognition shot through him. He clicked on her profile, a window to her world. His breath hitched as he scrolled through the snippets of her life, catching glimpses of the woman who had occupied his thoughts more than he cared to admit.

And then, he froze.

There, in a photo dated a few months back, was Olga, radiant as he remembered, standing beside a man with the casual protective air of a husband. They were waving at a child entering a school gate, the very picture of suburban contentment. But it wasn't the happy family scene that captured Alex's complete attention—it was the background. Lurking there, almost out of focus, stood a man beside a sleek black Mercedes. It was him—the man from Anton's hotel room, the same figure he had seen through the lens of his laptop's hidden recording, the same man he saw outside his Prague apartment.

Alex's heart hammered in his chest, the shock rippling through him like a physical blow. His mind raced, trying to connect the impossible dots. What were the odds? Was Olga somehow involved in this twisted web he was entangled in? Or was it just a coincidence? The idea seemed far-fetched, but his life had just become a string of the improbable and the deadly.

Questions cascaded through his mind in a relentless torrent. Was this man tracking Olga as well? Was she another pawn or a player in this dangerous game? Carefully analyzing the photograph, Alex came to an obvious conclusion: the two people, Olga and the man next to her, were a couple with their child entering the school's gates. The man in the background looked like a bodyguard, a driver, or an assistant to Olga's husband judging by the whole setting of the photograph, the distances between them, and the postures. He was standing behind Olga's man, not too close but not too far, displaying his practiced skills as a bodyguard.

Alex considered the implications, a sense of dread settling in his stomach. Every interaction, every chance encounter, could have been observed and cataloged. Could his association with Olga have led this predator to his doorstep—or had it already? The photo, innocent in its intent, now screamed of hidden threats.

The puzzle pieces began to align in Alex's mind, each revelation more chilling than the last. The bodyguard in the photograph wasn't a random individual - he was the key to a truth that Alex had never anticipated. He had thought he was a step ahead, but he was merely tracing the outlines of a shadow that loomed much more extensive than he had imagined. His chance meeting with Olga had now emerged as a dangerous mistake. The idea that he had meddled with the affairs of Olga's family was like ice in his veins. A few further clicks on Facebook confirmed that Olga's husband's name was Nikolai. His night was spent trawling through the digital underbrush, researching Nikolai Gromov, piecing together the scope of his empire, marked by his Cyprus company's hotel purchase in Paphos. Each click, each scrolled page, drove home the fatal error of his liaison with Olga.

***

The shrill ringtone of his mobile phone pierced the stillness of the next morning's air. Alex's heart skipped a beat as the screen lit up with an incoming call, the name "Olga" flashing innocently. A cold sweat beaded on his forehead, a visceral reminder of the world he was trying to escape, now calling out to him through a simple digital display.

His pulse throbbed in his ears, and his mind raced, painting scenarios of what could be said, the potential fallout, the sliver of human connection he so desperately craved yet knew he must avoid for safety.

Alex's hand hovered over the phone, torn between the urge to pick up and his disciplined survival instincts. He felt like a man standing on the edge of a cliff, tempted by the whisper of "what if?" With each ring, the chance to connect with Olga slipped further away. But his decision remained firm. He couldn't, and he wouldn't pick up.

Far at the back of his mind, Alex's inner voice whispered that it could be Olga setting up a trap for him, helping her husband and that man who was hunting down Alex to finally get to him. His intuition refused to accept it, and the hope that Olga was unaware of the situation flickered like a candle under the breeze.

The phone finally fell silent. But the silence in the wake of the ignored call was thunderous in its implications. The phone's screen went dark, and with it, the temptation extinguished. Alex didn't move, staring at the device, the weight of his choices anchoring him to the spot.

Chapter 12

It was a foggy morning in Paphos, the kind that hinted at secrets and hidden conversations. Following Alexa Marou's directive, Olga had become an observer in her own life, viewing everything with suspicion. It was just another ordinary day until murmurs from the study broke the silence, mentioning names and incidents that made Olga's pulse race.

Dmitri Orlov's gruff and urgent voice spoke first. "Nikolai, the situation with Paniv is precarious. He's vanished like a ghost in the night. There has been no trace since Monday late afternoon when he went out and did not return to his apartment."

With a tone sharpened by frustration, Nikolai Gromov responded, "He can't have evaporated. This Alex, he's clever, but everyone slips. Are you sure he had no idea about surveillance?"

"Positive," Orlov assured. "We were discreet until the end. He led quite a routine life in Nicosia, a regular tech entrepreneur. No extravagant expenses, no suspicious movements—until he disappeared."

Olga, perched against the cool wall near the slightly ajar door, felt the color drain from her face. Alex, the tech entrepreneur, the man from the cafe, the casual acquaintance with the warm smile. Could he be the same Alex Paniv now entangled in this mess?

"But how?" Nikolai's voice boomed, "Why would he disappear if he didn't suspect being watched? Have you found any traces at all, card transactions, anything?"

Orlov's reply was clinical, "I am working to answer that question, Nikolai. As for the traces, well, he left some, but only those he wanted us to find, like a ticket to Frankfurt. We followed it up and lost some time. He is not a professional, but he is intelligent and careful. I am positive he's doing the only right thing to be done in his situation – laying low somewhere, paying only in cash, and waiting. But we'll find him. Cyprus is way too small to hide. He can't have gone far without resources, and he'll slip up. They always do."

Olga's mind raced as she pieced together the puzzle with the scraps of information she had. Alex Paniv — tech entrepreneur, Nicosia, an unexpected disappearance. Her heart thudded with the realization that the man who had stirred an inexplicable sense of connection within her was more enigmatic than she could have imagined.

As silence fell in the study, Olga retreated to her room. She needed to know more, to confirm the identity of the man who now consumed her thoughts. She retrieved her phone, hands trembling slightly, and dialed the number Alex had given her—the number that might connect her to a man wanted by the most dangerous people she knew.

It rang, and with each tone, her heart leaped. But the call spiraled into the void, unanswered. Confusion and fear knotted in her stomach, but above all, a stubborn flicker of concern bloomed for Alex, whoever he was.

***

In a quaint cafe tucked away from prying eyes, Alexa Marou waited patiently, accustomed to the tangled webs of covert affairs. The cafe, chosen by Olga for its privacy, was small and intimate, with walls rich with the scent of ground coffee and whispers of countless confessions, offering a semblance of solitude in a world where secrets were a rare luxury.

Olga arrived, a mix of nerves and determination, her eyes scanning the room before settling on Alexa. The CID officer, composed and perceptive, noticed the tremble in Olga's hands and the flicker of fear in her gaze.

"I'm glad you called," Alexa began, her voice a low hum designed to comfort. "What's troubling you?"

Olga took a deep breath, and her story unfolded — a tale about her chance encounter and eavesdropped dialogues, the image of Alex threaded through its center.

"I met him by accident at a random cafe while waiting for you in Nicosia. Or at least it all looked that way. Then again, at the hotel. He was kind, calm, and intriguing..." Olga's voice wavered. "But today, I overheard Dmitri and Nikolai. They spoke of a man, Alex from Nicosia, who had vanished. They're hunting him, and there's talk of money — stolen or lost, I can't be certain."

Alexa listened intently, sifting through the narrative for grains of truth. "This man, Alex, do you think he's involved with Nikolai's... operations?"

"I don't know," Olga admitted. "He doesn't fit the image of a criminal, but then again, neither did Nikolai when we first met."

The conversation veered into the mysterious dealings in Nicosia. Alexa shared some of what she knew from the findings of Jack McBride about the peculiarities of crypto trading software and its sudden uptake by unsuspecting local developers. "It's odd," she confessed. "The software, the developers, none of it breaks the law on the surface. But it does feel like we're missing an important puzzle piece here."

Olga leaned in, her voice dropping to a whisper, "I believe Alex is in danger, possibly because of the money he took from Nikolai. I've tried calling him, but he won't answer."

"You have to be careful," Alexa cautioned. "If your suspicions are correct, getting involved could place you in tremendous danger."

"I need to know if Alex is the man they want and why. I can't turn a blind eye to this."

Their cups sat forgotten, the coffee cooling as the two women dived into theories and speculations.

Alexa said, "We'll continue this investigation carefully. I'll look into Alex's dealings in Nicosia further, and you... you keep listening, Olga. Stay close to Nikolai, but do not—under any circumstances—reveal your suspicions."

Olga nodded, a silent pact forming between them. They were two women, each strong in their own right, now allied by a shared thread of intrigue and the pressing need to uncover a mystery that was as puzzling as it was dangerous.

***

Jack McBride leaned back in his chair, the creased pages of the latest surveillance reports rustling in his hands. The report was thorough—a mosaic of events and possibilities painstakingly pieced together by his team. They had tracked Alex's movements with the precision of hawks, noting his escape to the quaint seclusion of Latchi. They detailed his online searches and web pages he visited, unmasking his interest in Olga Gromova.

He rubbed his temple, thoughts racing. McBride's team had done well to remain invisible to both Orlov and his prey, Alex, observing without interfering. The transcript between Nikolai and Orlov was a treasure trove, teeming with frustration and the bitter tang of desperation. Nikolai was desperate to find Alex Paniv, who seemed to be a key to his Pandora's box.

McBride's eyes narrowed as he connected the dots. Olga Gromova, Alex's unexpected interest, was the wild card. She didn't fit the profile of the criminal underworld they'd come to expect, and yet her presence was intricately woven into the fabric of this chaos. As relayed to Jack by Alexa, Olga's coincidental encounter with Paniv in a Nicosia café added an intriguing layer to the unfolding narrative. Was it really accidental? Maybe. Maybe not.

What if Alex wasn't the hardened criminal, they presumed, but another pawn caught in Nikolai's ruthless game? The notion settled in his stomach like a stone.

A transcript excerpt caught his attention:

Orlov: "He vanished like a ghost, Nikolai. But ghosts leave echoes. We'll find him."

Nikolai: "Do not patronize me, Dmitri! That money is mine. So be it if it takes spilling blood to get it back."

The raw hunger for retribution was felt in every word Nikolai spat out. This didn't sound like it was just about the money; it had a personal touch to it. And somewhere between the lines, McBride sensed fear—the kind that led men to drastic measures.

The report ended with the latest: Alex's Facebook search. The Brits had him in their silent crosshairs, and McBride knew this was the moment to move carefully. One misstep and Alex could be lost to them—or worse, found by Nikolai.

McBride's following actions would need to be calculated with the precision of a chess grandmaster. He needed to unravel the nexus of Nikolai's operations, and getting to Omar was his primary goal. The British team stumbled upon Alex accidentally due to Mr. Orlov's activities but couldn't place him in the right puzzle spot.

***

The glow of the secure line's interface was the only light in Dmitri Orlov's room. He held the encrypted phone to his ear, the voice of Leonid Varushev, his superior, a soft but commanding rumble on the other end.

"Dmitri, report." Varushev's voice was as cold as the Russian steppes in winter.

"Nikolai has become... unpredictable," Orlov began, "The situation with the stolen money—he's taking it personally. It's interfering with his main operations."

There was a pause on the line, a silence that spoke of decisions being weighed in the balance of clandestine power.

"Nikolai is a tool, nothing more," Varushev said, finally breaking the silence. "But a useful one. Our network in the Middle East relies on his... entrepreneurial spirit. It's vital for our cash flows to those we support. You understand the importance of plausible deniability?"

Orlov's jaw tightened, "Yes, and Anton Gorin—"

"—Is a loose end that you will tie up. The system must continue to work, Dmitri. If Nikolai's utility is at an end, that is your call to make, but do not forget—"

"—The greater purpose," Orlov finished the sentence, a phrase etched into his mind over years of service.

"Exactly," Varushev's voice was the iron hand within a velvet glove. "Omar is key. Through him, we maintain the charade of distance from these groups. Should the finger be pointed, it finds only the Russian mafia, not the state."

Orlov knew the subtext; Nikolai Gromov's criminal facade was a cover, a layer of protection for the FSB's more covert activities. The web was intricate, the stakes high. One mistake could see it all unravel.

"If Nikolai proves a liability, you have the authority to act. But do so with the finesse we expect of you. We can't afford a spectacle."

"Understood," Orlov said, the word a granite promise. "I'll ensure the operation continues smoothly."

The line went dead. Orlov placed the encrypted phone down, its secrets locked away once more, and stepped into the night. The hunt for Anton Gorin was no longer a matter of stolen cash retrieval. It was about maintaining the delicate balance in a world unseen by most, where money flowed in silent currents, and men like Nikolai Gromov were the expendable cogs in a much larger machine.

Dmitri Orlov was aware of the irony as he disappeared into the night. In this world of espionage, he, too, was but a pawn—albeit one with the power to decide the fate of others.

***

The Cypriot sun was at full throttle, baking the stone-laid paths of Nikolai's estate, as Olga watched her daughter, Christine, laugh and play with Karen in the garden, her trusted friend and occasional babysitter. Olga sent Christine back to the house to get her bag. With two cups of tea, Olga and Karen sat in a shaded patio.

"Karen, are you sure you are okay to take Christine to Kalopanayiotis for a few days?" Olga's voice trembled slightly, a telltale sign of her inner disquiet.

"Absolutely no problem, love. There's a lovely resort there, Myrianthousa. It's safe, secluded, we'll have fun."

Karen tilted her head, sensing the urgency in Olga's eyes. "Is everything okay, Olga? You seem... worried."

Olga managed a brittle smile, her eyes betraying a flicker of the storm within. "I just need to sort out some things, and I can't have Christine caught up in this," she said, her hands clasped tightly together.

Karen nodded, her eyes soft with understanding. "Don't worry about a thing. I'll take her to my place now, let the kids have fun, and we'll leave first thing in the morning for the mountains."

After Christine and Karen left, Olga found herself alone with her thoughts, the house's silence amplifying the pounding of her heart. She paced back and forth, the decision to contact Alex clawing at her conscience.

She drove to the town and walked into a small electronics shop, the bell above the door announcing her entrance. The clerk greeted her with a nod, and she quickly made her selection—an inexpensive mobile phone and a So Easy prepaid sim card—paying in cash to leave no trace.

Back in her car, Olga opened the phone's packaging with trembling hands, the plastic crinkling loudly in the quiet vehicle. She inserted the battery and SIM card and then powered on the device. It felt alien in her hand, a lifeline to a man she barely knew.

Drafting the message was a struggle. Each word had to be chosen carefully. She paused, her fingers hovering over the keypad. Her message had to convey urgency, a plea for alliance, and above all, it had to convince Alex to trust her.

She typed, erased, and retyped until, finally, the words on the screen made her nod.

Hi! This is Olga. I know my husband is after you, and I want to help. He is a dangerous man from the underworld. Call me back.

The message was a gamble, but one Olga was willing to take. She hit send before she could second-guess herself.

As the text winged to Alex, Olga felt a shiver pass through her. She was no spy, no player in the games of shadow and deceit, but she couldn't sit idly while lives were toyed with and her husband's machinations spun out of control.

She placed the phone on the passenger seat, her gaze fixed on the phone as if it might erupt into life at any moment. Every second that ticked by stretched into an eternity of waiting, the sinking sun marking the passage of time with its waning light.

***

Alex sat alone on a weather-worn bench on the beach in Latchi, the rhythmic beat of the waves against the shore offering a soothing soundtrack to the cacophony of his thoughts. The sea stretched out before him, a vast expanse of blue that mirrored the uncertainty of his own future. His mind was a hive of scenarios, each more complicated and dangerous than the last.

A soft ding from his phone cut through the seaside tranquility like a boat cleaving the water. Alex glanced down to see a message from an unknown number.

Hi! This is Olga. I know my husband is after you, and I want to help. He is a dangerous man from the underworld. Call me back.

His heart raced, and he felt a cold sweat despite the warmth of the Cypriot sun. Was this a lifeline or a lure? He pondered the possibilities, turning the phone in his hands as if it might reveal more answers. Could he afford to trust Olga, or was this another of Nikolai's traps?

An hour passed as Alex debated with himself, the pros and cons swirling in a whirlpool of doubt and fear. Finally, he made his decision. He would call her. It was a risk, but so was breathing and living—especially now.

"Olga?" Alex's voice was a cautious whisper as if he were testing the waters of a potentially treacherous river.

"It's me, Alex," Olga replied, her voice restrained, mirroring his caution - "I'm glad you called; I was worried for you. We need to talk."

"Yes…" – Alex's voice was hesitant. "But not over the phone." – he paused and added - "It is better if we meet".

The idea of meeting Alex in person stirred a whirlwind of emotions within her. There was an undeniable undercurrent of apprehension, a niggling doubt at the back of her mind. She couldn't shake off the feeling of stepping into uncharted waters, of leaving the safety of the known for an encounter shrouded in uncertainty. With a deep breath, she steeled herself, determined to face whatever lay ahead, and whispered: "OK."

"There's a taverna in Kathikas called Petradaki. It's usually busy but should be safe for us," Alex proposed, the words rushed but clear.

"I can be there in about two hours," Olga confirmed, her voice laced with a cautious determination.

Two British agents, pretending to enjoy the sea view from a tourist-plated car parked just ten meters behind Alex, smiled as they picked up his part of the conversation through their high-tech mic. The device automatically translated it into English and sent the report to their boss. Now, they knew where Alex was heading next.

**

As Alex's taxi waded through the winding roads leading to Kathikas, the scenery transitioned from the coastal vistas to the rugged charm of Cyprus' heartland. Kathikas, with its rolling hills and vineyards, was a village where time seemed to move five times slower than the rest of the world. The taxi's engine hummed a steady rhythm as they passed rows of ancient olive trees, their gnarled branches testifying to centuries of silent watch over the land.

The village itself was a picturesque mosaic of stone houses and narrow streets, each turn revealing quaint courtyards overflowing with vibrant bougainvillea and geraniums. With their rustic wooden tables and chairs spilling out onto the cobblestone, local tavernas promised authentic Cypriot cuisine and the village's renowned local wines.

As the taxi entered Kathikas, the air was perfumed with wild herbs and the earthy aroma of the surrounding vineyards. Elderly villagers engaged in leisurely conversations and paused to observe the newcomer with a blend of curiosity and friendly scrutiny. Children played in the narrow alleys, their laughter echoing off the stone walls, adding a lively contrast to the otherwise quiet atmosphere.

In the heart of the village, the central square was dominated by a small but beautifully preserved church. Its bell tower stood proudly against the clear blue sky, a silent guardian watching over the community. Around the church, local shops offered everything from handcrafted souvenirs to fresh produce, the shopkeepers greeting each customer like an old friend.

Stopping on one of the village's narrow side streets, Alex got out of the taxi. He spent the next hour and a half surveying the taverna from a distance. His eyes were sharp, scanning for any sign of pursuit, any hint of danger. When he saw Olga on the road slowly turning into the parking lot and was satisfied that she had not been followed, he finally allowed himself to walk towards the taverna. Inside, he found her seated at a secluded table, her posture tense, her eyes wary. He sat down opposite her, and for a moment, they just looked at each other, two strangers bound by a thread of shared peril.

" I did not expect you to call or send a text." Alex's voice was a hushed, urgent undertone.

Olga's voice trembled slightly, a mix of excitement and urgency evident in her tone. "I understand the situation is complex, and trust doesn't come easily," she began, locking eyes with Alex. "Our meeting in Nicosia was completely accidental, as if fate had a hand in it. But I realize how it might look to you, especially given my connection to Nikolai."

She leaned in closer, her words laced with earnestness. "You see, being Nikolai's wife puts me in a difficult position. People often have preconceived notions about who I am, but the truth is, I'm just as trapped in this marriage as you are in your situation with him, Alex."

Pausing to gauge his reaction, she continued, her voice growing more passionate. "I don't know the full story of what happened between you and Nikolai, but I've heard enough to know he's after you, something about money that was taken... or stolen."

Alex's expression hardened slightly, but before he could respond, Olga rushed on. "I don't see you as a thief, Alex. To me, you don't seem like someone who would steal. I believe this might all be a misunderstanding or... something more complicated."

Alex interrupted her, a note of resignation in his voice. "Well, Olga, it's not exactly as simple as a misunderstanding." He sighed, "There is indeed an issue with the money, a significant one at that."

Olga's eyes widened, a mix of surprise and intrigue in her gaze as she waited for Alex to continue. Her heart raced, sensing that the veil of mystery surrounding Alex was about to be lifted.

Alex shifted slightly, revealing a hint of hesitation before he spoke. "Olga, I trust you," he began, his voice laced with a cautious undertone. "This meeting, it's not something I would normally agree to. But a feeling inside me, perhaps my intuition, tells me you're being honest. And I sense you're risking a lot just by being here with me."

He paused, taking a deep breath as if gathering his thoughts. "I've done some social media digging, and I discovered that you're his wife," Alex continued, voice dropping to almost a whisper, " I also figured out that the money I had stumbled upon, quite unintentionally, belongs to him."

Olga's eyes reflected her surprise, her breath held in anticipation as Alex leaned in closer, ensuring their conversation remained private amidst the taverna's ambient noise.

"I thought initially it might have been someone else's, someone I saw stalking me, someone who, as I understand, works for your husband." - Alex's tone conveyed a blend of wariness and resolve. "But now, knowing who you are, it's time I shared the entire story with you." Olga nodded, her expression a mix of intrigue and concern, as she prepared herself to listen to the tale that had entwined their fates in such an unexpected way.

Alex's voice was low and tinged with a hint of melancholy as he recounted his past, "I was trapped in a marriage that was falling apart, and in a desperate attempt to salvage what was left, I planned a trip to Cyprus with my then-wife. It was a last-ditch effort to mend things." He paused, his gaze distant as he relived the memory. "But it all came crashing down spectacularly. After yet another argument, I grabbed my stuff and drove to the airport in a rented car. It was at a roadside kiosk that I made a startling discovery."

His tone shifted, a mix of disbelief and bewilderment coloring his words. "In the trunk of my car were three suitcases. Not mine, obviously; a mix-up, probably by the hotel's porter. But what I found inside them..." He trailed off, his eyes meeting Olga's. "They were crammed with cash, Olga. Stacks of euro bills. An unfathomable amount."

At this revelation, Olga couldn't help but gasp, her eyes locked on Alex. She leaned in closer, absorbing every word, her heart racing with the realization that his story was unfolding into something far beyond what she had imagined.

Alex's voice carried a mix of resignation and determination as he opened up to Olga. "When I discovered that fortune, it felt like the universe offered me an escape hatch. My old life, with all its failures and disappointments, suddenly seemed like a distant memory. I couldn't ignore the chance to reinvent myself, to break free from a marriage that had become a prison, to step into a world of possibilities," he said, his eyes reflecting the mix of emotions he had experienced.

He leaned forward, his expression intense. "I knew the money wasn't clean. No one leaves that kind of cash lying around unless it's tied to something dark, something illegal. But at that moment, the risk seemed worth it. I tapped into my skills, hacked into the hotel's security system online, and discovered the cameras were down. It was like fate was nudging me to take the cash and run," he explained, a hint of excitement in his voice.

"I took the biggest gamble of my life. I stashed the cash in a rented apartment, returned to Kyiv, and started crafting a new identity. Everything was calculated, and every step was planned. I moved to Prague legally, leaving the old me behind. Eventually, I emerged here, in Nicosia, as a different man," Alex continued his narrative, painting a picture of a carefully orchestrated escape.

"Then, one night, they found me. My past, or rather, the shadow of that cash, caught up with me, and I had to vanish again and lay low. And now, here I am, sharing this with you, Olga. It's a life I never imagined, constantly looking over my shoulder, but it's the path I chose," he concluded, a mix of regret and resolve printed on his face.

Olga sat there, visibly moved by Alex's candid revelation. His story resonated with her on a deep, personal level. She felt a whirlwind of emotions swirling within her—a mix of empathy, shock, and an unexpected sense of connection. Here was a man who, like her, dreamed of a fresh start, a new chapter free from the chains of a past that no longer served him.

His honesty in admitting his flaws and the boldness of his actions struck a chord in Olga. She, too, had often fantasized about breaking away from the shackles of her stifling marriage, dreaming of a life where she could be her true self, unburdened and free. As she absorbed every word, Olga realized how much she admired his courage to take control of his destiny despite its dangerous path.

Olga's hand gently found its way across the table, resting atop Alex's. Her touch was tender and firm - a physical manifestation of the emotional bridge being built between them. "I understand," she whispered, her voice a soft but resolute. "And I know one thing with absolute certainty, Alex - the money that somehow ended up with you, it's tainted. Illegal. Nikolai, my husband, is connected with the mafia, and now, the police are closing in on him."

As she spoke, her eyes, usually a vivid pool of emotions, brimmed with tears that threatened to spill. "I've made a decision," she continued, her voice gaining strength despite the tremble of emotion. "I've decided to cooperate with the authorities. It's about saving myself and my daughter. We deserve a life far removed from this world of crime and fear."

Olga's gaze locked with Alex's, conveying a deep sincerity and determination. "I want to help you too, Alex. And in helping you, perhaps, I can find some redemption for myself, for having been blind to the life I was dragged into."

Her hand squeezed his slightly, a silent pledge of solidarity. Their eyes met, and there was a silent pledge in that gaze—an unspoken agreement that they were in this together. They had both been unwittingly drawn into a dangerous game, but now they chose to play it, not as pawns, but as players determined to rewrite the rules.

***

After they left the taverna, Alex strode down the road, his mind replaying every moment of their exchange. Her eyes, fierce with determination, her voice trembling with fear and courage—all resonated within him. However, he pondered whether revealing so much to her was dangerous. Had he stepped too far in the intricate dance of trust and risk? How could Olga's involvement with the police backfire on Alex?

Her words about wanting to escape her marriage, to break free from the clutches of a life she never wanted, resonated with a sincerity that was hard to dismiss. The risk for her was high; the consequences could be dire if Nikolai discovered her betrayal. Alex knew too well the cruelty of men like Nikolai.

Meanwhile, Olga sat alone in her car parked behind the taverna, her thoughts a stormy sea. Her primary concern was Christine—her daughter, her world.

Every decision she made, every step she took, was to ensure a brighter, safer future for her child. This unexpected alliance with Alex had only solidified her resolve.

But as she lingered over the remnants of their meeting, she had to acknowledge the stirrings within her heart. There was a pull towards Alex, a man who had appeared as a stranger and had become an enigma, an unexpected source of hope. His earnestness, vulnerability, and shared connection over their dire circumstances resonated with her in a way she couldn't entirely rationalize.

As she finally started the engine, Olga admitted that something about Alex drew her in. It felt like a touch of admiration, a flicker of what might be, under different circumstances, the beginnings of something more profound. But with the stakes so high, she shrouded these feelings, knowing that any personal desires had to be secondary to the safety and future of her daughter.

***

Alison Dayus and Daniel Moore, MI6 agents, had perfectly played their part. They blended seamlessly with the tourists at the Petradaki taverna, posing as British tourists. After a long day under the sun, their keen eyes and ears tuned to the couple who were the subjects of their surveillance. The unsuspecting older British couple at the neighboring table, deeply engrossed in their holiday bliss, provided a perfect cover by chatting and discussing their day.

"Could you take our picture, love?" the lady asked Alison, nudging a camera toward her.

"Of course," Alison smiled, taking the camera. Daniel subtly adjusted a small device under the table as Alison clicked away. It was a high-sensitivity microphone that was cleverly disguised and aimed to capture every syllable between Alex and Olga.

Later, back in the van packed with monitoring equipment, they handed the recording to the translation team. The exchange between Alex and Olga was now a digital transcript awaiting Jack McBride's scrutiny.

Jack leaned back in his office chair, the transcript before him. He couldn't help but chuckle at the absurdity of the situation—suitcases full of cash, a love interest possibly blossoming in the middle of international espionage, a runaway crypto trading software guy, and a Russian mobster's wife with a conscience.

"So, the IT guy turned thief because he wanted a new life, and now he's got the mobster's wife on his side," Jack mused aloud. "Sounds like a twisted spy novel."

Alison nodded, "It's certainly not your everyday operation, sir."

Jack's amusement gave way to sharp analysis as he sifted through the details of the conversation.

"Alright, let's break it down," he began, tapping the transcript with a pen. "Paniv has the mob's money and is scared enough to keep it close. He's intelligent and resourceful, but above all, he's scared. That makes him unpredictable."

He continued, "Olga Gromova, on the other hand, wants out. She's trapped in a world she despises, with a daughter to protect. She could be our key to deeply understanding Nikolai's operations with Omar. More importantly, she's a potential asset if we can guarantee her safety—and that of her child."

Alison listened intently as Jack connected the dots.

"Paniv doesn't trust anyone, rightfully so, but he's gravitating towards Olga. There's an emotional element here we didn't anticipate. It could be leverage or," Jack paused, "it could easily blow up in our faces if not handled delicately."

"And the money?" Alison interjected.

"The money is a rope. As long as Paniv holds it, Nikolai and his friends will snap at his heels. We can use that to steer the situation to our advantage. As for the grand suitcases' saga," Jack's eyes twinkled with mirth. " It's a reminder that sometimes the truth is stranger than fiction."

Jack stood up, his mind racing with possibilities. "We need to keep close tabs on Paniv and Gromova. However, these two are just spectators in a bigger game that they haven't got a clue about. We must uncover what Nikolai, FSB and Omar are doing together."

Alison nodded, "We'll keep our ears to the ground, sir."

"Good. And Alison," Jack said, a severe tone replacing his earlier fun, "I also want the team to keep an eye on those nasty characters, Slavik and Zhorik. We should always know where they are and what they are up to."

As Alison left to relay the orders, Jack stared at the transcripts. The pieces were on the board, and the game was intricate. The following moves would be critical; he intended to ensure that he would get to the bottom of everything.

His intelligent sources in Beirut had passed information that Omar had just left the port in his private yacht with some friends and eager girls. It could be something, or it could be nothing – thought McBride. He picked up the phone and ordered his team to monitor the boat's movements.

Chapter 13

Stelios Georgiou, a man of medium stature with a receding hairline and a perpetual tan, was a well-known figure in the Cypriot community. Born into a modest family in Limassol, he had always been ambitious, driven by a desire to rise above his humble beginnings. His early life was marked by hard work and a keen business sense, which propelled him into a successful career in both the public sector and private enterprise.

His venture into the world of real estate began in his late twenties, shortly after completing his studies in business administration. Stelios quickly demonstrated a natural flair for property development, and by the time he was forty, he had established a modest portfolio of residential properties - a few apartment buildings around the Paphos area. His achievements in real estate allowed him to indulge in his passion for coffee, establishing a small chain of cozy, well-loved coffee shops across Cyprus.

Parallel to his business ventures, Stelios nurtured a career at the Cyprus Border Control. He joined the agency in his early thirties, drawn by the promise of a steady government paycheck and the respectability of a civil service position. He climbed the ranks over the years, and his affable nature and savvy negotiation skills made him a popular figure among his colleagues and superiors.

Stelios first encountered Nikolai Gromov at a high-end fundraiser on a warm summer evening. Nikolai, with his imposing presence and charismatic charm, had immediately caught Stelios' attention. They struck up a conversation over drinks, and Stelios was impressed by Nikolai's shrewd business acumen. It wasn't long before they discovered mutual interests and a shared vision for potential deals.

During one of their golf outings, their relationship took a defining turn when Nikolai casually proposed a lucrative arrangement to Stelios. Nikolai needed a reliable ally in Border Control to ensure smooth operations for so-called 'relocation' items that the local Russian community required to be flown in from Moscow in private jets. In return, he offered Stelios a substantial sum, far exceeding any bribe he had encountered in his career. Initially hesitant, Stelios found the offer too tempting to resist. The money would secure a luxurious retirement life for him and provide means for his secret lust for younger women, a thought that heavily influenced his decision to get involved with the Russians. Rationalizing it as a one-time affair, Stelios agreed. However, the 'one-time' arrangement soon spiraled into a series of transactions, each more lucrative than the last. Stelios was entangled in a web of deceit and illegality, far removed from the straightforward world of real estate and coffee shops.

As he approached his fifty-third birthday, the weight of his choices began to press on him. His two children, now young adults, were unaware of the darker aspects of their father's dealings. Stelios often caught himself wondering about the legacy he would leave behind if it came to light. Would his children be proud of the small empire he built, or would they despise the means through which it was acquired?

Stelios' palms were moist, and his fingers tapped a nervous rhythm against the steely railing as he watched the small Cessna descend. The aircraft, initially a tiny speck in the vast Cypriot sky, grew larger and more distinct. The plane's engines rumbled as it touched down, and Stelios swallowed hard, his throat tight. The afternoon sun cast long shadows across the tarmac, shadows that seemed to play tricks on his eyes, morphing into menacing figures. He wiped his brow with the back of his hand, attempting to steady his breathing.

Around him, the airport buzzed with the usual chaos of logistics and travel, oblivious to the drama unfolding in its heart. Stelios felt isolated in his foreboding, a lone actor on a stage set for an unknown play.

His mind raced with possibilities. Was it weapons? Stolen goods? His gut told him it was something far worse. The Russians didn't involve him in simple contraband, and the ease with which they operated spoke of deep and dark connections.

He glanced over his shoulder, half-expecting to see the police closing in or, worse, one of Nikolai's cold-eyed associates watching him. Paranoia clawed at his senses, making him see enemies in every passerby.

Stelios had been careful in the paperwork, labeling the containers as 'fragile furniture,' a veneer of legitimacy he hoped would be enough to avoid suspicion. He was no novice to bending the rules, but this time the bending felt like a fracture about to snap.

The fear was visceral, a leaden weight in his stomach. He had crossed lines before, but this felt different. He considered disappearing into the crowd and leaving behind this world of under-the-table dealings and silent threats. But the image of Nikolai's icy stare, the veiled warnings, anchored him in place. He was in it, too deep, and now, he was part of a game he could neither win nor afford to lose.

***

Jack McBride's silhouette loomed inside the operations room over a series of screens, casting a watchful gaze over the live feeds streaming in. He held the phone to his ear, Alexa's voice a thread of sound in the sea of electronic hums.

"Alexa, the bait's been set. Stelios is facilitating the transfer as we speak," Jack began, his British accent crisp and clear. The large screen at the front of the room flickered as it focused on a live satellite image of the Cessna making its descent.

Alexa, situated in her own intelligence hub, replied with equal measure, "The trail from Stelios could lead us to much bigger things. Are you sure we should just watch this unfold?"

Jack leaned in, his voice firm but controlled. "Absolutely. We're not after the minnows here. We need the sharks, and for that, we must let the food chain play out without interruption. We have to see who bites."

Alexa considered the consequences. "If this goes south, it could be on us. We're letting a substantial amount of money change hands, Jack. Provided we are right that this is all cash."

He chuckled softly, a sound without humor. "This isn't our first rodeo, Alexa. We've played the long game before. Remember, we're the spider, not the fly. The web's been spun, and now we wait. And I have a gut feeling it is cash."

Her voice was a murmur of acknowledgment. "I trust your judgment, Jack. What's our next move?"

"We monitor the transaction, follow the money, and keep tabs on Stelios.

"And what if they sense a trap?" she queried, the concern evident even through the encryption of the line.

Jack's response was calculated, a testament to years in the field. "We've been careful. They believe they're moving in secret, under the radar. As long as we keep our distance and our tech doesn't fail us, they'll remain in the dark. Let's not forget we have the best eyes in the sky, and our ears on the ground are unmatched. Finally, Alexa, they have no other way but to do something with that cash."

Alexa gave a small sigh, a blend of resignation and confidence. "Then we watch and wait."

Jack's eyes never wavered from the screen. "Exactly. We wait. And when the moment is right, we close the net. But for now, patience is our ally."

The conversation ended, leaving Jack with his thoughts and the soft buzz of electronics. In this game of cat and mouse, timing was everything, and Jack McBride was a clock master.

***

The Cessna touched down with a gentle bounce, rolling to a stop not far from Stelios. He could make out the figures of Zhorik and Slavik, two of Nikolai's most trusted men, exiting the plane. They were bear-like, their presence alone enough to deter any unnecessary curiosity.

As the ground crew began working on the parked Cessna, Stelios took a tentative step forward. The boxes were handled carefully and marked with the false promise of delicate contents. Each container that rolled past him on the conveyor seemed to echo with a silent accusation, a whisper of the betrayal of his own principles.

Zhorik and Slavik were busy unloading. They've done this before; it was just another workday for them. The illusion of normalcy was so convincing that, for a moment, Stelios allowed himself the luxury of belief.

The containers were loaded into an old truck, the kind you'd see making deliveries in any neighborhood. But these were no ordinary deliveries. Stelios handed over the papers, his signature a reluctant stroke of ink that could very well be signing away his freedom.

As the truck vanished into the distance, blending with the traffic, he swiftly stuffed fifty thousand euros into a package beneath the seat of his car, locked the doors, and returned to his office to continue his routine as an officer for the Cyprus Border Patrol.

***

The hum of Nikolai's encrypted phone interrupted the steady rhythm of the waves against the shore of Paphos. He glanced at the caller ID — Omar.

"Omar," Nikolai said as he answered the phone.

"The package, Nikolai. Has it arrived?"

Nikolai couldn't suppress the slight curve of his lips. "The eagle has landed," he replied, using the agreed-upon code to signal a successful delivery.

Silence stretched for a heartbeat on the line before Omar spoke again. "I will make the collection at the designated time and place."

"As we have arranged," Nikolai affirmed. He watched a solitary boat bobbing on the horizon. "The shadows will cloak your approach, as always."

"There's no need for poetry, Nikolai," Omar reminded him, his tone dry.

Nikolai's eyes narrowed slightly. "Of course. You'll find everything in order, as per our understanding."

"It had better be. Our friends in Moscow do not tolerate deviations," Omar's voice carried a hard edge, a reminder of the unseen hand that guided their covert operations.

Nikolai remained unfazed. "They have my assurances. Our arrangement has been profitable for all parties. I keep my side of the streets clean; in return, they turn a blind eye to... other endeavors."

"That is the nature of our business," Omar said. We take from here and give to there. It's simple."

"Indeed," Nikolai concurred. Their relationship was transactional, nothing more. He provided the means, Omar the movement, and the FSB pulled the strings somewhere in the depths of the shadowy web they created.

With an indifferent and rather cold goodbye, Omar ended the call. Nikolai sat for a moment longer with the fading light painting the evening in shades of amber. The cargo, a fortune in euros, was nothing more than fuel for a machine that churned somewhere beyond the sight of ordinary men. And he, Nikolai, was a mere cog in that machine.

The stakes were high; they always were. But to Nikolai, who had found a way to survive and thrive in the shadows cast by powerful forces, the risk was the price of his continued freedom and influence. Every successful transfer, every undetected movement of funds, was a victory in a game where the players remained hidden and unseen masters who wrote the rules.

***

Many years ago, in the backroom of an inconspicuous Moscow bar, Nikolai Gromov, then a small-time young mafia figure entrapped in the murky world of drug smuggling, found himself sitting across from two stern-faced men. They introduced themselves as agents of the FSB, Russia's principal security agency. The seriousness of the situation was not lost on Nikolai; his heart raced as he realized nothing good was coming his way out of this encounter.

One of the agents, a man with cold, calculating eyes, slid a thick file across the table. "Mr. Gromov," he began, his voice steady and devoid of emotion, "we have been following your... activities. Quite a risky business you've got yourself into."

Nikolai's mind raced as he flipped through the pages, each filled with detailed accounts of his crimes. The evidence was overwhelming. They had him, literally, cornered. He was facing a long prison term. The other agent, younger but equally stern, leaned forward, "However, we believe a man of your talents could be of use to us."

They laid out a proposition that would change Nikolai's life forever. The FSB needed someone reliable, someone who could operate in the shadows to smuggle electronics and home appliances into Russia. But that was only the beginning. They envisioned Nikolai as a key player in a larger scheme that involved relocating to Cyprus, establishing a legitimate business front, and, ultimately, facilitating the movement of large sums of cash into the country.

It was a lifeline thrown into the deep, dark waters that Nikolai was swimming in. The prospect of escaping the dangerous drug trade and the potential of prison for a more profitable and somewhat safer venture was too good to pass up. "What's the catch?" Nikolai asked cautiously.

"The catch, Mr. Gromov, is your complete loyalty and discretion. You will operate under our guidance, and in return, we ensure your protection and prosperity," the older agent replied with a hint of a smile.

Nikolai's decision to accept the offer marked the beginning of his transformation from a local gangster to an international businessman. His business adapted as political tensions rose and sanctions were imposed on Russia. The FSB's backing allowed him to circumvent restrictions, and soon, he was smuggling luxury items from the West into Russia – cheeses, wines, and other delicacies in high demand among the Russian elite.

His success was meteoric. Later, Nikolai established himself in Cyprus at the orders of his patrons from FSB, leveraging the island's strategic location and growing his network of contacts. He invested in property, became a well-known figure in local circles, and carefully crafted the image of a successful entrepreneur. However, beneath this veneer of legitimacy, the dark undercurrents of his operations continued, guided by the invisible hand of the FSB.

***

The Wave Cruiser sat majestically in Paphos harbor, its white hull gleaming under the Cypriot sun. In the early hours, before the bustle of tourists and the cacophony of vendors selling their wares along the dockside, the boat was a realm of quiet industry. Workers, clad in the bright blue polo shirts emblazoned with the Wave Cruiser's logo, moved with efficiency, preparing for the evening's excursion.

Aboard the vessel, the air was thick with the smell of the sea and the fresh tang of citrus from the cleaning fluids. Hoses snaked across the deck, expelling bursts of water that washed away the remnants of the previous night's festivities. Scrub brushes danced in rhythmic circles, pushed by hands that had done this many times before, restoring the wood to its polished gloss.

The bar area was a hive of activity, with crates of bottled beer, stacks of soft drink cans, and boxes of snack foods arranged neatly behind the counter. A young bartender, with a deft touch, carefully placed glass bottles onto shelves, creating a clinking melody.

But within the symphony of preparation, there was a subtle undercurrent of something else at play. Zhorik and Slavik, who were posing as a part of the stocking crew, carried a different kind of cargo with them. What was earlier disguised as furniture and household items on the plane quickly became regular beer cartons on the boat; their contents were anything but bundles of cash amounting to 50 million euros.

They moved casually, moving the heavy boxes. To any onlooker, they were just two more workers organizing the boat's supplies for the evening's cruise. The other staff paid them no mind, accustomed to the daily stock replenishment.

The beer cartons, cleverly resealed and indistinguishable from the genuine products, were placed behind legitimate supplies at the back of the storage room with restricted access. Slavik was concentrated and grim as he worked, aware of the importance of their task. Zhorik, on the other hand, seemed to carry an air of indifference, whistling a tune under his breath as if he were merely unloading another shipment of alcohol. Once the cartons were stacked, Zhorik wiped his hands on his jeans and scanned the area. "All clear?" he muttered to Slavik.

Slavik nodded, casting a cautious glance over his shoulder. "Yeah, just another day at the office. Just make sure no one gets here and takes anything without your permission." Zhorik smiled and nodded.

As the sun climbed higher, the harbor began to fill with life. The sound of laughter and chatter rescinded as the day's first tourists congregated near the Wave Cruiser, eager for the promised experience of a Cypriot sunset at sea.

***

A few years before the tumultuous events that would define his life in Cyprus, Nikolai Gromov, on the explicit instructions of the FSB, found himself negotiating with a Cypriot businessman to purchase a vessel named 'Wave Cruiser'. The FSB had clearly articulated the need for a robust cover for their secret operations, and this luxury entertainment boat seemed like the perfect choice.

Unaware of the vessel's intended use, the businessman was more than happy to discuss terms with Nikolai, a seemingly affluent Russian entrepreneur. Leveraging his refined negotiation skills, Nikolai struck a lucrative deal for both parties. The transaction was smooth, with Nikolai building the perfect image of a businessman expanding his leisure enterprise.

From the outside, the Wave Cruiser was the epitome of opulent sea-based entertainment. A large, sleek boat, it boasted modern amenities and a spacious deck for parties and was the ideal setting for sunset watching, dancing, and drinking sessions. It quickly became popular among tourists and locals alike, known for its lavish cruises and exceptional service.

However, the Wave Cruiser's real purpose was far from the public eye. The FSB had envisioned it as a key asset in their complex network of operations. It provided the perfect cover for clandestine meetings, discreet transportation of goods, and, as it turned out, a significant amount of cash. The boat's frequent trips and the ever-changing roster of guests and partygoers made it an ideal vessel for covert activities.

Nikolai, playing his part to perfection, often mingled with guests, his charm and charisma adding to the allure of the cruises. Yet, beneath his friendly exterior, he was always alert, constantly monitoring the activities that were the real reason behind the Wave Cruiser's existence. This boat, a symbol of luxury and leisure, had become a pivotal tool in a game of shadows and secrets, navigated by Nikolai under the watchful eyes of his FSB handlers.

Chapter 14

The evening air in the expansive living room of their Paphos home was charged with tension, an unsettling stillness that seemed to have settled between Nikolai and Olga. A solitary glass of red wine sat untouched on the marble countertop, reflecting the muted light of the overhead chandelier.

"Olga, my dear," Nikolai said, his voice a velvety purr as he stepped closer to her. Why don't we retire early tonight?" The suggestion carried an implicit command, and his hand reached out to trace her jawline.

Olga recoiled from his touch, her eyes steeling over with a resolve that had been building for months. "I'm not in the mood, Nikolai," she said, her voice steady but with an underlying tremor that betrayed her inner turmoil.

Nikolai's expression darkened, the softness in his manner evaporating. "I wasn't asking, Olga."

This was not the man Olga had married, or perhaps it was, but she had been too blind to see. "We need to talk," she said, clutching at the fabric of her dress in a desperate attempt to anchor herself. "About everything — the money, the strange men coming and going at all hours. What are you involved in, Nikolai?"

Nikolai's eyes narrowed into slits. "You are my wife. You don't need to worry about my business."

"But I do worry!" Olga's voice broke, a dam of silence finally yielding to the pressure of her fears. "I worry daily about what kind of life we're building here, what danger we're in."

Nikolai's hands balled into fists, his knuckles whitening. "You are safe because of what I do! The luxury you enjoy—"

"I don't want any of this if it comes with shadows and secrets!" Olga interrupted, her own hands trembling. "I can't do this anymore, Nikolai. I can't be the woman who smiles, nods, and pretends she doesn't see what's happening right in front of her."

Nikolai's face contorted with fury, his body tensing as if coiling to strike. "You will not speak to me in this manner," he spat.

Olga's chest heaved, her following words slipping out like a whisper of smoke. "I don't love you, Nikolai. I haven't for a long time."

The air seemed to crackle with the impact of her words. Nikolai's hand moved so fast, it was a blur —

and then there was a sharp sting on Olga's cheek, the sound of the impact slicing through the room's stillness. She stumbled, her hand flying to the reddening mark on her face, her eyes wide with shock and pain. Shaking, she headed for the door.

"You will not leave," Nikolai seethed, "You will not disobey me!"

But Olga was already moving, her survival instincts kicking in. She darted past him, her feet carrying her swiftly to the door, her entire body shaking. The opulent home that had felt like a cage for so long now seemed like a treacherous maze as she navigated her escape.

Once in her car, Olga's breaths came in ragged gasps, her hands gripping the steering wheel as if it were her lifeline. Her cheek hurt like hell. She turned the ignition; the engine roared in the silence she left behind.

Nikolai watched from the doorway, his face a mask of rage and disbelief. He pulled his phone from his pocket, his hand still trembling from the anger, and dialed with purpose.

"Slavik," he barked into the phone, "Olga's just left in her car. Find her. Bring her back to me."

The line clicked dead as Slavik acknowledged the order. Nikolai's gaze turned towards the night, where

Olga's taillights had already disappeared, leaving behind nothing but the chill of the Mediterranean breeze and the echo of a door slamming shut on a life Olga no longer wanted to live. The room was silent, but his mind roared with betrayal, anger, and the unrelenting drive for revenge.

***

Olga's escape had been a blur of streetlights and sharp turns. The rumble of the car engine mingled with her heart's erratic pounding. When she finally reached the Coral Bay Hotel, she parked under the flickering glow of a lamppost. Her hands, still trembling, clutched the phone as she dialed Alex's number. It felt like an eternity until his voice, a steady calm in the storm, finally answered.

"Alex," she whispered, a quiver in her voice betraying her panicked state, "I have run away and need your help." Olga quickly explained where she was.

"Olga, listen to me carefully," Alex's voice was firm, "Leave the car in the parking lot, take your personal belongings, and walk away. Find a place to hide and wait for me. I'll be there as soon as I can."

With every nerve alight, Olga followed his instructions to the letter. She slipped into the darkness, eyes scanning for any sign of pursuit. The night air was cool against her flushed skin as she found a spot in the shadows, waiting.

When a taxi silently rolled into the lot, and Alex got out, it seemed like a sliver of hope. She emerged from her hiding spot, and their eyes met — his filled with concern, hers with a haunting fear that clung like a second skin.

He ushered her into the back seat with a gentle hand on her back, and the taxi started driving away with Alex's careful eye on the rearview mirror. The drive to Latchi was quiet, save for Olga recounting the night's harrowing events.

Upon arriving at his apartment, he led her inside. He quickly moved through the kitchen, boiling water for tea as Olga settled onto the couch, her body folding into the cushions as if trying to disappear into them.

He handed her the warm mug, his fingers brushing hers, a silent exchange of comfort. "Drink this. It'll help," he said softly.

Olga sipped the tea, the herbal warmth spreading through her. Her eyes were fatigued, and her mind was a whirlwind of emotions. Sensing her distress, Alex decided to distract her attention from the current events and share a piece of his childhood, a story that always comforted him in times of turmoil.

He sat next to her. "You know, when I was a kid, I had a secret place," Alex began, his voice soft and soothing. "It was in my grandmother's house. She had this old attic full of forgotten treasures and memories. But it was more than a dusty room. It was my sanctuary."

Her eyelids fluttering, Olga listened intently, finding comfort in his words.

"A small corner of the attic was behind an old, creaky wardrobe. I found it one day while playing hide and seek. It was like discovering a new world. I cleared out the cobwebs and brought in an old lamp, old worn carpet and cushions, and a few books. It became my secret room," Alex continued with a nostalgic smile on his lips.

He stood, walked over to the window, gazing out into the night as he spoke. "Whenever I felt hurt or stressed with school or friends, I would escape to that room. It was my place where no one could find me, where I could just be myself, away from the expectations and pressures of the outside world. I would spend hours there, reading, dreaming, or just listening to the silence. It was as if the walls of that little corner held my fears and let me breathe, let me be just a kid with dreams and a wild imagination."

He sat down next to her again, his voice a mere whisper. "That room taught me the value of having a safe space, a haven where you can let go of your worries, even for a little while."

Olga reached out, her hand gently squeezing his. "Thank you, Alex, for sharing your attic with me and for being my safe space tonight."

As the night deepened and Olga's breaths evened out, sleep finally claimed her, the teacup resting empty on the coffee table. Alex draped a blanket over her, his fingers lingering for a moment on the softness of her hair. Settling into an armchair nearby, he remained awake, watchful and protective. He felt a connection that went beyond the fear and the danger — a connection that felt like a promise.

***

The first light of dawn slowly crept into the apartment. Olga stirred, her eyes fluttering open to find Alex sitting in the armchair, his eyes soft and caring.

"Good morning," he greeted her with a gentle smile, the worry lines around his eyes easing.

She managed a weary smile in return, the terror of the night melting away in the warmth of his gaze. "Good morning," she echoed, her voice still laced with fatigue.

"I've made coffee," Alex said, pouring her a cup. The rich aroma filled the room. He handed her the cup, their fingers touching briefly again. Olga took a deep breath, the steam from the coffee mingling with the salty sea air that wafted through the open window. She looked up at Alex, her eyes finding his.

"Thank you," she said, not just for the coffee but for the safety, the care, and the unspoken vow of protection he had given her.

In that quiet morning hour, as they sat together, a new day beginning, there was an unspoken understanding between them. They were two souls, cast adrift by their circumstances, finding anchor in each other's storm. The romance of the moment was not in grand gestures or passionate declarations — it was in the simple act of being there, the silent promise of "I've got you," and the shared solitude that spoke volumes more than words ever could.

Olga needed to freshen up. "May I take a shower?" she asked, her voice tinged with a vulnerability that resonated deeply with Alex.

"Of course," he replied, standing up. Alex then led her to the bathroom with fresh towels and other necessities. "Take your time," he said, "make yourself at home."

Emerging from the shower, Olga felt a sense of renewal. The warmth of the water had washed away the stress and fear, if only temporarily. Wrapped in a towel, her hair damp and clinging to her skin, she softly asked, "Alex, do you have a hairdryer?"

"Yes, just a second," he said, entering the bathroom with the hairdryer in hand. The confined space brought them closer together, their bodies just inches apart. Their eyes met as he handed her the hairdryer, and the tension known only to those who were falling in love with each other filled the air.

At that moment, all the barriers that had held them back seemed to dissolve. The air was charged with an electric current of attraction and desire. Olga's eyes, usually filled with sadness, now sparkled with a different emotion, one that mirrored Alex's own rising feelings.

Without a word, they moved closer, their breaths mingling, hearts racing. The towel slipped slightly as Alex reached out, gently tucking a strand of damp hair behind Olga's ear. The touch was light, but it ignited a fire between them.

Their lips met in a hesitant, exploratory kiss that quickly deepened into something more passionate, more urgent. With its steamy mirror and the sound of dripping water, the small bathroom became their secluded world where the chaos outside ceased to exist.

The towel fell to the floor, forgotten, as they embraced each other tightly, lost in the moment's intensity.

As they eventually stepped out of the bathroom, breathless and flushed, there was a silent acknowledgment of the significance of what had just happened. It wasn't a fleeting moment of passion but rather the beginning of something deeper that could potentially blossom into a profound and meaningful relationship.

Chapter 15

The bustling harbor of Paphos served as a picturesque spot for Theo's Restaurant, where the air was filled with the scent of the sea and grilled seafood. Jack McBride and Alexa found a quiet corner table, away from the lunchtime chatter, allowing for privacy amidst the clinking of cutlery and the occasional seagull's cry.

Alexa glanced across the table at Jack, noting the sun highlighting the angles of his face, giving him a more softened, approachable look than the stern expression he usually presented. "So, what's the play with Nikolai?" she asked, leaning forward, her elbows resting on the table.

Jack paused, his gaze fixed on the shimmering waters beyond the harbor. "We let him move, watch his steps. He's the key to a larger door, Alexa, and I'm betting it swings both ways – into our world and out to whoever he's dealing with."

His tone had a slight, almost imperceptible warmth that Alexa hadn't noticed before. It caused a flutter of something like anticipation in her stomach. She quickly masked it with a sip of water, feeling the coolness wash away the unfamiliar sensation.

The conversation shifted subtly from professional to personal stories as their meal arrived. Laughter mingled with strategy, and Alexa enjoyed Jack's company unexpectedly and slightly disarmingly.

Alexa Marou, now a seasoned police officer, had long learned to guard her heart, especially after her early years in the force had left a painful scar on her personal life. As a young detective, full of ambition and the naivety of youth, she had found herself drawn to a man who represented everything she thought she wanted.

He was five years her senior, a well-respected figure within the police force who seemed to epitomize leadership and strength. Their connection was instant, a spark that quickly grew into a flame. But there was a catch — he was married.

He told a story of an unhappy marriage, of being trapped in a relationship that had long since lost its love and warmth. Alexa, believing in the sincerity of his words and the intensity of their connection, fell deeply in love. He promised her a future and spoke of a time when they could be together openly, free from secrecy. But as the months turned into years, his promises proved empty. The divorce he spoke of never materialized, and Alexa realized she was nothing more than a secret being kept in the dark.

The end of their affair left Alexa with a deep sense of betrayal and a vow never to let her heart be so recklessly handled again. She built walls around her emotions, focusing on her career and on becoming the best in her field. The experience taught her the bitter lesson that not everyone who shows affection can be trusted and that promises can be as flimsy as smoke.

Now, years later, sitting at Theo's with Jack McBride, she felt the past quietly knocking at the doors of her carefully guarded heart. Jack was different. He exuded a sense of stability, an air of honesty she hadn't encountered in a long time. There was a genuineness in his eyes, a sincerity in his words that resonated with her. He didn't feel like another chapter in her life but rather a fresh beginning, a chance to finally let down her guard and explore the possibilities of a relationship built on mutual respect and trust.

As they talked, Alexa couldn't help but compare Jack to the man from her past. Where her previous love had been a storm, full of passion but ultimately destructive, Jack was like a calm harbor – safe, steady, and reliable. With him, she felt a sense of peace, an assurance that there was a man who valued honesty and integrity above all.

In Jack's company, the wounds of the past began to feel distant, like a storm that had passed, leaving the skies clear and full of hope. Alexa found herself smiling more, her laughter coming more easily. It was a feeling she hadn't realized she missed until now – the feeling of being genuinely happy.

As they were finishing their meals, the beautiful view of the harbor was interrupted by the sleek silhouette of a yacht maneuvering gracefully into a berth next to the Wave Cruiser. The vessel was a vision of opulence, white and gleaming under the Cypriot sun.

"That's her," Jack said, his voice dropping an octave as he watched the yacht with an eagle's focus. "The same yacht that left Beirut three days ago. If my hunch is correct, that's how they're moving the cargo."

Alexa's gaze followed the yacht as it docked, her instincts kicking into overdrive. "So, Nikolai's entertainment cruises are a front," she murmured, piecing it together. "And Omar—"

"—Could very well be the link to the cash flow we've been tracking," Jack finished her thought, their minds in sync.

Their eyes met, a spark of adrenaline-fueled excitement passing between them. They were on the brink of understanding a complex web that spanned across the Mediterranean.

The lunch crowd began to thin, and the clatter of the harbor faded into a distant hum as they sat, contemplating their next move.

"It's all coming together, isn't it, Jack?" Alexa said, her voice a blend of determination and an unintentional hint of admiration.

Jack nodded, his eyes still on the yacht, but his mind was aware of the woman in front of him—her intelligence, strength, and something else he was beginning to let himself feel. "Yes, it is. And we're the ones who are going to ride this wave to the shore."

They stood up, their lunch forgotten, their focus now entirely on the yacht and its hidden secrets.

***

Slavik stood in the shadow of the palm trees flanking the Coral Bay Hotel, phone pressed to his ear, his gaze locked on the parking space where Olga's car had been abandoned. The humidity clung to his skin, but the heat was nothing compared to his burning irritation at this unexpected complication.

"Boss, the car is at Coral Bay," he reported, his voice as rough as the gravel underfoot. "No sign of her, though."

Nikolai's response crackled through the line, cold and sharp as a winter in Moscow. "Check her friends, Karen and Elena. She must have run to one of them."

There was a pause, a moment where Slavik could almost hear Nikolai's mind working, calculating. "And Zhorik?"

"On Wave Cruiser, boss. He hasn't moved, he keeps eyeing the cargo like a hawk watching its prey," Slavik responded, keeping his tone neutral.

"Good. Keep him there. In two days, all this will be a bad memory," Nikolai said with a venomous chuckle.

Slavik hesitated before bringing up his next point. "Should I know anything about the cargo, boss? In case something happens?"

Nikolai's laugh was dark, devoid of humor. "You just follow orders, Slavik. That's all you need to do."

The line went silent for a beat before Nikolai's voice cut through again, edging with contempt. "As for Olga, that woman is as replaceable as the last season's fashion. I took her from a drab apartment in Odessa to this paradise, and she repays me with defiance?"

Slavik shifted uncomfortably. His respect for Nikolai was tainted with fear, not loyalty. "She's your wife, boss."

"A mistake I'll rectify soon enough," Nikolai snapped. "Find her, Slavik. And when you do, I will remind her of her place."

The call ended, leaving Slavik with the bitter aftertaste of the conversation. He had seen Nikolai's cruelty before, but his disdain for Olga was a chilling revelation. With a sigh that carried his own unspoken worries, Slavik turned away from the empty parking spot and began the next task, another link in the chain of his servitude.

Slavik tapped Zhorik's number into his phone. Across the airwaves, seagulls and distant chatter filled his ear before Zhorik's laid-back voice answered.

"Zhorik, you good with the cargo for two more days?" Slavik asked, his voice low despite the privacy the noise provided.

"Brother, I'm more than good. I'm living the life!" Zhorik's tone was jovial. "You should see the sunset from the deck; it's pure magic!"

Slavik grunted, unimpressed by the poetry. "Want to switch shifts?"

Zhorik laughed, the sound rich with amusement. "And miss all the fun here? Not a chance. The evenings are wild, my friend. Tourists love a man in uniform."

A couple of tourists, their skin reddened from the Cypriot sun, passed by Slavik, their laughter mingling with the clinking of masts in the gentle sea breeze.

"I'm glad you're finding time for leisure," Slavik said, the sarcasm in his voice as subtle as a sledgehammer.

"Oh, come on. Last night, I met this British beauty." Zhorik's voice dropped to a conspiratorial whisper. Let's just say she was fascinated by my knowledge of the local waters."

Slavik's eyes rolled so hard he could see the back of his phone. "Just be careful, don't let your 'knowledge' get you in trouble."

Zhorik chuckled. "Worry not. I've got it all under control. She's coming back tonight. Says she wants to learn more about the 'navigational techniques'."

Slavik couldn't help but crack a smile. "Just remember, we're not on holiday. Keep your eyes open."

"Aye, aye, captain!" Zhorik's tone was teasing. "Over and out."

Slavik couldn't shake off a twinge of envy as the call ended. Zhorik was out there playing Casanova while he was playing a detective in a game of hide-and-seek with a woman who likely didn't want to be found. He pushed the thought away, his gaze scanning the horizon. Work was to be done, and he couldn't afford distractions—not even the thought of a British tourist falling for Zhorik's less-than-sophisticated charms.

***

The Wave Cruiser, a splendid vessel, cut through the dark blue waters of the Mediterranean as the sun began its majestic descent into the horizon. The air was alive with the sound of laughter and chatter from the tourists who had come aboard for the sunset cruise. The deck was a kaleidoscope of activity – couples leaning against the railing, lost in the beauty of the setting sun, groups of friends taking selfies with the vibrant sky, and families enjoying the rare moment of togetherness.

Zhorik, posing as a crew member, moved among the guests with a tray of colorful cocktails. His eyes, however, were scanning the crowd, part of his job, but also out of curiosity. That's when he spotted her – a striking British lady with a contagious smile, standing alone and observing the festivities with an amused expression.

He approached her, his accent thick as he offered a drink. "Sunset cocktail, miss?"

Alison accepted the drink, her eyes sparkling with mischief. "Thank you," she replied, her British accent crisp. "I must say, your English is quite... unique."

Zhorik grinned, unoffended. "Ah, my English. She is not perfect, but she works hard, like me."

Alison laughed, a genuine, hearty sound. "Well, she's doing a fine job. So, are you part of the crew?"

"Today, yes. Tomorrow, who knows?" Zhorik quipped, playing along with the light-hearted conversation.

Alison raised an eyebrow. "A man of mystery, then? What's your story?"

Zhorik leaned closer, his voice a playful whisper. "If I tell you, I might have to... make you stay on this boat forever."

"Well, that's quite the commitment for a first meeting," Alison retorted, her tone laced with humor.

Their banter continued, with Zhorik telling exaggerated tales of his life at sea, each more outlandish than the last. Alison countered with her witty remarks, and soon, they were both laughing, the sound mingling with the soft music that filled the air.

As the cruise progressed, the sky transformed into a canvas of purples and oranges, the sun bidding its final farewell for the day. Zhorik and Alison found themselves in a quiet corner of the deck, their conversation turned more personal yet still laced with the easiness of two people enjoying a moment of unexpected connection.

"You know, your accent makes these stories even more fascinating," Alison teased, her eyes twinkling in the twilight.

Zhorik chuckled. "Maybe one day, I will tell you a story in perfect English, and you will find it very boring."

"I doubt that" Alison replied, her gaze lingering on him a moment longer than necessary.

Zhorik, with a mischievous glint in his eye, led Alison downstairs to the quieter, more intimate setting of the Wave Cruiser's lower deck. The gentle hum of the boat's engine provided a soothing atmosphere as he uncorked a bottle of fine wine. Pouring two glasses, he handed one to Alison, their fingers brushing momentarily.

"To unexpected meetings," Zhorik toasted, raising his glass.

Alison smiled, clinking her glass against his. "And to stories that are probably too good to be true."

As they sipped their wine, the conversation flowed effortlessly. Zhorik, usually guarded, found himself opening up about his past. He spoke of his time in the army, the transition to special forces, and the adrenaline-fueled world of private security. Alison listened, genuinely intrigued, her eyes never leaving his.

"I never thought I'd end up on a boat like this," Zhorik admitted, a note of reflection in his voice. "But here I am, making sure tourists don't go overboard after one too many drinks."

Alison chuckled. "A noble cause indeed. But I sense there's more to you than just playing the role of a glorified babysitter for inebriated holidaymakers."

Zhorik smirked. "Maybe there is. But tonight, I'm just a man enjoying good wine with a beautiful woman."

The air between them was charged with an attraction. Zhorik leaned in closer, and their conversation gave way to a more primal language. Soft whispers eventually turned into kisses.

Yet, just as Zhorik's desires were racing him towards more, Alison skillfully steered the moment back to the promise of tomorrow. "I think the best stories are worth waiting for," she whispered, her lips inches from his.

Reluctantly, Zhorik agreed, a mixture of frustration and anticipation building within him. He excused himself to fetch another bottle of wine from the bar, leaving Alison alone for a few minutes.

Seizing the opportunity, Alison slipped away to the storage area where Zhorik had hinted the crew kept extra supplies. Her heart pounded as she quietly approached the hidden boxes of beer. She was familiar with the boxes from video footage Jack showed her of Zhorik and Slavik unloading them from the truck. With a swift, practiced motion, she pried one open, her eyes widening at the sight of the neatly stacked euro bills. Quickly, she closed and sealed the box back, ensuring everything looked undisturbed, and made her way back, her expression carefully neutral.

When Zhorik returned, wine bottle in hand, Alison greeted him with a smile. "I think this night will make for an interesting chapter in your memoirs," she teased, accepting the glass of wine.

Zhorik raised his eyebrows in amusement. "Only if you promise to write the foreword."

Their laughter mingled with the sound of the waves as the boat continued its gentle journey through the Mediterranean night, returning toward Paphos Harbor.

***

Away from the prying eyes and ears of the public, Jack McBride sat across from Alison at a secluded corner table in a quaint coffee shop. Its old-fashioned decor gave off an air of being stuck in time, much like the information they were about to exchange.

"So, tell me about your evening," Jack began, his eyes scrutinizing Alison as she took a sip from her espresso.

Alison leaned in with a playful smirk on her lips. "Well, Jack, let's just say I went deep undercover," she teased, tucking a loose strand of her hair.

"Under the covers or undercover, Alison?" Jack quirked an eyebrow, his tone half-amused, half-reproachful.

She chuckled, the sound light and unapologetic. "Whatever it takes to get the job done. Zhorik is quite the charmer when he forgets he's supposed to be a hardened criminal. And it turns out he has a soft spot for British accents."

Jack ran a hand through his hair, a gesture of resigned tolerance. "And this 'soft spot' led to actionable intelligence, I presume?"

Alison nodded, the smirk blooming into a full grin. "I can confirm your deductions that the Wave Cruiser is carrying a hefty sum in euros disguised in those beer cartons. A whole stash of them is sitting in the storage guarded by my Russian friend.

Jack breathed a sigh of relief as his suspicions of cash smuggling were confirmed. He leaned forward, his voice lowering. "And what about tonight? Are you going back to the boat?"

She nodded. "I have to. We can't let Zhorik think he's scared me off. Plus, he promised me a lesson in 'navigational techniques,'" Alison said, her eyes twinkling with mischief.

Jack couldn't help the reluctant smile. "Just make sure that's all you get a lesson in. We need you sharp and not compromised."

"Don't be such a prude, Jack. A girl's got to have a little fun," she replied, laughing.

Jack's expression turned serious. "I don't need to tell you this, but be careful, Alison. Things could get messy if he suspects you're more than a tourist."

"Don't worry about me," she waved off his concern. "I'm just a harmless girl, lost in the waves of Cyprus."

"Fun is not in the job description," Jack retorted, but his smirk betrayed his stern facade.

They both stood and as they walked out of the coffee shop, the sunlight caught the highlights in Alison's hair. For a brief moment, Jack allowed himself to see her not only as a fellow operative but as the vibrant woman she was.

"Stay safe, Alison," he said.

"Always do," she replied with a wink before they parted ways, melting into the crowd, each heading back to their world of shadows and deception.

Jack felt like he needed a walk, a breath of fresh salty air to clear his thoughts and connect the dots. As he left the bustling atmosphere of the Paphos Harbor behind, his mind was a whirlpool of thoughts. His pace was steady, each step leading him further along the scenic walkway stretching towards St. Nikolas Church, a route parallel to the shimmering Mediterranean Sea.

The path was lined with palm trees that swayed gently in the sea breeze, their leaves rustling softly like a whispered secret. The air was filled with the salty scent of the sea, and the rhythmic sound of waves lapping against the shore provided a soothing comfort to his thoughts. As he walked, Jack's mind methodically pieced together the puzzle that Alison's revelations at the Wave Cruiser had presented. Nikolai Gromov, operating under the directives of the FSB, had orchestrated a cash smuggling operation right under the noses of the Cyprus authorities. The Wave Cruiser, a vessel teeming with tourists seeking sunsets and carefree parties, was the perfect cover for such illicit activities.

The idea that such large amounts of cash were being smuggled regularly, seamlessly blending into the daily operations of a tourist boat, was almost unfathomable. Yet, it made perfect sense. The Wave Cruiser's very public nature served as its best defense. Who would suspect a pleasure boat, loud with music and laughter, of being a cog in an international money smuggling scheme?

The visits from Omar's yachts to pick up the cash were another piece of the puzzle that fit perfectly into this intricate system. These discreet rendezvous, likely coordinated with precision, were the final step in a chain of events that started in the silent corridors of power in Moscow and ended in the sun-drenched waters of Cyprus.

Reaching the quiet serenity of St. Nikolas Church, Jack paused, his gaze settling on the gentle waves. The beauty of the scene before him was the total opposite of the dark undercurrents he was uncovering. The information he had now was crucial, a key that could potentially unravel this entire operation. It was time to act, to finally bring this hidden world of corruption and espionage into the light.

***

The sun had just begun to dip below the horizon as Jack McBride hurried to his rendezvous with Alexa Marou. His usually punctual nature battled against the unpredictable flow of Cypriot traffic with unexpected road works, resulting in his delay.

Upon realizing Jack was late, Alexa sent him a message with an alternative plan, "Why don't you come over to my place? It's cozier for planning, and I have a decent Merlot begging to be opened."

Jack couldn't help but smile at the message. "Cozy and Merlot do sound like a good combination. Be there soon," he typed back.

At forty-three, Jack McBride had lived a life marked by a dedication to his career and a personal history full of heartache. His journey had begun in the warm glow of young love, marrying his high school sweetheart at twenty-one. They were the golden couple, full of dreams and promises for a future together. But as the years passed and Jack's career in intelligence took him to the far corners of the world, the golden bliss of their marriage began to fade.

By the time Jack was thirty-two, eleven years into their marriage, the distance had taken its toll. His wife, feeling abandoned and lost in his absences, found reassurance in the arms of a college professor. The news of her leaving, taking their son Michael to the States, hit Jack like a storm he hadn't seen coming. The woman he had loved, the family he had built, crumbled in the wake of her departure. She claimed she couldn't endure the endless waiting, the uncertainty of his return from missions covered in secrecy.

The ensuing years were a blur for Jack, a period of throwing himself into his work, using the adrenaline of his assignments to numb the pain of his loss. It wasn't until Michael returned to the UK for university studies eight years later that Jack felt a semblance of family again. Reuniting with his son at forty and rediscovering being a father was a balm to his wounded heart. They restored their bond, finding joy in each other's company, filling the void that had grown between them.

Jack never ventured back into the embrace of romantic love. He had remained a bachelor, his heart cautiously guarded, focused on his career and his role as a father.

But meeting Alexa Marou stirred something in him, something he thought could no longer be reached. She was a force of nature—intelligent, beautiful, and fiercely independent. Her spirit and strength captivated him, and he was drawn to her in a way he hadn't felt for anyone in years.

There was an undeniable chemistry between them, a connection that went beyond the professional. In her presence, Jack felt alive in a new and thrilling way. He saw the possibility of a new chapter, a chance at love and companionship that he hadn't dared to dream of.

It was a prospect that both excited and scared him, but one thing was clear – Alexa Marou had awakened something in Jack McBride that he was now eager to explore.

When he arrived, Alexa greeted him with an easy smile and a glass of wine. Her apartment was tastefully decorated, blending modern and traditional Cypriot aesthetics.

"Sorry, I'm late. The charm of Cypriot punctuality seems to be rubbing off on me," Jack quipped as he stepped inside.

"Only the best habits, I see," Alexa retorted with a wink, handing him the glass of wine.

They settled on the balcony, the wine complementing the view of the starlit Mediterranean Sea. As the evening wore on, they laid out the details of their operation, occasionally interspersed with laughter and personal anecdotes.

"So, we'll have Alison continue her 'tourist activities' tomorrow to keep an eye on the Wave Cruiser while we coordinate with the local authorities to track any movements from Nikolai's associates," Jack outlined, marking points on a city map.

Alexa nodded, her focus on the operation razor-sharp. "And we'll need to monitor the harbor. That yacht is definitely involved. We can't afford to lose sight of it. I'll make sure our guys are on it."

The conversation gradually shifted from strategies to lighter topics, and before they knew it, the bottle was empty, and the clock showed a time neither expected.

Jack looked at his watch and laughed softly. "Well, I didn't plan on a sleepover, but it seems the wine had other ideas."

"The couch is comfortable," Alexa offered, her gaze holding a playful glint. "But there might be more comfortable options."

Jack met her gaze, the chemistry between them obvious. "I suppose, for operational security, I should accept that offer."

Their lips first met in a soft, exploring kiss before quickly deepening with passion. It was as if a dam had been broken, years of loneliness and unmet desires pouring out in that one kiss. Jack's arms wrapped around her, pulling her closer, his touch both protective and yearning.

Once a symbol of professional collaboration, the couch now cradled them as they explored this new, unexpected aspect of their relationship. They moved together with a rhythm that was as natural as it was thrilling, each kiss, each touch deepening their connection.

The night gave way to warmth and intimacy. Lying there in the soft embrace of dawn, Alexa watched Jack sleep beside her, a contented smile playing on her lips. The room was quiet, save for the gentle breathing, a soothing sound that filled the space with a sense of peace she hadn't felt in years. The faint light of morning filtered through the curtains, casting a warm glow on his features, softening the lines that spoke of his life's battles.

As she gazed at him, her mind wandered through the whirlwind of emotions she had experienced since they met. Alexa had always embodied strength and resilience, a fortress in adversity. Yet, in Jack's presence, she found something that allowed her to let down her walls to be vulnerable without fear.

Her thoughts drifted to how he had looked at her the previous evening, a look that conveyed desire, a depth of understanding and respect. In that look, she had seen a glimpse of a future where the loneliness that often accompanied her in a demanding career could be filled with shared moments of joy and companionship.

Jack stirred beside her, his eyes meeting hers. In the quiet comfort of the room, no words were needed. Their shared glance was a silent conversation, speaking of a connection that had grown stronger in the space of a night. It was a connection that promised more than fleeting passion.

As Jack's hand found hers, entwining their fingers together, Alexa felt a surge of happiness, a sense of rightness in this unexpected turn in her life. Here, in this serene morning moment, with the man who had unexpectedly stolen her heart, Alexa felt hopefulness for the future—a future that, just a day ago, seemed like a distant dream.

By morning, as they shared a quiet coffee, the previous night's closeness lingered in their smiles. Jack reached across the table, his hand covering hers. "I must admit, this is the most pleasant debrief I've had in years."

Alexa's laughter was light and genuine. "Who knew that planning an operation could lead to... this?"

He stood, pulling her into his arms. "It's the best plot twist I've come across," he murmured before their lips met in a kiss that promised more.

Chapter 16

The daylight light filtering through the blinds was gentle, but the undercurrent of tension in the room was anything but. Alex sat on the edge of the sofa, his gaze fixed on Olga, who paced back and forth with her phone pressed to her ear.

"Karen, can you keep Christine for a few more days?" Olga's voice trembled despite her attempts at steadiness. "It's just… things are complicated right now."

Karen's cheerful voice crackled through the speaker. "Of course, Olga. Christine is having a blast with the kids. Don't worry about a thing."

But worry was still deep in Olga's heart as she ended the call. She turned to Alex, her eyes filled with fear and determination. "I can't stay here, Alex. I need to go and at least see Christine and talk to her so she knows I am around and will pick her up soon."

Alex nodded. "We need a car, but we can't rent one. Any ideas?"

"Actually, yes!" – Olga replied – "Let's grab a taxi and go to my friend, Elena. She can help us with a pair of wheels".

Alex went out to get a taxi, and an hour later, they were driving an old beat-up Toyota, heading to Karen's.

Karen's townhouse was located within the quiet, family-friendly residential complex in Kissonerga, a quaint village on the outskirts of Paphos. The townhouse, painted a warm, sun-bleached yellow, stood harmoniously among similar houses, each with its own small, manicured garden blooming with local flowers—bougainvillea, hibiscus, and jasmine—that perfumed the air.

Karen's life as a single parent was a delicate balance of work and family. She cherished her role as a math teacher at the local British school, finding joy and purpose in shaping young minds. Her teaching style was a blend of patience and enthusiasm, making her a favorite among her students.

Living in Kissonerga was a strategic choice for Karen, not just for the tranquility the village offered but also for its proximity to her parent's home. Her retired parents lived leisurely in their comfortable villa nearby and were Karen's primary support system.

They adored their granddaughter and were always eager to have her over, providing Karen with much-needed respite and peace of mind. This arrangement allowed Karen to dedicate time to her profession while knowing her daughter was in loving, capable hands.

However, her personal life was a different story. Karen was still healing from the wounds of her previous marriage – a chapter of her life that had ended in heartache back in the UK. The experience had left her cautious, her heart guarded against further emotional turmoil. She had devoted herself to her daughter and her career, leaving little room for romance. Her weekends were often spent with family or indulging in her love for gardening and reading, finding joy in life's simple pleasures.

With its laughter and love, Karen's townhouse was a sanctuary for Christine and Karen's daughter, Lily, to have a fantastic time together. Returning from the mountain resort where they spent three days, Karen organized the kids to have fun at home: board games, movies, ice cream, everything was at their disposal.

The drive to Karen's was quiet. When they arrived, Alex's instincts screamed at him to be cautious. He scanned the area, but nothing seemed amiss — until they turned into the narrow street leading to where Karen lived.

Suddenly, a sleek black sedan slid to a halt, barricading their car from the front, and another car blocked them from behind. Slavik stepped out of the car in front, his eyes cold and calculating.

Olga's heart sank as she stormed out of the car, "Slavik, what the hell is this?"

"I'm sorry, Olga," he said, though his tone suggested anything but sorrow. "Nikolai's orders."

Exiting the car, Alex assessed the scene — there was no immediate escape; Slavik's hand was inside his coat, most likely on a gun. His car was barricading the entrance to the driveway. Two other people got out of the car that was blocking the exit. Surrounded, Olga and Alex had no chance to escape.

Slavik's stern facade shattered like fragile glass when he recognized the man standing beside Olga. It was Anton Gorin himself, a ghost from the surveillance photos, the cash suitcases grand master, a man Slavik had been ordered to find at all costs. And there he was, not hiding in the shadows, but here with a protective arm around Olga.

For a moment, Slavik felt the ground shift beneath him. This wasn't part of the plan. The sudden adrenaline rush mixed with treasure hunt excitement overwhelmed him.

"Anton Gorin," Slavik muttered under his breath, the name tasting like poison on his tongue. His eyes darted to Olga, now with a new layer of betrayal — not just the wife of Nikolai but the ally of a marked man.

Stepping back, his eyes locked on Alex, who stood like a calm island in the storm of Slavik's overwhelming encounter. Slavik's fingers fumbled with his phone, the numbers of Nikolai's direct line almost a blur. The phone rang, with each tone echoing in his ears like a countdown.

"Nikolai," he began, his voice in an overexcited whisper, "we have a situation. It's not just Olga — Anton Gorin is with her. Yes, Gorin himself."

He could hear Nikolai's breathing change, a sharp inhale that cut through the line. Slavik waited. The silence on the other end of the phone was more terrifying than any reprimand.

"Get them both to the safe house," Nikolai's voice finally came through. "It changes everything. Call Petros on the way. We need to borrow his fishing boat."

As Slavik ended the call, his mind raced. How had Anton Gorin, a target so high on their list, so elusive, ended up here in this ordinary suburban trap? He was no longer just a captor but a guardian of a prize that could turn the tides in his favor and at least a serious money promotion from Nikolai. The fishing boat, however, meant one thing – one or both of Anton and Olga would be dead in a few hours and buried in the depths of Akamas waters with iron balls locked around their necks. And Slavik knew it would be him who would have to kill them, an unpleasant ordeal.

They were separated in two vehicles, Slavik driving with Olga and the other two thugs driving Alex. Just before they left, Olga and Alex were stripped of their phones, handbags, and car keys. The drive was a blur of twisting roads leading to a secluded house in Kathikas.

The house, unremarkable in its exterior, was located among a row of similar upscale homes on a quiet side road at the end of the village. To the casual observer, it blended easily into the landscape of affluence and tranquility. But as Alex and Olga were escorted through the heavy, reinforced front door, the illusion of suburban normalcy immediately disappeared.

Inside, the atmosphere shifted dramatically. The foyer was stark, the luxury of the exterior giving way to a clinical efficiency that chilled the air. The walls, without any decoration, were cold, sterile white, making the space feel more like a high-security prison than a home. The plush carpeting underfoot did little to soften the ambiance.

Cameras, mounted in every corner, watched their every move with an unblinking gaze.

Their footsteps echoed as they were led down a narrow hallway, amplifying Alex's growing sense of foreboding. His mind raced, imagining the countless scenarios that could unfold in this place. The walls seemed to close in around him, each step forward tightening the invisible knot of danger.

With her heart filled with fear and uncertainty, Olga stayed close to Alex. Their hands brushed briefly, a fleeting touch that spoke volumes. They exchanged glances, a silent communication of mutual concern and unspoken questions about their fate.

The hallway opened into a staircase leading to a basement room, its purpose unclear, but its aura unmistakably intimidating. The space was sparsely furnished, with only a few useful chairs and a small, unadorned table. The lack of windows only added to the claustrophobic feel, the only light coming from harsh, fluorescent bulbs overhead.

Neither of their captors said a word while escorting them down to the basement room. As the heavy door closed behind them, the reality of their situation sank in. They were prisoners. Their lives hung in the balance, subject to the whims of a man consumed by a relentless thirst for revenge.

"Olga..." Alex began, reaching for her hand, their fingers intertwining as they faced the unknown.

Fear had solidified into resolve in Olga's eyes. "We'll get out of this, Alex. We have to."

***

Jack McBride's phone buzzed insistently against the worn wood of his makeshift desk. He glanced at the caller ID — Steve, one of his field operatives. His pulse quickened. Steve was their eyes on the ground, and if he was calling, it wasn't for pleasantries.

"Talk to me, Steve," Jack answered.

"Right, boss," Steve's voice crackled over the line. I've got a situation, and it's not good. I followed Slavik, like instructed, keeping a discreet tail on him. He led me to Coral Bay Hotel and later to a place in Kissonerga village where there was a takedown."

Jack straightened up in his chair, every muscle tensed. "A takedown? Who?"

"Alex Paniv and Olga Gromova," Steve continued. "It was professional, quick. I barely realized what was happening before they were spirited away."

"Where, Steve? Where did they take them?" Jack demanded, reaching for a pen and notepad.

"A house in Kathikas. I've confirmed the location. I'm set up half a klick away, keeping watch. No movement since they were brought in," Steve reported, his voice a low hum of controlled urgency.

Jack scribbled the address down. "You've done great, Steve. Keep your head down and maintain surveillance. If they've taken Paniv and Gromova there, it's for a reason. This could be the break we've been waiting for."

"On it, Jack. What's our play?"

"We're going to need backup. I'll make some calls. In the meantime, don't engage. We can't afford to spook them. Not now."

"Understood," Steve replied. "I'll report any changes immediately."

Jack McBride leaned back in his chair, his mind racing with the implications of Steve's report.

He analyzed the situation, piecing together the puzzle with methodical precision. "If Slavik took Alex and Olga to a house in Kathikas, it's more than just a random location. It's a calculated move," Jack mused aloud, tapping the pen against his notepad.

Firstly, he considered the players involved. Alex Paniv, an accidental thief caught in a high-stakes game, and Olga Gromova, entangled by her marriage to a man deeply rooted in criminal activities.

Jack's mind then shifted to the potential motives. Nikolai is desperate to retrieve his money. Alex is the key to it. Olga could be in danger, too, as Nikolai might have caught wind of his wife's betrayal and cooperation with Cyprus police. But what exactly is Nikolai planning? Interrogation, intimidation, or something more sinister?

He contemplated the broader picture, the network of Nikolai's operations, and the connections to figures like Omar. There was a much bigger game at play for Jack. Alex and Olga were pawns unknowingly interfering with his planned operation. Jack knew he needed to act, and fast.

Focusing on the immediate action plan, he called Alison, who was the head of the field operation unit. "Steve's surveillance is our eyes on the ground. We must keep tabs on any movement in and out of that house. Any visitors could lead us to Nikolai or his associates. And we must be ready to strike at a moment's notice," he instructed.

"Meanwhile, I will coordinate with Alexa and the local authorities. We've got a small window to turn this situation around before something bad happens." Jack paused, feeling the weight of responsibility. Alison, make sure nobody dies, all right? But also, we shouldn't rush things. We don't want to spook Nikolai and his deal with Omar. "

"Got it, boss," was the immediate reply.

The line went dead, and Jack stared at the scribbled address. The suitcase saga could seriously disrupt his operation. He was not going to let it happen.

***

In the dimly lit basement, the air felt heavy. As they sat side by side, Olga turned to Alex, her eyes reflecting a blend of fear and resilience.

"You know, I've always been afraid of basements," Olga began, her voice carrying a tremor of old fears being stirred. It goes back to my childhood. One summer, I was playing hide-and-seek at my grandma's house and accidentally locked myself in her basement. It was dark and cold, and it felt like forever before they found me."

Alex turned to her, noticing the distant look in her eyes as if she had been momentarily transported back to that time and place.

"That experience... it stayed with me. I guess that's why being here, in this basement, feels particularly unsettling," she added, trying to offer a weak smile that didn't quite reach her eyes. Sensing her unease,

Alex moved closer, touching her and kissing the hair cascading down her cheek. "Don't worry, I won't let anything happen to you."

"You know," she said, her voice soft but clear, "I have never really talked about my childhood with anyone, not even Nikolai."

Alex nodded, encouraging her to continue. Despite the dire circumstances, he was genuinely interested in knowing more about this enigmatic woman who had become a part of his life.

"I was born in Odessa," Olga started, a faint smile touching her lips as she recalled her early years. "A beautiful city by the sea, filled with vibrant colors and sounds. My parents were loving but strict, always pushing me to excel in my studies."

She paused, her eyes gazing into the distance as if visualizing her past. "My father was an engineer, and my mother a schoolteacher. We didn't have much, but we had each other. My childhood was simple but happy."

As Olga spoke, Alex noticed the warmth in her voice, a silent indicator of her happy memories. He could picture a young Olga, running along the sunny beaches of Odessa, her laughter mingling with the sound of the waves.

"But things changed when I turned six," Olga continued, her smile fading. "The Soviet Union collapsed, and with it, our lives. My parents struggled to make ends meet. The economic turmoil hit us hard."

Alex listened intently, his heart aching for the young girl who faced such hardships.

"I started modeling at sixteen," Olga said, her voice tinged with pride and regret. "It was a way out, a chance to help my family. But it wasn't what I expected. The industry was harsh, and I... I saw things, experienced things that no teenager should."

The pain in her voice was palpable. Alex gently took her hand in his, offering silent support.

"Eventually, I pulled myself out of the abyss and left Odessa for Moscow, where I worked as a housemaid. It was tough, but it allowed me to save enough money for university. I wanted to change my life, to escape the path I was on."

Alex admired her strength and determination, qualities he had come to associate with Olga.

"In Moscow, I met Nikolai at a club. He was different from anyone I'd ever known – charismatic, wealthy, and... I was drawn to him, mistaking his attention for love. I thought marrying him would secure my future, and in a way, it did. But at a cost, I hadn't anticipated."

Olga's voice broke, her eyes brimming with unshed tears. "I never loved Nikolai. It took me years to admit that to myself. I was in awe of his world, but I later learned it was built on secrets and dangers. And now, those secrets have caught up with us."

In the silence that followed, Alex felt a profound connection to Olga. Her story, a mix of struggle, resilience, and regret, resonated with his own experiences. They were two souls, brought together by fate's cruel twist, yet finding comfort in each other's presence.

***

Nikolai's car stopped on the gravel driveway of the safe house, a modern fortress, an imposing structure hidden behind a high fence and surrounded by lush greenery. The dust settled around the car like an ominous mist as he opened the door and walked toward the main entrance.

He entered the house with the authority of a man who commanded fear and respect. His eyes, cold and calculating, found Alex and Olga, in the center of a basement room.

"Olga," Nikolai's voice slithered through the room as he addressed his wife with an evil sneer. "My, what a tangled web we weave when we conspire to deceive."

Olga's response was a silent glare. The fire in her eyes hid the chill that had settled in her heart.

Nikolai turned his attention to Alex. "And Anton, or should I say, Alex. How touching that you've come to rescue the damsel in distress. But you seem to have forgotten something."

"There's nothing I've forgotten, Nikolai. Let her go," Alex said, his voice steady, betraying none of his fear.

"Let her go?" Nikolai laughed, a sound devoid of humor. "You think you're in a position to make demands? I want my money, every last euro of it."

"I'll give you the money," Alex shot back, "all of it, in exchange for Olga's freedom."

Nikolai's expression twisted into a cruel smile. "You're in no place to bargain. But I do enjoy the theatrics."

He then nodded to Slavik, who stepped forward and delivered a punishing blow to Alex's stomach. A grunt escaped Alex's lips, but his gaze never wavered from Nikolai's. Olga screamed and instinctively attempted to shield Alex with her body. Slavik retreated a couple of steps, watching Alex closely.

"I have business to attend to, but I will be back in 24 hours," Nikolai said, his tone now laced with a deadly promise. "You will tell me where the money is and then take me to it. After that, you and I, let's say, will go fishing. I love fishing. Do you, Alex?" Nikolai laughed but did not expect any answer. He then turned his attention to Olga.

"And as for you, Olga," he continued, turning towards her with disgust, "you'll stay where you can't cause any more trouble for now."

Slavik grabbed Olga roughly by the arm, dragging her upstairs to another windowless room — a cell — within the house. She stumbled into the darkness, the metal door locking behind her, echoing like a final verdict.

The room was suffocating, the air stale and unmoving. Fear gnawed at her, but underneath it all was a burning anger, a resolve not to let Nikolai see her break.

In the basement, Nikolai stared at Alex, a predator sizing up his prey. "Tick-tock, Alex. Your time is running out. I have finally found you."

With those parting words, Nikolai strode out of the room, leaving Alex alone with the sound of his labored breathing and the tick-tock of an unseen clock, marking the passage of time and the approach of his death.

***

The Paphos Harbor was a palette of dusky blues and grays as the night's darkness began to retreat before the approach of dawn. The first whispers of light were brushing the horizon, painting it with the softest strokes of pink and orange. It was that suspended moment when the world held its breath, waiting for the day to begin.

Zhorik moved with a silent efficiency, a ghost in the predawn shadows. The cartons, marked with the logos of various beer brands, were anything but alcoholic beverages. He loaded them onto the sleek yacht where Omar stood, flanked by two heavy-set bodyguards. Their eyes scanned the harbor, alert to any disturbance.

Unseen, in the embrace of the harbor's nooks and crannies, Alexa, Jack, and their team lay in wait. Alexa's eyes were sharp, missing nothing, her hand resting lightly on her holstered weapon. Jack stood close by, his focus as unwavering as the beams of light from the lighthouse that cut through the morning mist.

When the last carton was loaded and the yacht's engines hummed to life, coordinated chaos erupted around the harbor. From the south, a fishing boat chugged towards the yacht's path. Omar's yacht attempted to maneuver around, but the fishing boat was too quick, cutting off its escape with the precision of a practiced hand.

In the same heartbeat, the harbor came alive with action. Armed agents and police officers materialized from their hiding spots. A shout went up, "Police! Freeze!"

Zhorik, caught off guard, spun around, his eyes wide with panic. Before he could react, Alexa was upon him, her training evident in how she swiftly disarmed and subdued him.

"Mr. Abramov, you are under arrest," she declared a hint of satisfaction in her voice. The harbor, once a scene of serene beauty, had transformed into a stage for justice.

On the yacht, the surprise was absolute. Omar and his guards raised their hands instinctively as more officers swarmed aboard. Jack boarded with the fluidity of a seasoned agent; his eyes locked on Omar.

"Omar Sayed, you're under arrest for money laundering and illegal transportation of currency," Jack announced, his voice cutting through the commotion.

The arrests were executed with such precision and speed that it was all over by the time the yacht's crew even realized what was happening. Handcuffs clicked into place, securing the wrists of those who had believed they were untouchable.

From various vantage points, cameras continued to roll, capturing every detail. The evidence was undeniable, irrefutable.

As the sun broke free from the horizon, bathing the harbor in golden light, a sense of victory washed over the team. The Wave Cruiser sat empty now, its sinister cargo was gone, and the yacht was towed back to the dock, a captive itself.

Alexa turned to Jack triumphantly, saying, "Nice work, partner."

Jack grinned back, "We make a pretty good team, don't we?"

The operation had been a success. Jack knew they had struck a severe blow in FSB's Middle East operations, but the grand battle was far from over.

***

The sun had climbed a few degrees higher when Inspector Savvas' team pulled up to Stelios' lavish villa. The first rays of light caught the edges of marble columns and glinted off the crystalline waters of a swimming pool that lay undisturbed by the morning's events. The peace of the affluent neighborhood was about to be shattered.

With a nod from Savvas, the officers strode toward the entrance. The heavy wooden door stood imposingly until Stelios, alerted by the firm knock of an officer, opened it a couple of minutes later.

"Stelios Georgiou?" Commander Savvas' voice was stern, his face unreadable behind mirrored sunglasses. Stelios nodded, his usual bravado gone.

"You are under arrest for conspiracy to launder money," Savvas announced, his words slicing through the thick air.

Stelios' lips quivered in a feeble attempt at forming words that refused to come. His glance shifted from Savvas to the officers flanking him and back again, a caged animal seeking an escape that didn't exist.

"But how did you... I mean, there's been some mistake..." Stelios' voice trailed off, the usual authority it commanded reduced to a trembling whisper.

"There's no mistake, Stelios," Savvas replied, his voice devoid of emotion. "The evidence is quite conclusive."

One of the officers stepped forward with handcuffs ready. Stelios' gaze finally settled on the metal restraints, the reality settling in. There was no swagger now, no cocky retort. "But... My reputation..." Stelios mumbled, his voice breaking, "What will people say?"

"People?" Savvas echoed, his tone almost philosophical. "They will say that justice doesn't discriminate. They will say that no one is above the law."

As the cuffs clicked around his wrists, Stelios bowed his head. Gone was the ostentatious confidence, replaced with the heavy, sinking realization that the life he had known—the power, the control—was over.

Commander Savvas signaled for his team to escort Stelios out of his home. The neighbors peered through their curtains, the silence pierced by the soft murmur of speculation and the song of distant sirens marking the end of an era.

Stelios was placed in the back of an unmarked police car. Defeated and alone, Stelios Georgiou was nothing more than a footnote in the ongoing battle against corruption that today had claimed a significant victory.

***

Dmitri Orlov was in his hotel room. The silence was oppressive, heavy with anticipation. His finger hovered over the call button on his phone, the number for Leonid, his superior, already dialed in.

He pressed the button, the line connected with a click, and Leonid's voice immediately came through, sharp as shattered glass.

"What is it, Orlov?" Leonid's tone was clipped, brooking no incompetence.

"Leonid, there's been a complication," Orlov began, steeling himself against the eruption he knew was coming.

"A complication?" Leonid's voice was deceptively calm, the kind of calm before a storm. "Explain."

"The Cypriot police made their move. Omar has been arrested. They've seized the cash. Nikolai's antics have drawn too much attention," Orlov said, his voice flat, detached.

There was a momentary silence, a pregnant pause where the air itself seemed to freeze.

"You're telling me that our operations are compromised because Nikolai's personal cash vendetta has gone out of control?" Leonid's voice lost its calm, replaced by a fury that cracked through the line.

Orlov hesitated for a split second, choosing to withhold details of his venture in Nikolai's money retrieval affair. He wasn't keen on revealing his sideline aspirations to his superior. While overseeing the Middle East operation and liaising with Nikolai was part of his routine duties, actively working for him was a separate matter. Keeping this side project under wraps from his boss seemed like the smart move for Agent Orlov.

"Yes," Orlov confirmed, the word hitting like a bullet. "He prioritized his money over the operation. He kept pressing and pressing to find this guy. I believe, somehow, the police got wind of it. The worst is that the British are involved now. It's unraveling quite fast."

There was a sound that might have been a fist slamming against a table. "Nikolai is a dead man. But he just doesn't know it yet," Leonid snarled. "And Omar?"

"Omar is in custody. It's only a matter of time before they trace it all back to us. We need to act," Orlov said.

Leonid's next words were icy, each one articulated with lethal precision. "You know what needs to be done, Orlov. Clean it up. All of it. No traces. No loose ends."

Orlov felt the weight of the command settled on his shoulders, a mantle of death. "Understood. It will be handled."

"And Orlov," Leonid's voice dropped to a dangerous whisper, "if you fail, you know the consequences. Do not disappoint me."

"I won't," Orlov replied, the finality in his voice mirroring the darkness that crept around the edges of his soul.

The line went dead, and Orlov was left in silence, the ghosts of his orders echoing off the walls. He stood up, his movements precise, the gears of his mind already turning with plots and plans. There was work to be done, a cleanup of colossal proportions.

As his car cruised through the winding roads towards Kathikas, the dusk's bruised sky mirrored the turmoil within Dimitri. Leonid Varushev's orders were clear and chilling, resonating in his mind like a death knell. Failure was not an option, not for someone in Orlov's position, not for someone with his ruthless reputation. However, Orlov felt uneasy about killing innocent people who happened to be entangled in Nikolai's mess.

Kathikas, usually a quiet village, now harbored a storm beneath its serene appearance. The safe house was about to become the epicenter of Orlov's cleanup operation. He parked a safe distance away in the shadow of an old olive tree.

From his vantage point, Orlov watched like a predator assessing the terrain. His sharp and calculating eyes missed nothing. Then, he noticed the subtle signs of an impending strike—a flicker of movement in the periphery and the disciplined positioning of unknown operatives.

Years of experience in the field had sharpened Orlov's instincts to near perfection. He recognized a professional operation when he saw one. The realization dawned on him: he was not the only player on this chessboard. Someone else was making a move, and they had the advantage.

Orlov's mind raced, evaluating his options. The attack on the safe house was imminent, and his presence there now posed a significant risk. His mission was compromised to eliminate any loose ends, including Olga and Alex. The situation demanded a tactical retreat, which Orlov made with cold, emotionless logic.

As the first sounds of the assault echoed through the quiet village, Orlov was already in motion, slipping away into the night like a ghost. His car merged with the darkness, leaving behind the chaos that was about to unfold.

Orlov knew Nikolai wasn't in the safe house. Slavik, a connection from their days in the FSB, always updated him, which Nikolai never suspected. Orlov's next objective was clear—find Nikolai Gromov. The man was a liability, a loose cannon that must be silenced for good. The entire operation was already exposed, and he couldn't afford any more surprises.

***

Dawn had not yet broken when a convoy of unmarked vehicles snaked silently through the sleepy streets of Kathikas. The safe house sat unsuspecting as the agents disembarked with military precision. They moved quietly under the waning moon, communicating with hand signals and silent nods. Every step was measured, every breath controlled—the culmination of countless hours of training.

Jack McBride, his face a mask of focus, led the first team. They approached the back entrance while the second team, led by another British agent known for her tenacity, crept towards the front. Each agent knew the situation—two lives hung in the balance inside.

With a signal, a countdown began, unseen but felt by all. 3... 2... 1...

The front door exploded inwards as a breaching charge detonated, shattering the silence of the night. Flashbangs followed, their disorienting blaze of light and sound designed to confuse and incapacitate.

"Go, go, go!" the lead agent shouted, her voice harsh in the sudden chaos.

The teams flooded in, sweeping through the house with the unstoppable force of a tidal wave. They moved from room to room with practiced ease, guns ready, eyes sharp for any threat.

In the basement, Slavik and his compatriots scrambled, taken aback by the ferocity and swiftness of the assault. They reached for their weapons, but it was too late.

Jack's team descended upon them like avenging spirits. Slavik's hand was barely on his gun before he was disarmed, an agent's knee pinning him to the ground.

"Clear!" voices echoed, the call rippling through the house as rooms were secured one by one.

In a windowless room, Olga Gromova huddled, her heart hammering against her ribs. The door flew open, and she flinched, expecting her husband's goons. Instead, she saw a woman, her stance authoritative, her eyes kind.

"You're safe now," the agent said, offering a hand. "Olga Gromova?"

"Yes," Olga breathed. Tears of relief ran down her cheeks as she took the offered hand.

Meanwhile, Alex Paniv was in the basement room, dazed but unharmed. As he was led out into the first light of day, the joy of their liberation began to sink in. They were free, the nightmare seemingly over.

Outside, the rising sun painted the sky in a tentative color of victory and hope. The Russians, now handcuffed and subdued, were lined up on the ground as the agents secured the perimeter.

Jack McBride stood among his team, his gaze taking in the scene with a grim satisfaction. The operation was a success and this little Cyprus war seemed to be over. This was the final strike in the fight to dismantle FSB's covert financing operation. It was just a part of a lifelong battle the MI6 were now one step closer to winning. He smiled when he saw Alexa approaching. She was responsible for covering all exits from the village with her Cypriot team, and Jack was happy to see her safe. As the agents began to debrief, the sound of sirens announced the approach of the local authorities, ready to take over the scene.

***

The temporary Paphos office of Jack McBride was an example of order amidst the chaos that had engulfed the lives of Alex Paniv and Olga Gromova.

Alex, still sporting the roughened look of recent captivity, sat at the conference table. Opposite him, Olga clutched a steaming cup of tea, its aroma a small comfort against the cold dread that had been her companion for too long. Between them, Jack McBride loomed like a steadfast captain, ready to navigate through the storm of their revelations.

"Let's hear it then, Alex." Jack's calm voice carried an undercurrent of urgency.

Alex cleared his throat, a small gesture betraying the moment's gravitas. "The suitcases," he began, his voice a touch hoarse, "appeared in my rented car, a lucky fluke—or so I thought. It was filled with cash, which I recently learned was the product of Nikolai's less-than-legal enterprises."

Jack's eyes, sharp and assessing, never wavered from Alex's face.

"And Ms. Gromova's entry into this tale?" Jack prompted, with a glance toward Olga.

"That was the hand of fate," Alex said, offering Olga a supportive look. "Our meeting was accidental—an unexpected encounter at a café in Nicosia."

Olga's eyes met Jack's, her nod silent but full of shared understanding.

"I just wanted a coffee while I was waiting for Alexa," she said.

Jack leaned forward, the investigator in him fixated on the threads of truth. "And the laundering operation you got tangled in?"

Alex's lips quirked in a wry, humorless smile. "I have a knack for numbers and algorithms—crypto, specifically."

"Go on," Jack encouraged.

"My software," Alex explained, "it capitalizes on the volatility of cryptocurrencies. I built it myself, an automated system for crypto arbitrage. It's legal and surprisingly lucrative. I've made some serious money with the help of the software, and I am ready to return Nikolai's cash I stumbled upon in full. I'll pay all taxes on the profits generated." – Alex smiled.

Jack's expression softened ever so slightly. "Your willingness to cooperate and repay this money is commendable. And if your claims hold water, it'll be a boon to our case."

Olga, who had been quietly absorbing the conversation, spoke up. "I can attest to Alex's... integrity," she said. "And I implore you, Mr. McBride, to understand that my marriage to Nikolai has long since dissolved into nothing but regret and a desire to protect my daughter."

The room was still for a heartbeat, the only sound the distant hum of the bustling precinct beyond the door.

"Your cooperation with the police and MI6 is extremely valuable, Ms. Gromova," Jack said. "We will do our part to ensure your safety and your child's. Meanwhile, both of you will be debriefed by my agents in detail."

The dialogue inside Jack McBride's office was nearing the end when the door opened. Inspector Savvas and Alexa Marou stepped in.

"Jack, we've got a situation," Inspector Savvas began. "Nikolai has slipped through the net. We've got units on high alert, but as of now, he's still at large. We keep looking."

"Guys, it's essential we apprehend Nikolai by any means," Jack said. They all went silent.

"And there's the matter of the funds," Savvas said, breaking the moment of silence, his eyes sweeping over Alex and Olga. "Our legal team has been wrestling with the implications of the money in Alex's possession."

Jack gestured to the chairs. "Sit down. Let's hash this out."

Once seated, Inspector Savvas continued, "The money held by Alex, as it stands, has not been arrested or proven illegal. We all know how it came about, but from the legal point of view, it is a very tricky issue as it might be next to impossible to prove that the money is illegal in the first place. In legal terms, should there be any witnesses able to attest that the funds discovered in Alex's vehicle are indeed the property of Nikolai, it would be incumbent upon us to return these funds to Nikolai's estate. Subsequently, an investigation would be warranted to ascertain their origin and any pertinent details. Conversely, in the absence of any testimony from Nikolai's associates regarding the money – a scenario which seems likely given their probable reticence – the funds are categorized as inadvertently acquired by Alex. As such, they would be considered his income, subject to declaration as per the pertinent legal and tax regulations.

Everyone, including Jack, couldn't grasp where Inspector Savvas was going with his legal and accountant jargon.

"So, what's the plan?" – asked Jack.

"Well, if we are all in agreement here, I suggest we forget about the suitcase saga, skip the legalities, and let Alex return the funds to Olga as the legal representative of Nikolai's estate in Cyprus. Nikolai, if found, will face a long prison time anyway. Olga will promise to declare all of it and pay taxes to the government. Everyone goes home happy."- offered Inspector Savvas and added: "I've come to realize over the years that strictly adhering to legal technicalities can sometimes lead to more harm than justice. It's a path that might ultimately leave Olga empty-handed and benefit no one".

The entire scenario now unfolded with unmistakable clarity before them. Key elements of the suitcase blunder converged to reveal the true events: the anonymous tip implicating Stelios in aiding Nikolai's illicit cash smuggling, the peculiar encounter Alexa had with Nikolai involving the swimming gear suitcases, Stelios' prior warning to Nikolai about police scrutiny, likely prompting Nikolai's hasty and ill-fated attempt to conceal the cash in the hotel. This revelation cemented their understanding: the substantial sum Alex discovered was the same cash spirited away from Russia on the day of Nikolai's return. In a web of illegality and fraud, the money, technically Nikolai's, had found its way into Alex's car. Returning the money to Olga was the correct course of action despite the legal complexities involved. Legalizing and declaring it now fell squarely upon Olga's shoulders.

Jack was unsure how legal Inspector's offer was in its very nature, but he thought it was humane. If the Cyprus government is willing to close its eyes and have a deal with Olga, Jack wouldn't mind.

Alex, who had listened intently, nodded. "I understand. It's only right that the funds are returned in full to Olga."

Olga said quietly but determinedly, "I will do what's necessary. It's the least I can do to correct some wrongs."

"I promised to return every euro of it, and I will. Alex affirmed, his gaze steady. "Olga's been through a lot because of Nikolai's choices. She should have the means to start anew, especially for her daughter's sake."

Inspector Savvas gave a nod of approval, his usual stoic expression softening. "It's a complicated case, but your cooperation makes navigating it easier. We appreciate your openness and willingness to resolve this matter."

Alexa added her support, "We're making headway, thanks to all of you. Let's keep the momentum going and close this case once and for all."

Once thick with tension, the room breathed a collective sigh of relief. The path forward was clearer now, paved with good intentions and the promise of closure.

Olga's eyes met each person in the room, silent gratitude glowing in her gaze. "Thank you," she whispered, the two words heavy with emotion.

They stood up, almost in unison, the meeting ending. Olga's hand found Alex's, their grip firm, not just a comfort but a silent vow of solidarity. Three hours after full and detailed debriefing, Olga and Alex picked up Christine and, with the help of Steve, the British agent, they landed in a safe house in the small town of Polis.

Chapter 17

The vast concourse of Larnaca International Airport thrummed with the hum of travelers and announcements, a symphony of transience that served as the perfect stage for clandestine conversations. Three days after the successful operation in the harbor of Paphos, Jack McBride leaned against a column with an air of casual indifference, his eyes scanning the crowd until they landed on the figure of Dmitri Orlov.

Jack McBride's stance might have seemed calm to any casual observer, but his keen eyes were fixed on Orlov with the intensity of a seasoned hunter. The air between the two men was thick with history, a mix of encounters woven across the globe in the shadowy realm of international espionage.

Their paths had first crossed years ago in the tangled alleys of Marrakech. It was a covert operation gone awry, where Jack, then a young MI6 field agent, found himself at the mercy of Orlov's unexpected intervention. That day, in the sweltering heat of the Moroccan sun, a grudging respect was born in Jack's heart for the FSB operative. With his uncanny ability to blend into his surroundings, Orlov displayed a level of cunning and resourcefulness that Jack couldn't help but admire.

Over the years, their careers had propelled them into a series of intricate dances – sometimes as adversaries, occasionally as reluctant collaborators, but always as rivals. From the chilly streets of Moscow to the humid hustle of Bangkok, Jack had come to recognize Orlov's handiwork: precise, ruthless, and without a trace of remorse.

Jack respected Orlov's professional prowess, strategic mind, and dedication to his country's objectives, no matter how murky they were.

As Orlov approached, his gait confident and measured, Jack said:

"Dmitri," as he greeted Orlov, his tone neutral.

"Jack," Orlov replied with a nod, his eyes as unreadable as ever and his faint trace of a Russian accent coloring his words. "I didn't expect to find the British Lion himself prowling around a Cypriot airport."

Jack's lips twitched into a wry smile. "I'm sure you understand the necessity of unexpected encounters in our line of work."

Without another word, Jack steered Orlov to a quieter corner of the airport, away from prying eyes and ears.

Once they were relatively alone, the temperature of their conversation dropped several degrees.

"I'll be brief," Jack started, his gaze locked onto Orlov's. "Your operation is blown. Omar is singing, and the tune is all about the FSB financing radicals in the Middle East. My advice? Tell your bosses to cut the strings. We've got all the evidence we need."

Orlov's face tightened a subtle shift that betrayed his irritation. "McBride, you overestimate your position. My bosses are not the men who scare easily."

"But they are men who understand when they've lost," Jack countered sharply. "This time, the loss is on you. The game's up, Orlov."

There was a pause, filled with understanding of the stakes at play. Orlov's expression hardened.

"And what about Nikolai? He seems to have... vanished from the board," Jack probed, observing Orlov for any telltale sign.

Orlov's lips curved into a mirthless smile. "Nikolai has gone fishing, McBride. You might say a sudden passion for the solitude of the sea."

The implication hung heavily in the air, a dark cloud of finality. Jack's jaw clenched, understanding the euphemism all too well. Nikolai Gromov was no more, dealt with by his own for the failure he represented.

"A convenient hobby," Jack remarked dryly. "One that often ends with the fish being the only ones who know your whereabouts."

The two men stood in a momentary standstill, a silent acknowledgment of the life-and-death nature of their roles.

"Give your superiors the message," Jack said, his tone laced with steel. We'll be watching. If there are any more games, we'll be ready to leak all the evidence to the international press."

Orlov straightened his tie, his eyes cold and calculating. "I will convey your... concerns. But remember, McBride, the board is always set for another game."

"You know, Dmitri, there was a time when I thought we were on the same side. A time when Russia seemed to be stepping into the light, becoming a part of the Western world after the collapse of the USSR. We worked together, remember? MI6 and FSB, side by side, averting threats of international terrorism. We had a common enemy, a common goal."

He paused, the weight of his words hanging between them. "But now? It's like watching a tragic fall from grace. Russia, a nation with such a rich history and such potential, supports extremism and fosters anti-Western rhetoric. Why, Dmitri? Why turn your back on progress? Why choose this path?"

Orlov's expression was stoic, his stance rigid. "I serve my country, Jack. I follow orders. That's what I do. That's what we all do in this line of work."

Jack shook his head, a rueful smile touching his lips. "But it's not just about orders. It's about choices. Every man must decide for himself if the orders he follows are for the greater good. We're not machines, Dmitri. We're men with the power to decide what's right and wrong. Tell me something. We both know your bosses high up and their kids who are leading luxury lives in London, Miami, and LA... how come there is this anti-Western stance? I haven't seen a single Russian oligarch settling down in Teheran. What kind of politics is that? Skiing in Courchevel, playing in Monaco, living in Soho and at the same time funneling money to those who might well strike in the heart of London! Tell me, Dmitri, how does that all add up?"

A flicker of something undefinable passed through Orlov's eyes for a moment. Was it doubt? Reflection? However, it was gone as quickly as it had appeared, his mask firmly back in place.

"You see things in black and white, Jack," Orlov replied, his voice firm. "But the world is a spectrum of grays. My loyalty is to my country, to Russia. That is the only truth I follow."

Jack studied him for a long moment, seeing the resolve in his eyes, the unwavering commitment to his orders. "I hope one day you realize, Dmitri, that blind loyalty can lead to a path of no return. A path where the cost might be too high, even for a man like you."

With that, Orlov turned on his heel and merged with the crowd, leaving Jack to contemplate the endless cycle of move and countermove.

As Jack watched Orlov disappear, he knew this was far from the end. It was merely a respite. Pawns and kings alike were sacrificed in the grand chessboard of international espionage. And for now, the FSB had lost a pawn, perhaps even a rook, but the game was far from over.

In Orlov, Jack saw the mirror image of what he might have become in another life under different circumstances. It was a thought that both intrigued and repelled him. As they parted ways, Jack couldn't shake off the feeling that their mutual story didn't end there. In the world of shadows they inhabited, people like Dmitri Orlov didn't just fade away. They lingered, like ghosts, long after the final move was played.

Jack couldn't shake off a sense of regret. Regret for what could have been, for what still might be, if only men like Orlov chose to question rather than blindly follow. And as Jack walked away, he knew he would see Dmitri Orlov again.

***

In the stark, unforgiving light of the interrogation room, Jack sat across from Omar Sayed.

Handcuffed and visibly weary, Omar avoided Jack's steady gaze. His posture, once defiant, had wilted under the weight of his capture. The room was silent, save for the faint hum of the air conditioning.

Finally, Jack broke the silence, his voice even and probing. "Omar, we both know why you're here. But what I want to understand is why you chose this path. What's your end game in all of this?"

Omar's eyes flickered, meeting Jack's for a fleeting moment before dropping away. "If you think I am into some kind of terrorism or extremism, you are wrong. It was never about ideology for me, Mr. McBride," he began, his voice a mix of resignation and relief as if unburdening a long-held secret. "It was always about the money, the means to an end."

Jack leaned forward slightly, sensing the shift in Omar. "And what end is that?" he asked, his tone encouraging further confession.

Omar exhaled slowly as if the act of breathing itself was a burden. "I've been planning to disappear," he admitted. "I have documents, a new identity... I wanted to escape to Canada and live as a Syrian refugee. I've had enough of the Middle East, the endless games, the violence..."

Jack observed Omar intently, processing his words. "So, you're telling me you've been playing both sides to secure your escape? No loyalty to the cause, no grand vision for the future of terror?"

"There's no future in what I was doing," Omar said, a hint of bitterness creeping into his voice. "Just endless cycles of violence and retribution. I've seen enough death and destruction to last many lifetimes. I yearn for peace, Mr. McBride, a quiet life in a land far from here."

Jack leaned back, his expression contemplative. "And all the while, you've been funneling money to extremists, fueling the very violence you claim to despise?"

Omar nodded, his eyes downcast. "A paradox, I know. But in my line of work, moral clarity is a luxury I couldn't afford. I've done what I needed to survive: secure my way out."

Jack's gaze hardened. "And at what cost, Omar? How many lives have been destroyed in your pursuit of a quiet retirement?"

Omar looked up, his eyes meeting Jack's with a newfound intensity. "I've asked myself that question every single day, Mr. McBride. And I'll carry those burdens with me, wherever I end up. I'm no hero, nor do I claim to be a victim. I'm just a man who got caught in the gears of a machine much larger than himself."

The room fell into silence following Omar's admission, a brief pause in the interrogation that allowed Jack to digest the words. Then, Omar continued, "You know, Mr. McBride, the world of extremist groups and their financing isn't always what it appears to be," Omar began, leaning back in his chair, his hands still cuffed. "Many of these groups... they're less about ideology and more about profit. It's a business, a very dark one."

Jack's eyebrows furrowed in interest. "Go on," he urged, sensing the significance of what Omar was about to reveal.

Omar exhaled, a wry smile playing on his lips. "These groups get funding from sources like the FSB, right? Big money for big promises. But here's the thing: many have no intention of fulfilling those grand visions of jihad or whatever cause they claim to champion."

He paused, ensuring he had Jack's full attention. "What they really do is stage their own demise. A well-timed explosion here, a supposed firefight there.

All very dramatic, very convincing. And then, suddenly, they're martyrs for the cause. But in reality, they're on a beach, sipping cocktails, enjoying their retirement funded by Russian money."

Jack's expression was one of surprise mixed with understanding. "So, you're saying a significant portion of these extremist groups are essentially scamming their financiers? Faking their own deaths to escape with the money?"

"Exactly," Omar confirmed, nodding. "It's the perfect con. No one questions the death of a fighter; it comes naturally with the business. And in the chaos of places like Syria or Iraq, it's easy to disappear. New identities and lives are far from the reach of those who funded them. That was my plan, too."

Jack leaned forward, his mind racing with the implications of Omar's confession. "And the money you received was intended for these groups?"

Omar shrugged. "Some of it, yes. But once I realized the game, I started diverting funds for my exit strategy. I saw a way out, and I took it. I'm not proud of it, but I saw an opportunity to escape this endless cycle of violence."

Jack sat back, processing the revelation. Omar's story was a reminder of the complex and dark world of international espionage and terrorism financing—a world where truth and deception danced a dangerous tango, and survival often meant playing both sides of a deadly game.

Jack leaned in, his eyes sharp and focused. "Omar, do you know other channels the FSB might use to funnel money to these groups? Anything beyond what you were involved with in Cyprus?"

Omar shook his head, a hint of frustration in his expression. "The FSB is careful about compartmentalization. However, my role was broader than the operation with Nikolai in Cyprus. I managed others as well, channels from Turkey, Armenia, and Egypt.

He shifted in his seat, the chains of the handcuffs clinking softly. "But I'm certain there are other channels and people like me. The FSB wouldn't rely solely on one operation in their grand scheme. They have a far-reaching network and are very cautious about distributing information and responsibilities."

Jack rubbed his chin thoughtfully. "So, your dealings were directly with Nikolai, facilitated by your ability to speak Russian?"

"Yes," Omar confirmed. "My education in Moscow was an asset that made communication smoother. Nikolai and I, we could converse without translators, which was crucial for maintaining secrecy. It was easy to set up the operation with him. He was eager, ready to do whatever it took to keep his business afloat and expand it."

Jack nodded, understanding the depth of the situation. Omar's insights provided a glimpse into a vast and shadowy network orchestrated by the FSB.

"All right, Omar. Your cooperation could help prevent a lot of future harm," Jack said, standing up. "You will be fully debriefed in London, and if you cooperate and help MI6 further to round up your other channels of cash, they might consider your Canadian plan."

As he left the interrogation room, Jack's mind was abuzz with the information Omar had provided. The challenge now was to piece it all together, uncover the other channels and disrupt the FSB's intricate web of funding their goals.

***

Agent Moore, a seasoned MI6 operative, sat across from Zhorik, whose hands were clasped tightly on the metal table. Moore's expression was unreadable, his eyes sharp and focused as he prepared to unravel the story of Zhorik's association with Nikolai Gromov.

Zhorik, a man more accustomed to the shadows than the spotlight of an interrogation, shifted uncomfortably. When he finally spoke, his voice was a mix of resignation and defiance. "I was just a bodyguard, nothing more," he began, his accent thickening under stress. "Nikolai needed someone to watch his back, and I was there."

Moore listened intently, jotting down notes. "And these... 'shadowy things' you mentioned. Can you elaborate on that?"

Zhorik exhaled slowly, choosing his words with care. "I helped him move things... cash, mostly. Large amounts. It was never clear where it came from or where it was going. I just did the lifting, made sure no one interfered."

"So, you're saying your role was purely logistical?" Moore pressed, seeking clarity.

"Exactly," Zhorik replied, a note of earnestness creeping into his voice. "I've never hurt anyone, never been part of any... any violent activities. I'm sure Nikolai had his dealings, but my hands are clean of blood."

Moore's gaze hardened. "And you expect us to believe that? A man like Gromov doesn't hire a bodyguard to move boxes."

Zhorik met Moore's gaze, his own eyes revealing a hint of the turmoil within. "I was there for protection, not participation. Yes, I knew things weren't entirely legal, but I stayed out of the details. I had my reasons for staying with Nikolai, but none of them involved harming others."

Moore leaned back, assessing Zhorik's demeanor. "What were these reasons, then?"

"A man's got to make a living," Zhorik shrugged, his voice laced with a bitterness born of regret. "Nikolai paid well, and I had little else to fall back on. It was a job, nothing more. I was a soldier following orders, not a criminal mastermind."

The agent nodded slowly, closing his notebook. The interview had painted a picture of a man caught in circumstances beyond his control, a pawn in a game played by kings. Whether Zhorik was as innocent as he claimed remained to be seen, but for now, Moore had a clearer understanding of the man before him—a bodyguard ensnared in the web of Nikolai Gromov's dark empire.

"Someone wants to talk to you," Agent Moore said before leaving the room. In walked Alison.

Zhorik looked up, his expression a mix of fatigue and apprehension, only to find Alison standing there, her gaze severe yet sympathetic.

"Alison," Zhorik's voice held a note of surprise, "I didn't expect to see you here."

She took a seat across from him, her eyes holding a complex blend of emotions. "I guess I owe you an explanation," she began. "I was there on Wave Cruiser undercover. I had to find out what was going on."

Zhorik let out a humorless chuckle. "So, that was all just a part of your job? Making me think... well, you know."

Alison sighed, her gaze softening. "Yes, it was part of the job. But it doesn't mean I didn't enjoy your company, Zhorik. You're not like the others."

He looked down, a mixture of relief and sadness in his eyes. "I never wanted any of this. I'm not a criminal, Alison. I just got caught up in Nikolai's world."

"I know," she replied gently. "And that's why I believe you won't face the same fate as Slavik. He was caught with a weapon, holding hostages. You were just... there moving the boxes."

Zhorik met her gaze, hope flickering in his eyes. "So, what happens to me now?"

"You'll likely be deported back to Russia. It's not ideal, but it's better than a prison cell," Alison explained.

Zhorik nodded slowly, absorbing her words. "And what about you? Will I ever see you again?"

Alison hesitated, then smiled faintly. "Maybe. Once all this is over, you might just find your way to the UK if you'd want that. I did like you, Zhorik, despite the circumstances."

His face lit up with a mixture of surprise and happiness. "I'd like that. And Alison... thank you."

She stood up, ready to leave. "I'll talk to my boss, see what I can do to help. Take care, Zhorik."

With that, she left the room, leaving Zhorik with a glimmer of hope in a situation that had seemed utterly hopeless.

***

In Moscow's cold, imposing office, Dmitri Orlov stood before his boss, Leonid Varushev, a man whose presence alone commanded respect and fear in equal measure. The grey, wintry light filtering through the windows starkly contrasted the warmth of the office's wood-paneled walls.

"Report, Dmitri." Leonid's voice was sharp, cutting through the silence.

Orlov straightened, his expression impassive. "Nikolai Gromov has been dealt with, as per instructions. He's no longer a concern."

Leonid nodded, a flicker of approval in his eyes. "And the others?"

"Olga Gromova and the individual known as Alex Paniv are now under British protection. It was impossible to proceed without risking significant exposure and diplomatic fallout," Orlov reported his tone even.

Leonid leaned back in his chair, steepling his fingers. "It's an unfortunate complication but not unexpected given the involvement of MI6. We must assume they have full knowledge of the Cyprus operation."

Orlov nodded in agreement. "It's a logical conclusion. Cyprus is compromised. We need to suspend our operations there, at least for now."

Leonid's gaze hardened. "Agreed. We cannot afford further scrutiny from MI6, especially in our current position. Our operations in the Middle East must continue, but we'll have to find alternative routes and methods. Cyprus is off the table."

Orlov considered this, his mind already racing through possible alternatives. "I'll begin working on new strategies immediately. We have other assets and contacts that can be utilized."

Leonid's expression remained unreadable. "No, Dmitri. I want you on something else. Soon, we will begin a major operation in Ukraine. All my resources are concentrated there as what is coming, Dmitri, will shake the world. You are going to Kiev next week. You will be briefed shortly on the details."

Orlov gave a curt nod. "Understood, sir."

In that pivotal moment, a wave of emotions surged through Dmitri Orlov, a cocktail of fear, panic, and a rare sense of vulnerability that he seldom allowed himself to feel. His stoic facade faltered as a barrage of thoughts raced through his mind hundreds of miles away to a small, unassuming city in Ukraine - Kherson.

Unknown to the world, there lived a fragment of Orlov's personal life that he had kept hidden—his nine-year-old daughter, Sophia. Her existence resulted from a brief but passionate affair with Inna, a woman he met during a nine-month assignment in Budapest. Inna, who had unknowingly fallen for the enigmatic Dmitri Orlov, returned to her hometown after her pregnancy, carrying a memory of him with her.

Orlov, the master of shadows, had kept an invisible yet watchful eye on his daughter. Always from a distance, he observed her growing up, her laughter and play through the lenses of his camera. He had amassed a collection of photographs of Sophia, each snapshot secretly taken during his covert visits to Kherson. Even his superiors were unaware of these clandestine trips, proof of Orlov's ability to vanish when necessary.

The thought of Inna remarrying and of Sophia calling another man 'Dad' was something Orlov couldn't bear. So, in a move befitting his clandestine lifestyle, he orchestrated a seemingly random but lucrative job offer for Inna. Through one of his many shadowy contacts in the digital underworld, he ensured that she received a substantial salary working for an online software company. It was his money, funneled discreetly to provide for them. Inna worked hard and lived a comfortable, independent, and financially stable life, diminishing her need to seek a partner for support. True love eluded her, and she remained a single mom, much to Orlov's relief.

As Orlov sat there, absorbing his superior's words about the upcoming operation in Ukraine, an inexplicable shiver ran down his spine. The fear that gripped his heart was uncharacteristic of the man known for his icy composure. For the first time in many years, Orlov's instincts screamed a warning of impending doom. Something terrible was on the horizon, potentially shattering the fragile world he had built from afar for his daughter and her mother.

As Orlov turned to leave, Leonid's voice stopped him. "And Dmitri," he said, his tone carrying a weight of unspoken warnings, "This new assignment is of paramount importance, failure is not an option. Remember that."

Orlov's response was a simple, determined nod. As he exited the room, the weight of his responsibilities and the dangerous game he was a part of settled on his shoulders like the heavy snow outside the windows. "Blind loyalty will take you nowhere, Dmitri," Jack McBride's words echoed in Orlov's mind with the force of a pre-storm thunder, reverberating powerfully as he was making his way through the labyrinth of FSB Headquarters corridors in the heart of Moscow.

Chapter 18

Nestled on the tranquil edges of Armou village, a quiet street ending in a cul-de-sac basked in the enchanting glow of a Cypriot morning. The air was filled with the sweet scent of citrus and the rhythmic sound of snipping shears as a young man dressed in shorts and a shirt, wearing garden gloves, shaped the verdant life that adorned his front yard. Each careful cut he made was a testament to his dedication, the bushes and trees standing as proud sentinels around the modest property that had been in his family for generations.

The house itself was an essence of rustic charm, its white-washed walls kissed by time and weather, and the terracotta tiles of the roof holding stories of the decades they'd stood watch over under the Mediterranean sky. It was small and unassuming, yet every tile, and every stone in its garden path, was meticulously cared for, reflecting the pride of its owner.

The calm of the morning was disrupted by the crunch of gravel as a car made its way into the cul-de-sac. It came to a gentle stop near the gate, the man straightened up, wiping a bead of sweat from his brow as he regarded the newcomer with a mix of curiosity and the easy hospitality that the villagers were known for.

The driver's door opened, and out stepped a woman, her presence as commanding as it was graceful. She offered a smile as warm as the sun overhead, her hand extended in greeting as she approached.

"Good morning," she said, her voice carrying the melody of the local dialect mixed with the authority of her position. "Mr. Panicos Constantinou?"

"That's me," the man replied, taking his gloves off and extending his hand in a handshake, noting the strength in her grip that contradicted her elegant appearance.

"I'm Alexa Marou, from the Criminal Investigation Department." She presented her badge, which glinted briefly in the morning light. Her eyes met his with an intensity that spoke of purpose.

Panicos' eyes lingered on the badge before returning to her gaze, a flicker of understanding passing through his features. He nodded, a gesture of acknowledgment and respect.

"How can I help you, Ms. Marou?" he asked, the shears hanging idly by his side.

"I'd like five minutes of your time. It won't take long," she replied.

Panicos gestured towards the back of the house, the branches parting to reveal a sun-dappled patio embraced by climbing bougainvillea. The vibrant purples and pinks contrasted beautifully against the white walls, creating a secluded oasis that promised a respite from the world's prying eyes.

"Let's talk here, if you don't mind," Panicos suggested, leading the way. The patio was arranged with a quaint charm, the chairs inviting in their simplicity, arranged around a small table that bore the marks of countless morning coffees and evening reflections.

As they settled down, Panicos excused himself briefly and returned with two steaming cups of coffee, the aroma rich and welcoming. He handed one to Alexa, who wrapped her fingers around the warm ceramic, grateful for the comforting heat against her skin.

"Thank you," she said, taking a careful sip, the robust flavor of Cypriot coffee grounding her. She placed the cup on the table, her gaze meeting his cautious, yet open expression.

"I'll come straight to the point," Alexa began, her voice even. "It's about that call. I am aware it was you who made it."

Panicos' eyes held a flicker of unease, a shadow crossing his features before he nodded, the weight of his decision apparent in the tightness around his eyes. He was a junior Border Control officer working at Paphos International Airport and the one who placed an anonymous call to the police about unlawful business with the Russian private jets.

"Yes, it was me," he admitted, his voice barely above a whisper, laden with a mix of fear and resolve. "I couldn't just…" Panicos did not finish his sentence.

Alexa leaned forward, smiling, her eyes softening. "Your call has been instrumental, Mr. Constantinou. Because of people like you, we can make a difference. You did the right thing. I came to thank you personally."

Panicos looked away for a moment toward the sprawling olive groves bordering his property. When he turned back to Alexa, his gaze was determined, and his steely sense of purpose didn't quite match the gentle nature of the gardener she'd just met.

"I just want to live in a place where honesty isn't overshadowed by… by corruption," he said, his voice firmer now. Panicos paused, his gaze wandering over the greenery of his garden before returning to Alexa with an earnest intensity. "I made that call not out of envy, Ms. Marou. Stelios… he may have wealth, but it's the kind that soils the soul," he said, his voice tinged with a mix of sadness and conviction. "I chose to remain anonymous, Ms. Marou, I have a family, a young daughter who is only two. I was afraid of the consequences. I never know who I can trust. And the worst thing is that I am in my own country, and I am scared to tell the truth."

Alexa listened intently to Panicos' emotional speech.

"You see," he continued, "this island is more than just land and sea. It's the heart of our history, our culture. It's the legacy we leave our children. But men like Stelios they trade that legacy for coins, betraying everything we stand for. Our pride, our dignity, they're not for sale. We should be the keepers of our destiny, not puppets dancing to the tune of the highest bidder."

He took a deep breath, the air around them charged with his vibrant energy. "I can't stand by, watching our country become a marketplace where everything is transactional. Our values and identity are auctioned off to those who care nothing for what it means to be a Cypriot."

His eyes blazed with fire, his every word a testament to the love he bore for his homeland. "No, I couldn't just watch. Because, in the end, it's not just about preserving our land. It's about safeguarding the soul of our nation for the generations to come."

Alexa listened, moved by the passion in his words. She could see the depth of his commitment, the love for his country that propelled him to act.

She nodded, the gravity of his words resonating deeply with her own principles. "And that's exactly what we're working towards, Panicos. With your help, we're one step closer." They shared a moment of silent understanding, the clink of their coffee cups a subtle salute to the courage and integrity that had brought them together on this tranquil morning.

Leaving, Alexa asked Panicos if he was going to work on Monday.

"Yes. Sure," he replied. She winked at him and said,

"Great. You are in for a surprise. Good luck!"

Panicos Constantinou would soon discover that the minister had signed the directive to appoint him as the new Head of the Border Control Services of Paphos Airport.

***

The Nema Restaurant, within the elegant Anemi Hotel in Paphos, radiated a serene ambiance that contrasted with the significance of the conversation unfolding at one of its private tables. Soft lighting bathed the area in a warm glow as waves from the nearby sea provided a soothing acoustic backdrop. Jack, Alexa,

Olga, and Alex were sitting at the table with glasses and a freshly opened bottle of Cypriot white wine.

"Nikolai's story is not uncommon," Jack began, his voice low and measured. "Recruited by the FSB during his brash mafia days, he became a valuable asset. His criminal activities were overlooked as long as he played his part in their grander scheme."

Olga, who had been following along intently, interjected with a bitter edge to her voice. "So, his wealth and power, it was all underwritten by the FSB?"

Jack nodded. "Exactly. They allowed him to amass a fortune through smuggling—tax-free and beyond the reach of the law. In return, he became the hub of their operations here in Cyprus."

Olga clasped her hands tightly together, her knuckles whitening. "So, all this time, Nikolai was funneling money to Omar. Is that it?"

Jack's gaze swept over the group. "Yes. Through Nikolai's plane and his extensive network, vast sums of money were delivered to Omar. He was the financier, the lifeblood of their covert operations. His dealings funded... unsavory activities in the Middle East."

Alexa, silent until now, added, "And we disrupted this flow when Nikolai became desperate to retrieve his lost funds and drew unwanted attention. It was a fatal error."

A waiter approached, refilling their glasses.

"To think," Olga murmured, "that the man I married was at the heart of this... I was living with a monster." She turned to Jack and asked him: "Do you know where he is now?"

Jack reached across the table, his hand briefly covering hers in a gesture of comfort. "The Nikolai you knew was a mask that concealed his true role as a linchpin in a much larger and more dangerous machine. He has disappeared, Olga, and he is not coming back. I have no proof that he is dead or alive."

"I'm figuring out how I should approach all of this with Christine," Olga said quietly.

Alex frowned, processing the depth of the conspiracy. "So, what happens now? With Nikolai gone, will it all just... stop?"

Jack's eyes held a shadow of regret. "Nikolai was a cog in a vast operation. With him gone, they'll find another way to continue. Our job is to stay vigilant to disrupt their activities wherever we can. As for you, Olga" – Jack looked into her eyes – "the situation is the following: you have played a valuable part in the operation. You are entitled to protection from the

British government. We will offer you a new identity and a shortlist of places where you can settle down."

As Jack's words settled in, Olga felt a rush of conflicting emotions. Relief washed over her at the thought of escaping the tangled web that had become her life, yet it mingled with a deep sense of loss. The idea of leaving everything behind, her past, her identity, even her name, was daunting.

In her heart, Olga knew the offer of protection was more than an escape. It was a chance to start anew, to build a life free from the shadows of fear and manipulation that had loomed over her for so long. As she contemplated Jack's offer, Olga's thoughts drifted to Christine. The prospect of her child's safe and stable future brought a sense of calm.

In the aftermath of Jack's offer to Olga, Alex sat deep in thought. The idea of Olga starting a new life, potentially in a far-off place under a new identity, filled him with fear and sorrow. His feelings for her had blossomed unexpectedly, a ray of light amid chaos, and now the thought of losing her was almost unbearable. His mind replayed their recent moments together, the connection they had forged under the most unlikely and challenging circumstances. He looked at Olga, and a silent vow formed in his mind. He would respect her decision, whatever it might be, but he also knew he couldn't let her go without expressing his feelings, without letting her know that he was willing to face any challenge, any uncertainty, as long as it meant being by her side.

Alexa, filling the void at the table, leaned back in her chair, her gaze lingering on the horizon where the sky had turned to a velvet blanket punctuated by the first twinkling stars. She continued with the story:

"Nikolai's network has been thoroughly dismantled," she began, her voice holding a note of finality. "Stelios, the Border Control office, the ever-complacent accountant, his shady banker, the staff members who doubled as informants—everyone has been rounded up."

Jack interjected with a sardonic twist of his lips, "Quite the clean sweep. Must feel good to put a full stop to that chapter, eh?"

Alexa's lips curled into a faint smile, "It's satisfying, certainly, but in this line of work, we rarely get to write the ending. We just... turn the page."

Alex listened, nodding appreciatively. "You're both like chess players, always thinking several moves ahead."

Olga had been quiet, reflecting on the sweeping changes in her life, but Alexa's next words drew her back to the present.

"And you, Olga," Alexa's tone softened slightly, "where do you see your future? What do you think of Jack's offer?"

The question hung in the air, and Olga felt the weight of all eyes upon her. She took a moment to collect her thoughts before responding.

"My future," she started, pausing to glance at each person at the table, "feels like a book whose pages are yet unturned. I was married to a lie, entangled in a web I couldn't see. Now, with freedom I never anticipated, I want to rediscover who I am—beyond the shadows of Nikolai's deceit."

There was a fire in Olga's voice, a steely determination that resonated with her listeners. "I intend to start anew. I will go with Jack's offer because I want safety and security. I want to build something that is truly my own, untouched by corruption or espionage. And I want to ensure that Christine grows up knowing the value of truth and integrity."

Jack raised his glass to her, a gesture of respect. "To new beginnings then, and to a future defined by our choices, not our circumstances."

They toasted, the clink of glass echoing softly. Alexa's gaze was thoughtful as she watched Olga, a nod of approval gracing her features. "There's a resilience in you, Olga. I've no doubt you'll carve out the future you desire."

Olga reached across the table, her hand finding Alex's with a gentle tenderness. "You know, Alex," she said, her voice carrying a new note of hope, "we've both been given a second chance. Maybe it's fate or just fortunate timing, but I think we could make something great out of this mess."

Olga turned to Jack, her smile reflecting the soft flicker of candlelight. She looked happy.

"Would the British government extend the offer to my boyfriend?" she asked joyfully.

Jack chuckled, lifting his glass again, "To second chances then, and to finding peace—or maybe even love—in unexpected places."

Their glasses chimed in the still evening air, sealing the sentiment. With a knowing smile, Alexa added, "Let's drink to us, the unexpected architects of a new future. May our designs be strong and our partnerships enduring."

There was laughter and lightness at the table, the Mediterranean breeze sweeping around them, almost like a blessing on their newfound bond.

Olga's curiosity couldn't be contained. She felt a hint in Alexa's words. She glanced at Alexa and then at

Jack, a curious arch to her brow. With a twinkle of mischief in her eye, Olga leaned forward and regarded Jack and Alexa with an exaggerated squint. "You two seem to be pairing up like the olives and feta on this table—undeniably a good match. Should we expect any joint operations shortly that aren't strictly business?"

Alexa and Jack burst into laughter. Jack glanced at Alexa with a playful smirk, then turned to Olga, raising his eyebrows in mock surprise. "Well, Olga, I must say, you're as sharp as the sea breeze on a Cyprus morning. Let's say, Alexa and I have decided to merge our 'assets' and 'intel' on a more... personal level. We're now officially on a joint mission titled 'Operation Sunset Romance' — and no, it's not code for anything clandestine, unless you count the secret recipe for Alexa's legendary moussaka as top-level intelligence.

"So, are you heading back to the UK with Jack?" Olga asked, her voice a mixture of playfulness and genuine interest.

Alexa opened her mouth to respond, but Jack called in, his voice laced with humor and a hint of mischief. "Actually, I've decided that Cyprus has a certain... charm that I just can't seem to find anywhere else. And well, I think I might need a personal guide to appreciate it fully," he said with a wink.

"And who better than an insider from the local law enforcement to show me the ropes, right?" he added, nodding toward Alexa, who was trying to suppress a grin.

Alexa finally spoke up, her eyes alight with shared amusement. "Well, it seems I've been recruited for an extended tour of duty. Something about being absolutely essential to the cultural education of a certain British agent."

Olga laughed, the sound light and free. "I think that's a mission you can't refuse, Alexa."

The two couples shared a moment of contentment, their faces lit by the stars above and the prospects of their new beginnings. They raised their glasses one last time that evening.

"To new horizons," Alexa declared.

"And to Cyprus," Jack added, "the island that brought us all together and refuses to let us go."

Their laughter mingled with the clinking of glasses, and the soft murmur of the sea seemed to whisper its approval. In the company of stars and the warmth of shared connections, they all embraced the promise of what was to come.

As they strolled out of the restaurant, Olga and Alex lingered behind their steps in sync.

Olga looked up at the stars, then at Alex. "Do you believe in fresh starts?" she asked quietly.

Alex stopped and turned to face her, his eyes earnest. "After everything? Absolutely! I think we've earned it, don't you?"

Olga nodded, her hand squeezing his. "Together then?"

"Together," Alex affirmed, and that word had a universe of possibilities. They walked on, side by side, united in a shared vision of what could be—a life built not on the ruins of the past but on the promises of a shared future.

***

Milton, Ontario, greeted the early days of spring with a burst of life and color. Situated at the backdrop of the Niagara Escarpment, this charming Canadian town was a mix of picturesque landscapes and cozy suburban streets. As the snow melted away, revealing the first hints of green, the town awoke from its winter slumber.

The streets of Milton were lined with a mix of traditional and modern homes, each with neatly trimmed lawns and budding gardens. The community was close-knit, with neighbors greeting each other warmly and children playing in the parks that dotted the area. The air was filled with the sounds of life – birds chirping, kids laughing, and the distant hum of daily activity.

Downtown Milton was a blend of historic charm and contemporary convenience. Main Street, the heart of the town, was lined with quaint shops, cozy cafes, and family-owned restaurants, each offering a warm welcome to locals and visitors alike. The historic Mill Pond and Rotary Park provided a scenic backdrop for weekend picnics and leisurely strolls, while the nearby conservation areas offered a haven for nature enthusiasts.

The community was known for its vibrant arts and culture scene, with various festivals and events dotting the calendar. The Milton Centre for the Arts was a hub of creativity, hosting exhibitions, performances, and workshops that celebrated local talent.

Education was a cornerstone of the town, with excellent schools and community programs fostering a nurturing environment for young minds. The local library was a popular gathering place, offering resources and a space for learning and connection.

As spring ushered in new growth, the residents of Milton embraced the season with open arms. The town's parks and recreational spaces came alive with activity – from joggers and cyclists on the trails to families enjoying the playgrounds.

In one of the peaceful streets of the town, nestled within the tranquility of suburban life, a charming house stood out with its well-tended garden. There, a young woman named Olena was diligently planting spring flowers, her hands gently pressing the earth around each new addition. Her husband, Andjei, arrived home from the store, arms laden with bags of gardening essentials. Together, they worked harmoniously, a picture of contentment and domestic bliss.

Their presence in the neighborhood had been a pleasant surprise to the locals. The couple, recently arrived from Poland, had quickly endeared themselves to their neighbors with their friendly demeanor and willingness to embrace community life. Their 7-year-old daughter, a bright and cheerful child, had adapted seamlessly, her laughter often mingling with the other children's as they played outside.

As Easter approached, Olena and Andjei were busy preparing their garden, eager to see it bloom with the colors of the season. It was a time of renewal and hope, a sentiment that resonated deeply with them. The couple shared knowing glances and smiles, a silent acknowledgment of their journey to reach this point of peace and normalcy.

To their neighbors and new friends, Olena and Andjei were just another immigrant family building a new life in Canada. No one suspected that behind their new Polish identities lay a history intertwined with espionage, danger, and a dramatic escape from a life that once threatened to swallow them whole.

Relocated to Canada with the help of Jack McBride and MI6, Olga and Alex, who were now Olena and Andjei, found not just safety but a chance to reinvent themselves, to live without the shadows of their past looming over them. Here, they were just a family eager to embrace the future and all its possibilities.

As Olena and Andjei continued their work in the garden, their conversation flowed easily, punctuated by shared smiles and laughter. They paused for a moment, leaning on their garden tools, and looked around at their new home with a sense of gratitude and disbelief.

"I still can't believe we're here, in Canada, starting anew," Olena said, her eyes reflecting the bright sky above. "Sometimes I wake up and have to remind myself that it's not a dream."

Andjei smiled, reaching out to squeeze her hand. "We've come a long way, haven't we? Who would have thought that we'd find such peace after everything that happened?"

Olena nodded, her thoughts drifting back to Cyprus. "I'm forever grateful to Jack and Alexa. Without their help, I don't know where we would be right now." Her voice was tinged with sincerity and appreciation. "They ensured our safety and helped me move all the assets out of Cyprus. Selling the property, tying up all those loose ends. They did so much for us."

Andjei agreed, "Yes, they did. And I am so happy they're coming to visit us this month. It will be nice to see them again, under much happier circumstances." The thought of hosting their saviors in their new home brought joy and excitement.

"It's incredible, isn't it?" Olena mused. "We have a chance to build something beautiful here, free from the shadows of our past. Christine has a future here, safe and full of possibilities."

"Yes," Andjei replied, looking fondly at their daughter playing in the yard. "A future where she can grow up without fear, where we can live as a normal family. We've been given a second chance, and I intend to make the most of it."

As they worked in their garden, with Christine playing nearby, there was a sense of completion, of a chapter closed and a new one joyously begun. The hardships they had faced seemed like a distant memory, overshadowed by the bright promise of the life they were now living. In the simplicity of their daily routines, their child's laughter, and the quiet moments they shared, Olena and Andjei found the peace they had longed for, a peace they once thought was unattainable.

Little did they know that precisely ten months from now, on February 24, 2022, their world would be shaken by the pre-dawn missiles raining down on Ukraine, plunging their families into peril, triggering fear and bloodshed, setting Olena and Andjei in a desperate bid to save their loved ones.

***

Playground:Ukraine

Chapter 1

February 19, 2022

In the subdued heart of February, Kyiv found itself in the embrace of an unusually mild winter. The city, with its historic monuments and grand churches, stood under a heavy sky, low and thick with clouds that promised snow but seldom delivered. The Dnipro River, often a frozen spectacle by this time of year, flowed unfettered, its banks flanked by the bare outlines of trees awaiting spring.

Winter's chilly grasp was loosening, heralding the arrival of early spring with its earthy fragrances felt in the air. February held the city in a gentle pause, with the earth starting to stir from its rest, hinting at the eventual explosion of life and color yet to come. It was a period of transformation, where winter began its gradual retreat, making way for the first signs of green to tentatively break through. The city's beautiful right-bank hills, a mix of still bare trees, winding trails, and golden domes of Pecherska Lavra, were poised on the cusp of bursting into life. They pledged to awaken fully in just a few weeks.

Maidan, the city's vibrant soul, usually a canvas of snow this season, remained untouched by winter's white mantle. Instead, it was covered in a cloak of dreariness, the grey pavements and solemn statues reflecting the gloomy skies above. Despite the gloom that enveloped the surroundings, the air was alive with the spirit of resilience, reverberating with tales of courage and an unwavering pursuit of freedom that once ignited this very square in the flames of revolution. It was a place where the past's echoes of struggle and triumph mingled with the present's whispers of hope, a sacred symbol of unity and courage in the face of adversity.

Even with the veil of a grey winter, life in Kyiv throbbed with a steady, colorful rhythm. The city streets bustled with the energy of its residents. Cafes, those cozy refuges from the chill, buzzed with activity; their warmth a haven for conversations over coffee, the steam rising like breaths into the cool air. The city lived its everyday life, waiting for winter to finally surrender.

Dmitri Orlov, one of the most adept operatives of the Russian secret service, found himself on an all too familiar road. His mission, one of utmost importance, had brought him to Kyiv. Sent by his FSB patrons, Dmitri was to prepare and execute an operation that danced on the edge of danger, its outcome potentially altering the geopolitical landscape. The assignment was bold and daring, once again placing Dmitri in a world where the lines between right and wrong blurred into obscurity. As he drove his car along the Dnipro River, heading towards the city's northeastern district – Obolon for a secret meeting, he couldn't help but feel the shadow of approaching danger. It felt like everything around was on the edge of a significant change that would soon shake this city's peaceful existence. Yet, the shift wasn't spring knocking on the door. The sense of ordinary, regular life outside his car window on one side and the understanding of what was coming on the other pressed on Dmitri, reminding him of how quickly things could change and how fast the line between life and death could disappear.

With each mile in slow Kyiv traffic, his mind wandered to another Ukrainian city, Kherson, where his daughter, Sophia, and her mother, Inna, lived, oblivious to his existence. A heavy burden troubled Dmitri's heart, knowing his superiors' dangerous games could soon threaten his most cherished.

Dmitri's memories came to life, taking him back a decade to Budapest, bisected by its grand river, much like Kyiv. It was the time when Dmitri found himself in Hungary for nine long months. The mission involved the FSB, CIA, and MI6 working together against a looming terrorist threat in Europe. Those days still echoed a time when alliances were forged to combat a common enemy. Between the clandestine meetings and shared intelligence gatherings, a quaint café in Budapest became the setting for a fateful encounter. Inna, a luminous presence from Ukraine, had just concluded her local university studies. She lingered in the city through the summer, serving café guests to gather her savings before returning back home to Kherson. Her vibrant spirit was undeniable, igniting a romance that swept Dmitri into a whirlwind of emotions he had never known.

In spite of the demands of his mission, Dmitri found happiness in stolen moments with Inna—nighttime walks through amazing parks, kisses shared on secluded benches, and dawn crossings over the Danube, bathed in the nascent light of day. Love, a stranger till then, wrapped him in its tender embrace. She was the antithesis of everything he embodied— their contrasting worlds colliding in a beautiful paradox. Her radiant joy and boundless energy filled the voids he had long accepted as immutable.

As their bond deepened, duty called Dmitri away to the dangerous terrains of Africa, leaving his promise of return hanging in the balance. When fate brought him back to her fourteen months later, Dmitri found Inna quietly living in Kherson. Just as he was about to approach her, he froze, his heart-shattering at the sight of her from afar, cradling an infant in her arms. At that moment, Dmitri knew without a doubt that the child was his. There, before him, was the example of what could have been—a family, a future, a life far removed from the dangers that trailed his every step.

As he watched from the shadows, the weight of his decision bore down on him. His last mission in Africa had earned him a roster of vengeful enemies, placing Dmitri squarely on the hit list of several ruthless drug cartels. The realization of the danger he posed to his child made his blood run cold, filling him with dread. The very act of revealing himself, stepping into the light and acknowledging his presence carried a risk too great to impose on the unsuspecting pair. His heart ached, longing to reclaim the lost time, introduce himself to the child he had never known, and rekindle the love that had once set his soul ablaze.

Yet, in the silence of that moment, Dmitri made the excruciating choice to retreat into the anonymity from which he had come. He vanished into the dusk, leaving Inna to the peaceful life she had built, untouched by the dangers of his world. She would be forever oblivious to his silent return and the unspoken goodbye that lingered between them.

His life, a mix of missions and dangers, posed a significant risk to both of them. Numerous unhappy people, ranging from government officials in some third-world countries to major terrorist organizations, were eager to learn more about Dmitri Orlov and seek revenge for his many deeds. The thought of enemies leveraging his most profound bonds against him was a gamble too dangerous to entertain.

Months later, Dmitri orchestrated a labyrinth of companies and fronts to provide for Inna and their daughter, Sophia, from afar. A software development company hired Inna online as a web designer and offered her a spectacular salary. Even though the money issue was settled, Dmitri's heart still ached at the thought of another man stepping into the role meant for him. But year after year, Inna remained alone. It was a bittersweet comfort for Dmitri.

Known by many names, bearing passports as varied as the languages he spoke, Dmitri was a grand master of the clandestine. His existence was always covered with secrecy and silence. Even those who commanded his loyalty were oblivious to his pilgrimages to Kherson. Three, sometimes four times a year, he would ghost through the city, a silent protector watching from afar. Through his camera lens, he captured the milestones of Sophia's life - her first tentative steps in the park, the joyful abandonment of games with neighborhood children, and the proud march into school on her first day. These stolen moments, frozen in time, were treasures hidden in a digital online vault, a secret gallery of love's quiet testament.

***

As he navigated the streets of Kyiv, Dmitri felt the weight of looming events, a prelude to chaos that tugged at his focus. For the first time, the man who had been the personification of precision and detachment found his thoughts adrift, trapped by the ties of his heart to Sophia and Inna.

His turmoil began long before his mission to Ukraine. The seeds were sown in the office of his superior, Leonid Varushev, where Orlov, fresh from Cyprus, was briefed on his next assignment. When he learned that his next destination was Kyiv, Dmitri understood all too well the ominous undertone of his boss's words. He was aware of the nefarious plans his country harbored toward its neighbor. However, despite his high level of information access, Dmitri couldn't believe until the very end that the government he served was capable of launching something so unimaginable - a war between nations so deeply intertwined in their history, families, and relationships.

What troubled Dmitri most deeply was the safety of his daughter. The coming war threatened to engulf everything in its path, including the life of his child, whose existence remained a secret to Dmitri's world. The realization that his daughter's well-being hung in the balance only served to intensify his internal conflict. Deep down, he recognized the impossibility of fulfilling both of his obligations – the service to his country and the need to shield his daughter from harm. In his internal battle, Dmitri was caught between duty and desire, a man at war with his own heart.

***

Nestled within the busy neighborhood of Obolon stood an apartment complex, a blend of contemporary elegance and city charm. Orlov eased his vehicle into a parking spot nearby and checked his inside pockets, ensuring his driver's license and passport — the identity of Pavel Lukovich from Brest, Belarus, was safely zipped within his parka. With his phone and tablet in hand, he locked his car, stepping into the role of a businessman poised to venture beyond Belarusian borders with aspirations of a software empire in Ukraine. Below the surface, however, lay his true mission - leading a group of FSB operatives into the most daring of plots.

Entering the apartment, Dmitri found his team assembled. Casting aside his parka, he settled into the heart of their makeshift command center. "Let's go over it again," he commanded, his gaze sharp. "On day X, our window will open with a signal — a mere couple of hours notice. In the coming chaos, our moment strikes. The inside man at the SBU will set the stage, orchestrating a meeting that will promise crucial intelligence for the Ukrainian side. Here is how: a call from the Belarusian Secret Service to SBU will set things in motion approximately three to four hours after the main operation begins. The call will request a face-to-face between the Ukrainian president and a special messenger bearing a so-called super-secret message from the Belarus president himself. The fact that the message comes through unofficial channels makes it easy to believe for Ukrainians, knowing Belarus' president is totally controlled by Russia but secretly wants to help. The messenger is going to be me. That's the initial setup."

Dmitri unfurled a detailed map of Kyiv, its streets and buildings like chessboards awaiting their next move. "Once the meeting is confirmed, Anatoly and I will get into the presidential office here while you, Sergei," — a pencil tapped decisively—" and Oleg secure our retreat here and here." Acknowledgement was swift, the plan a living entity among them.

"The device," Orlov inquired, the room holding its breath.

Anatoly carefully pulled out an iPhone from a stainless steel box, its sheen concealing a lethal purpose. "Prepared. But the challenge remains: how do we bring it past security?"

"We don't. Devices are to be surrendered," Dmitri clarified, a strategist foreseeing every move. "But in the heat of negotiation, with towering stakes and frayed nerves, protocols will fall to the wayside. Desperation for what we 'offer' will blind them to caution. I will ask for the phone to be brought in later to show the proof of the message. Given the circumstances, the importance of the message, and the enormous level of stress, their judgement will be clouded, and security will not be an issue at that moment. They will be jumping at any opportunity." He paused for a second and continued, - "I will put the phone in front of them on the table. The screen with the message will trigger the device, and in four seconds, it will go boom. So, Anatoly, once the message is displayed on the screen, you count to three and dive for cover as far to the side as possible. After that, we'll have to deal with whoever comes running. It'll be quick and dangerous, but we've planned for this. In case the iPhone plan fails for any reason, there is a plan B where, for Anatoly and I, this mission is going to become a one-way ticket. You know what to do in that case, Tolya."

Anatoly quietly nodded. His heart was heavy with the prospect of dying so soon. His eyes briefly lingered on Orlov's right hand, where a thick golden ring encircled his finger. While it appeared as an ordinary piece of jewelry to an outsider, Anatoly knew better. This ring, with its deceptive simplicity, had a lethal secret. Constructed with precision, it contained a tiny needle, invisible to the unsuspecting eye but as sharp as the finest syringe. A simultaneous press on both sides of the ring could spring the needle into action. With just a mere handshake, a fatal dose could be delivered, its venom seeping into the bloodstream upon the needle's subtle penetration of the skin. Anatoly was aware that Orlov required only a moment's proximity to the president to execute his mission. He knew what was at stake, including the very real possibility of not making it out alive.

Sergei, one of the operatives, shifted in his chair and declared, "Let's hope it all works out, and in a week or so, this whole country will be on its knees." His tone carried a chilling certainty.

Orlov met his gaze with a long, measured look. "We must concentrate on our mission. Let's not be distracted by politics."

"That's not politics," Sergei shot back. "It's a pure necessity to eliminate this nation. They are traitors, American pets, who will never be loyal to Russia."

The room fell into an uneasy silence. Orlov, the head of the operation, decided to let the comment slide, though it gnawed at him. Sergei and Oleg were SVR officers assigned as a backup team to Orlov and Anatoly, who were both FSB. Dmitri, who had just been introduced to them, didn't know them well. They were highly professional, but their personal views were another matter.

Sergei's harsh stance towards Ukrainians made Orlov uncomfortable. He couldn't help but project Sergei's ruthless words onto the image of his own daughter, who happened to be a Ukrainian. Throughout his long career as a spy, with numerous missions in various countries - even those involving the assassination of some truly unsavory characters - Orlov had always taken pride in never harming civilians. He felt that the days ahead would test his beliefs, loyalty, and humanity. With operatives like Sergei in the mix, Orlov feared that their path might lead them into darker, more dangerous territory than he had ever anticipated.

Printed in Dunstable, United Kingdom